FULL THROTTLE

A TOM ROLLINS THRILLER

PAUL HEATLEY

INKUBATOR
BOOKS

Published by Inkubator Books
www.inkubatorbooks.com

ISBN (eBook): 978-1-83756-354-8
ISBN (Paperback): 978-1-83756-355-5

For Aidan

PROLOGUE

Lainey Wylder's eyes burn.

She's been to her fair share of funerals, especially when she was younger. She's lived all her life in Detroit. She grew up in Belmont. Back then, death was practically a daily part of life. She's seen so many friends and acquaintances die – shootings, stabbings, beatings, suicide – that after a while she became numb to the funerals. Tears that used to come freely dried up in her ducts. She saw too much of the same thing – young lives, full of potential, snuffed out and buried.

She got herself out. She worked hard. She went to college on a scholarship, aided in getting there by teachers who saw her drive, and determined themselves to assist her promise and her ambition. She studied law. She went to law school. Graduated top of her class. Became a lawyer. She could have worked anywhere.

She chose to stay in Detroit. She got out, but she never intended to leave entirely. No one ever helped a place get better by running away.

Lainey kept working. She was always pushing herself. She never stopped. It felt like she never slept, yet she never allowed herself to become tired. There was too much to do. She started making waves. She got big cases. She won more than she lost. She took pride in this. She was getting bad people off the streets of her city. Of her *home*. Making the difference she always wanted to. The difference she aspired to be a part of.

Eventually, she saw an opportunity to do more good. The chance arose to become District Attorney. She went for it. Her exemplary record spoke for itself, but still she had to fight. There had been only one other Black female D.A. for Wayne County, Michigan. Lainey was undeterred. She'd fought for everything she'd ever earned – she wouldn't back down from this challenge.

She won. She became the District Attorney for Wayne County. For Detroit. In that moment, she'd never felt elation like it. A sense of optimism and hope flowed through her like she'd never known before. From a position of such power, she could enact *real* change. She could make *real* differences. She could change things for the better.

Or so she thought.

And now she finds herself at a funeral, her eyes burning. She's not numb to this. She won't let herself be. When a tear rolls down her cheek, she doesn't wipe it away.

Lainey stays back, away from the other mourners. She's dressed all in black, with a wide-brimmed hat and sunglasses to disguise her face. People have glanced her way, no doubt wondering who she is, but no one has recognised her. She has her arm hooked through her bodyguard's, and people probably think they're together. She told him to be inconspicuous. She's come here to pay respect, not to stand out. He stands with his hands clasped in front of himself, and his back ramrod straight. Lainey supposes there's only so much she could expect from him. Some habits cannot be shaken. He does, however, wear a woollen hat pulled down low to conceal the radio in his ear.

The bodyguard's name is Terry. He's Black. Lainey made sure to bring Terry and not Max, who is white. The people being buried are Black. While there are white people present, the majority of their family and friends are Black. Lainey did not want anything about her to stand out, or draw attention. This funeral isn't about her.

It's her fault, though.

She closes her eyes. No one can see her do it, not behind her thick shades. She closes them tight and takes a deep breath. She has seen a lot of death, but this is the first time she has been responsible for it. And not just one – two. Man and woman. Husband and wife.

More than that, she has destroyed a family. She looks across the open graves of Colby and Etta Styles toward their children. Ruth and Calvin. Lainey has never met either of them, but she knows exactly who they are. She knows what she has caused for them. What the future holds, because of *her*.

Ruth is twenty-five. Calvin is only fourteen. Ruth has suddenly found herself the legal guardian of her younger brother. All of her plans for herself and her future have suddenly come tumbling down. Colby had told Lainey that Ruth is training to be a nurse. He told her it's all she's ever wanted to do. That dream will be on pause, now. It will take a backseat to more pressing concerns. The siblings stare down into the graves of their parents. Calvin cries openly. Ruth holds his shoulders. She's trying to be strong, though tears run down her face and her lips tremble. Her jaw is clenched. She holds her brother tight.

Staring at them, Lainey's legs begin to feel weak. Terry notices. He keeps her upright. He lowers his face close to her ear and whispers. "Are you okay?"

Lainey takes a deep breath. "I'm fine," she says.

"Do you want to leave?"

Lainey forces herself to stare at Ruth and Calvin, to see and to understand and to *know* what she has done to them. She has to live with this, same as they do. "No," she says. "I'm seeing this through."

1

Tom has been walking for six miles.

It's early March, and it's cold, despite the thick jacket he's wearing. He's passing through Kentucky. His car broke down. The engine overheated. He saw the temperature gauge start running up a while back, but there was nowhere for him to stop. He pressed on, seeing how far it would get him, and holding out hope he would reach the nearest town or gas station. He did not. Steam burst out from under the hood. He pulled over and opened it up and saw water pissing out from an undetermined point. He could hear a sound, too, like a high-pitched whistle. It sounded like it was coming from inside the engine. Tom didn't bother taking off the oil cap, or checking the levels. If he'd done that, he was likely to get himself burned by an eruption similar to all the water. He didn't linger on it. The car was dead, and that was that. He grabbed his bag off the passenger seat and started walking.

At the time, he was on a backroad. It was quiet and there was no one passing by. There were trees either side of him.

No homes, no businesses, and no other vehicles. No signs for any upcoming towns, either. Through the trees to his left, he could hear the distant sounds of traffic. He made his way through, and found himself on an interstate. A sign told him it was I-75. Another sign told him that Mt Vernon was ahead, but it was going to be a long walk.

Tom presses on. Six miles down, only five more to go.

The interstate is busy. He sticks to the shoulder, close to the grass. He's stuck his thumb out a few times, but no one has stopped. The drivers look straight ahead and pretend they don't see him.

It's going to be late when he reaches Mt Vernon. The sun is still high for now, but a few more hours and it's going to be dark. It's going to be cold, too, colder than it is now. Winter clings to the year with icy tendrils, refusing to let go. Tom keeps his hood up. With his bag on his back, it feels like when he was in the Army. Trudging on, the destination still far, no other choice but to press forward. And that's what he does – he walks. There's no alternative. He could veer off into the woods again and think about making himself a shelter for the night, but so close to a busy road it's unlikely he'd be able to capture anything to eat. As it is, he's in no real rush. He's not running from or to anything. He can push on. He'll reach Mt Vernon when he gets there, and when he does he'll find a place to eat, and a place to rest, and then he'll find a place he can buy a cheap car. Hell, if he likes the look of Mt Vernon, he might hang around for a little while. See if there's any work. So long as he's frugal, he still has savings from his Army and CIA days to live off, not to mention from the odd-jobs he's picked up here and there, but he's always careful. He knows money is easy-come, easy-go, and it's too easy to lose when you're not paying attention.

Behind him, a horn sounds.

It's not aggressive. It doesn't blare. It's a short, sharp honk, designed to get his attention. Tom turns, pulling back his hood. A long-haul truck flashes its lights at him and puts on its signal light. Tom steps back onto the grass. He watches as the truck passes by, the driver raising his hand in a wave. The truck passes, slowing. It comes to a stop on the shoulder. Tom walks to the passenger door and hauls himself inside.

"Been walking long?" the driver says. He looks to be in his fifties, slightly overweight in the middle from days spent sitting on his backside while he drives cross-country. His hair is white and a little wild around the sides. He smiles. His face is friendly. He looks glad to have some company.

"Just a couple of hours," Tom says. It's warm in the cab of the truck. Tom pulls his hood down and unzips his jacket. "My car broke down."

The driver signals, then pulls back onto the interstate, rejoining the traffic. "Down the road? I didn't see any breakdowns for a while."

"Other side of the trees," Tom says, tilting his head toward the woodland on their right. "Figured I had a better chance of getting picked up here."

"You keep in mind where your car is? If you've been walking a couple of hours you might struggle to find it again."

"It's dead," Tom says. "I'm not coming back for it. Some tow truck will come by eventually and take it away. All it's good for now is scrap."

The driver grunts. "I take it you're not going anywhere in a hurry then, huh?"

"Nowhere I need to be."

"Do you have a destination in mind?"

"I was walking toward Mt Vernon, but I'm not beholden to it. I just needed somewhere I could find a car dealership, maybe a place to rest up for the night, get something to eat."

The driver is silent a moment. "You on some kind of road trip? Or are you just a drifter?"

"More of the latter, I guess. A road trip would imply I'm trying to get somewhere."

The driver smiles wide suddenly. "Just enjoying your freedom, huh? My dad, he was a hippy. When I was young, he would tell me all these stories about how he would hitchhike everywhere. Just him, his bag, and his thumb out by the side of the road. How he met my mom, in fact. She picked him up one day, and he just ended up staying in the passenger seat. But he said you could guarantee people would *always* stop back then. Said for ten years he didn't need to own a car. It's not like that anymore. People are more careful now, and for good reason."

"*You* stopped," Tom says.

"I like to think I'm a good judge of character."

"From the back of my head?" Tom says. "Wearing a hood?"

The driver laughs. "When you came on up to the cab, if I'd got bad vibes I would've kicked you out back to the shoulder and been on my way."

"Then I'm glad the vibes were good," Tom says.

The driver laughs. "Maybe something about you reminded me of those stories my dad used to tell. Seeing you walking along made me think of him, and the pictures he showed me from when he was a younger man. Except your hair's a lot shorter." He laughs again. "I'm Lewin, by the way.

Lewin Spinks." He twists his body and offers an awkward handshake.

The angle is more accommodating to Tom. He turns his shoulders and returns the shake. They keep it brief so Lewin can return his hand to the wheel. "Tom Rollins," Tom says.

"Pleased to meet you, Tom. Couple of hours and it's going to be dark. I'm going past Mt Vernon, but I'm planning on spending the night in a rest-stop just beyond it. There's an all-night diner and a motel. You'll be able to spend the night then you can ask directions to a dealership in the morning. How's that sound?"

"Sounds good to me, Lewin."

2

It's dark when they reach the truck stop. It's not late, but it feels like it might as well be.

"You planning on eating now, or later?" Lewin says.

Tom looks at the well-lit diner, its neon sign burning into his eyes. His stomach grumbles. "Now," he says, looking around the lot to see where the motel Lewin mentioned earlier is. He spots it, across the lot, past the parked trucks. The sign closest to the road says there are vacancies.

"Then I'll join you, if you don't mind," Lewin says. "So long as you haven't had enough of my company."

"I'm sure I can tolerate you for a couple more hours," Tom says. "Where you spending the night? In the motel, or back there?" Tom nods at the sleeping compartment behind where they sit.

Lewin turns and slaps a hand down on the mattress. "No fancy motel for me," he says. "I'm a man of the road."

They go into the diner and order food. It's busy inside. The clientele are mostly truck drivers, some of whom Lewin knows and exchanges brief pleasantries with. While he talks to someone he knows, Tom takes a seat in a booth at the rear of the room, keeping his back to the wall. Lewin follows and slides in opposite him.

The food takes a while to come, but it's busy and Tom doesn't hold it against them. He and Lewin make small-talk while Tom scans the area. The atmosphere is loud, borderline raucous. He sees a couple of families present, too, stopping off to eat before they get back on the road. He notices how they look warily at the truckers, but they don't dare ask them to keep the noise down.

Tom gets a chicken salad. Lewin has a steak. They eat in comfortable silence. Tom doesn't mind being around Lewin. He's friendly. A nice guy. Clearly lonely on the road, no doubt thinking about his wife back home. He hasn't spoken of his wife, but Tom has seen his wedding ring.

Tom has seen movement out on the parking lot as the hour has grown later. A congregation of women, barely dressed despite the cold. They wear shorts or skirts, and tops that show off their shoulders and midriffs. A couple of them have coats, but they keep them open. Tom sees them talking to the truck drivers.

Lewin follows his eyes. He chuckles. "The lot lizards are out."

Tom doesn't need to ask him what he means. He already knows what they are. Hookers.

"Thinking about getting yourself some company?" Lewin says. "They don't just cater to truckers."

"I don't pay for it," Tom says.

"I do," Lewin says, but when Tom looks at him he points at his wedding ring. He laughs. "Feels like it, anyhow. You ever been married?"

Tom shakes his head.

"Then maybe you don't know what I'm talking about. Try and keep it that way, young man."

Tom doesn't answer. Lewin isn't looking at him. He's looking at his ring still. There's an expression of guilt on his face. When he looks back up, his voice is earnest. "I *do* love my wife, though. I was just messing. She means the world to me."

"I don't doubt it," Tom says.

"She says that sometimes, when I've been on the road for too long and the only other people I've seen have been truckers, she says that my jokes can run a little coarse. I think maybe that was one of those times."

"Since you sound so apologetic, I won't tell her," Tom says.

Lewin laughs. "I appreciate that."

When they finish eating, Tom pays for Lewin's meal to thank him for the ride. Lewin protests, but Tom ignores him. They leave the diner and shake hands as they say their goodbyes.

"Thank you for the company, Tom," Lewin says. "And for the food."

"Thanks for the ride."

They go their separate ways. Lewin heads back to his truck. Tom makes for the motel. Snow is lightly drifting down, but it's too light to lie. The ground is wet and offers no support to the falling flakes. The wind is strong, however, whipping the snow around. It has a hard-edged bite, and Tom pulls up his hood to protect against it as he crosses the lot.

A couple of the women he saw earlier emerge from the shadows of a truck. A blonde and a redhead. "Hey there," the blonde says. She wears fishnets and denim shorts, and a black tube top. She's flat chested and doesn't fill the top out. Her exposed stomach ripples with muscle. The redhead has a little more meat on her bones, though not by much. She wears a pleather skirt that glistens in the dark, and totters on high heels. She holds onto the blonde for support. Her white blouse is tucked into a bow at the front, the top buttons undone and showing off her deep cleavage.

Tom nods. He's not interested, but he's not rude, either. "Evening," he says, not slowing.

"You wanna party?" the blonde says.

"Not tonight," Tom says. He's past them, now. They can take the hint. They don't follow.

It's dark down the spaces between the trucks. There are street lights in the lot, but they're mostly on the outskirts, with a couple closer to the motel and back at the diner.

A noise catches Tom's attention. It comes from down between two trucks. Tom pauses, turning his head to listen. The scraping of shoes. A scuffle. A muffled voice, something clamped over a mouth.

There is movement. The sounds become faint. They're moving off.

Tom stays where he is. He can't leave. The sounds were concerning. He follows them, heading into the darkness, sticking close to the truck on his left and stepping lightly. He hears a door open. He hears voices now, hushed and threatening.

"*Shut the fuck up, will ya?*"

Tom keeps his footsteps light, but he moves faster toward the sound. He reaches the end of the two trucks and sees another parked nearby. Its cab door is open, its interior light on. The shine allows Tom to see what is happening better. He sees one of the lot lizards, and two men. One of them has her by the ankles, and the other has her under the armpits from behind, hand clamped over her mouth. The woman struggles against them, but the two men are burly, each of them at least twice the size of her. Her strength and weight cannot match up to theirs.

"I'm sure the two of you are planning on paying that woman," Tom says, stepping out from behind the trucks so they can see him. "But it looks like you're going a strange way about it."

The two men wheel on him.

"Mind your business," says the man holding her ankles. He has a bushy beard that hangs down to his chest.

"Get outta here," the other man says. He doesn't have a beard, but his stubble is thick, covering his heavy jowls and pudgy cheeks. "Just keep moving. You didn't see nothing."

"You *deaf*?" the bearded man says when Tom doesn't leave. "Get fucking gone!"

The woman takes advantage of the distraction. She bites down on the stubbled man's hand. He gasps and almost drops her. "*Help me*!" she says.

The bearded man drops her ankles and grabs her by the hair. He shoves her toward the truck's open door.

Tom moves on them. Stubble sees him coming. He's shaking his bitten hand. He balls it up and throws it at Tom. It's sloppy, poorly aimed. Tom easily ducks it and throws a right punch of his own into the man's solar plexus. He follows through, spinning, and planting a left into the man's kidneys. He goes down, coughing and gagging.

The bearded man turns, swinging. Tom blocks it, protecting his head, then drives his forehead into the man's face, feeling his nose break. Blood squirts down the front of the man's shirt and into his beard, matting the hairs together. He drops down to his knees, clutching his face. Tom places a boot in the centre of his chest and pushes him over onto his back.

The woman steps forward, rubbing at her scalp where the bearded man grabbed her by the hair. "Hell," she says, looking at the two truckers on the ground. "You made quick work of them."

"What happened here?" Tom says.

"Sons of bitches didn't want to pay," she says, spitting toward the bearded man. "Decided they were going to *take*. Cheap bastards. Thanks for coming along. Don't know that many others would've."

"Let's go," Tom says. He escorts her away from the two fallen men, down between the trucks and back to the lot. As they step out into the light and the swirling snowflakes, Tom notices a group of truckers nearby. Three of them. They're standing around, drinking beer and smoking cigarettes. They glance over toward Tom and the woman.

"Well," the woman says, "I appreciate what you did. I gotta get back to work."

"Maybe stay where it's light for the rest of tonight," Tom says. "And find someone who can watch your back."

She nods. As she's about to turn, Tom hears movement behind them. The bearded trucker stumbles out of the darkness and from between the trucks, spitting blood. His nose badly swollen, already twice its normal size. He sees the other three truckers standing around. "This motherfucker just jumped me and my buddy!" he says, pointing at Tom.

The three truckers straighten at this. They roll their shoulders, loosening up. Tom assumes there's some kind of unspoken brotherhood between the truckers. They don't need much encouragement. They take the bearded man at his word.

"Ignore him," the woman says. "This guy helped me out. He and his buddy were getting rough – they weren't gonna pay. You wanna see the bruises?"

"Pretty sure we know where you get your bruises from," one of the three truckers says. They move on Tom and the woman. The man in front brandishes his bottle. Tom positions himself in front of the woman. These men are big, same as the two he's just dealt with, but they don't concern him. He recognises them from inside the diner. They were loud, drawing attention to themselves. They've been drinking, and they've just eaten heavy meals. They'll be slow. Tom waits for them to get closer. He turns to the woman. "Get out of here," he says. "You don't need to hang around for this."

She hesitates, but not for long. She hurries away on her platforms, running toward the diner where some of the other women are.

Tom doesn't watch her go. He has more pressing concerns. The three are getting closer. As close as he needs them to be.

"I'm gonna give you one chance to walk away," Tom says. "You keep coming at me, I'm going to treat you the same way I treated this bearded asshole and his buddy. Do you want to get yourselves hurt protecting a couple of attempted rapists?"

The men don't falter. They sneer at him. They're undeterred.

Tom makes the first move. There's no sense in waiting for them to swarm him. He steps forward, teasing the bottle wielder in the lead to take a swing for him. He does, and

Tom easily ducks under, then drives his boot into the side of the man's knee, dislocating it. He screams going down. Tom grabs the bottle from him as he falls, and holds it by the neck. He spins, ducking another attack from the man on his right. As he suspected, they're slow. Tom is too fast for them. As he completes his spin, he swings the bottle toward the man on his left. The base of the bottle, where the glass is thickest, cracks him across the jaw. It knocks him down. The bottle breaks, the body coming away from the neck in Tom's hand. The body of the bottle flies away, shattering on the ground.

Tom lets go of the neck and turns to the man still standing. The man throws a right, then a left. Tom dodges them both, ducking and weaving. He steps in close and blocks another right with his left arm, then hooks the arm and pulls the man in closer. Tom jabs at his throat with his hand, driving the air out of him. The man drops to his knees, coughing. Tom pushes him down onto his face.

The bearded driver is still close by. He's on one knee, watching what has happened with wide eyes. Blood is smeared across his cheeks where he's wiped at his broken, bloodied nose. Tom zeroes in on him. He hauls him to his feet by his collar and slams him up against the nearest truck.

"Maybe my first message didn't get through to you," he says. He punches the man across the face, opening a cut high on his cheek. "How many more messages will it take?" He shows his bloodied fist.

"That's enough," the man says, "I swear. I get it. I promise."

"If you didn't pay her, then it's rape," Tom says, holding his bloodied knuckles under the man's eyes. "You wanna know what I do to rapists?"

"I get it!" the man says. He's terrified. "I promise, I do!"

Tom shoves him to the side. "Make sure your buddy does, too." The man falls, then scrambles to his feet and hurries away into the darkness, back toward the truck where Tom first found him. Tom turns and sees the other three men on the ground. The man with the dislocated knee cries out, while the one with the broken jaw groans and whimpers. The man who Tom hit in the throat lies on his back, clutching at his neck and gasping. He'll be able to breathe properly again soon, though his throat will hurt for a few more days, maybe weeks.

"That was impressive," a familiar voice says.

Tom looks. It's Lewin, crossing the parking lot and coming closer. He stops when he reaches the fallen men, looking down at them.

"Think maybe you went a little overboard?"

"They were warned," Tom says. "And I've got no mercy for anyone stepping in to protect a pair of wannabe rapists."

Lewin whistles low. "That what was going on here? I wondered." He stands with his hands on his hips, looking around. He looks at Tom, thinking. There's something on his mind. He points back at his truck. "I was just getting settled down for the night when I saw you disappear off between the two vehicles. Thought something must have been up, so I kept watching. Truth be told, a part of me was worried you were going to try and steal one of them." He bites his bottom lip, still thinking. "Listen," he says. "Let's go back to the diner. I wanna talk to you about something."

Tom looks toward the fallen men. "What about them?"

"Sounds like they know what they did wrong. They're not gonna call the cops or anything. They're gonna drag their sorry asses back to their rigs and patch themselves up and never speak of this again."

"All right," Tom says. "What is it you want to talk about?"

Lewin is clearly still thinking. He hesitates, though not for long. "I wanna offer you a job," he says.

3

Tom waits while Lewin prepares to explain the job.

They're back in the diner, sat in the same booth as before. Lewin drinks decaf coffee. Tom has a glass of water. It's quieter now than it was earlier. Most of the truckers have left, returned to their vehicles to rest for the night. Outside, a couple of the lot lizards continue to roam. Most of them are gone, though, likely busy in either the trucks or the motel.

Lewin clears his throat and takes a drink of his coffee. "Basically," he says, "I need protection."

Tom cocks his head, surprised at this.

"It's nothing like *that* – I'm not in trouble or anything. It's work-related. I'm transporting electrical equipment – televisions, laptops, things like that. I'm taking them to Detroit."

"So what's the problem?"

"The problem is, there've been some jackings lately, going back the last couple of months. There's a gang up in Detroit. They've been targeting trucks that carry cargo like mine, and by that I mean anything of value. They're not going after trucks carrying produce, nothing that doesn't have any real resale value. They're coming after the good stuff, and I'm carrying good stuff right now."

"What's the net worth of what's in the back of your truck?"

"Hell, I don't know. Thousands, tens of thousands – maybe more. Point is, though, if they're selling on electrical equipment that they've paid nothing for, then that's one hundred percent profit no matter what they charge. Shit, they could charge a buck, and it's all profit. Of course, they'd be stupid if they did that. I highly doubt they're giving the stuff away for chump change."

"How many trucks have been hit?"

"I've heard about four, all the company I work for, but there could be more. Other companies could be getting hit too."

"Anyone been hurt?"

"There's been some beatings, yeah. One guy lost his truck – they just drove the damn thing off and burnt it out. Took his livelihood away, just like that." Lewin clicks his fingers.

"Your truck's unmarked," Tom says. "If they're being as selective as you say, how could they know what's inside it?"

"I don't know."

Tom raises an eyebrow. "Yet whoever is jacking you knows what you're carrying. You know what that sounds like, right?"

"Yeah, I guess I do," Lewin says. "It sounds like someone in the company is selling the route information. Probably getting a cut of the sales for themselves. Guy I get the routes from, who I work for, he's suspicious of it, too, but he's struggling to find out who it is."

"Does it happen anywhere else?"

"Just Detroit."

"The cops don't care?"

"They say they can't police every truck route that passes through their city. I hear they're stretched pretty thin up that way, though, so I don't hold it against them, personally. I get it. They already got a lot on their plates. My boss says we should arm ourselves and be careful – all we can do."

"And have you?" Tom didn't spot a gun in Lewin's cab.

Lewin grins. "You remember I said my dad was a hippy, right? I wasn't brought up in that kinda household. I've never owned a gun." He breathes deep. "Considered it, though. Since this all started."

"You been up to Detroit since it began?"

Lewin shakes his head. "First time," he says. "I've been losing sleep over it, if I'm honest. When I saw the route I had, and the cargo I was carrying, my stomach sank. It's gotta be done, though. I can't try and hoist it off onto someone else. If I got someone else to take my route and they got hurt... I wouldn't get over that. I wouldn't be able to forgive myself."

Tom takes a drink. "So what's the job you want to offer me?" he says, though he already has a good idea what it is.

"I saw how you handled yourself out there," Lewin says. "Against *four* guys. Hell, maybe more – I didn't see what happened when you went down into the dark and before you brought that woman back out. You know how to fight. You know what you're doing. I'm guessing you've had some kind of training. Military, right?"

Tom nods once.

Lewin leans closer over the table. "I need protection up there in Detroit. *That's* what I wanna hire you for. Protection. Get me and my cargo to our drop-off in Detroit."

Tom takes another drink. "How much are you offering?"

It's clear Lewin has been expecting this question. "I'm making just over two grand on this route. I'll pay you half."

Tom's impressed. "That's more than I was expecting."

"It's an investment in my wellbeing. And I'll pay upfront, too. You come to my truck tomorrow morning, I'll pay you soon as we're on the road."

"I haven't accepted yet," Tom says.

"*If*," Lewin says. "*If* you come to my truck." He waits a moment. He clears his throat. "Well? How's it sound?"

Tom considers. He has nowhere else he needs to be. No pressing concerns that he needs to attend to. A trip to Detroit for a thousand bucks is as appealing an offer as he's had in a while.

"All right," Tom says. "I'll see you in the morning."

4

Greg is a confidential informant.

Greg is sweating. He wipes at his forehead and mouth with the back of his hand. He's trembling. His left eye is blackened. There's a contusion on his forehead. His lips are split in various places. These wounds are not brand new. They're healing, but they look fresh enough to still be hurting.

Carter Brown stares hard at Greg. Greg struggles to meet his eye and hold his gaze. He keeps swallowing. Carter's arms are folded. His biceps bulge at his shirt sleeves. The veins there pop huge, the thickness of one of Greg's fingers. Greg is sitting, but even if he wasn't Carter dwarves him in every way. He could break Greg over his knee like a dry branch, and Greg knows it. Carter clears his throat, and he sees how Greg flinches. The sight makes him smile, but only briefly. A scowl quickly returns to his face. This isn't an interrogation. This isn't an interrogation room. They're in a back room of HQ, only two chairs present, no table, and a bare bulb dangling above them.

Darren Wong sits on a chair close to Greg, their knees almost touching. Darren's expression is more sympathetic. His eyebrows are raised, he's leaning in close. His arms are unfolded – he keeps his body language open and inviting. "Greg, come on, man," Darren says. "You have to give us *something*. Greg – Greg, look at me."

Greg forces himself to look up. He's shaking like he's coming down from something, but that's not what it is. He's scared. He's scared because he doesn't have what Carter and Darren want.

"You remember how we first met, right?" Darren says, sitting back, smiling like they're going to discuss a fond memory.

Greg swallows. Carter hears a dry click in his throat. "Y-yeah," he says. "Yeah, I remember."

Darren continues as if Greg hasn't spoken. "You had a pocket full of yellowjackets – no, wait, you had *two* pockets full of yellowjackets. You remember – it wasn't all that long ago. What, one year? Year and a half?"

"Two and a half," Greg says.

Darren whistles low. "Time flies, huh? But you had two pockets full to bursting with yellowjackets, and you *claimed* they were all for personal use, but come on, man. None of us were buying that. There was more than enough on your person to put you away with intent to sell – but we didn't do that, did we?"

Greg doesn't respond. Carter leans closer, like he's expecting an answer. Greg flinches. "No," he says. "No, you didn't."

"That's right. Now, don't get me wrong, my buddy here, *he* wanted to put you away. He wanted to put you away for a *long* time. See, way he sees it – and these are his words, not mine – *scum like you shouldn't be allowed to walk the streets*."

Carter grunts.

"If he had his way," Darren says, "he'd lock you – and everyone else like you – lock you up and throw away the key. He'd make it so you'd never see the light of day. Carter here, he says, *what if they're feeding them to kids*? And that's a reasonable fear to have. Because what *if* you had been planning on selling those yellowjackets to kids? Anyway, anyway," Darren holds up his hands like he's been going off topic. "I didn't believe you were going to sell those pills, Greg. *I* don't think you're scum. *I* don't believe that anyone is beyond redemption. They gotta work for it, though. And that's what I said to Carter here. I said that I believed you could be redeemed. So why don't we give him a second chance, huh? Give him a second chance and put him to work. And now here we are, two and a half years later, and you've done good by us so far, Greg. You've been proving me right, and I appreciate that. But now, lately, today, you've been breaking my heart, man. You really expect me to believe you've got nothing for us? You really expect me to believe that the well has run dry?"

Greg can't look back at him.

"We're out in these streets every day, Greg," Darren says. "We *know* the well ain't run dry. Nowhere near. But you've got nothing for us, huh?"

Greg looks like he wants to curl in on himself and disappear.

Darren takes a moment. Inhales a deep breath. He lets his words sink in. "I can see those cuts and bruises, Greg. You've taken a beating. Now, I don't think word's got out about what you do for us. That was the case, I reckon you'd be dead instead of sitting here in front of me. But there's a rumour, isn't there? People are getting wary of you. They're careful what they say around you. And that's got you spooked, ain't it?"

Greg manages to nod.

"That's a real shame, Greg," Darren says. "I'm real sorry to hear that. But, listen, you've jammed yourself real tight into a corner here. You see, if you've got nothing to tell us, then that means you're no longer our confidential informant. If you're not our CI, then you're no longer under our protection. You know what our protection offers you, right? It gives you immunity, Greg. If you ain't got that, then that means it's time to finally pay for those yellowjackets we found on you two and a half years ago."

Greg's head snaps up. His eyes bulge and flicker, understanding what Darren is saying.

"Yeah, Greg, that's right. That didn't just magically go away. If you're not our CI, then you're going to jail, buddy. Hate to say it, but that's what's gonna happen. And because you've been talking to us, you're gonna go in there with a snitch jacket. You know what'll happen to you when people find out about that invisible garment? And they *will* find out, Greg. They always do, no matter how much we try to keep it quiet."

Greg swallows. Carter hears the dry click in the back of his throat. He watches as the CI closes his eyes tight. Carter can see moisture catching in his eyelashes. Greg clears his throat. He looks up at Carter again, still terrified.

"All right," Greg says. "I might...I might have something. It's not big, but it's something."

"What are we talking?" Darren says.

"A new stash house."

Darren looks to Carter. "What do you think, boss man? A new stash house big enough to keep Greg here on the streets?"

"It's a start," Carter says, and then he leaves the room, leaving Darren to take the details.

They're not at the station. Carter and his people don't operate out of the station. They're in the field. They're in an old tyre factory just off 7 Mile Road. The Gang Control Task Force have called this building HQ for almost as long as they've been in existence. The room where Carter and Darren were talking to Greg was an old storeroom. Many a perp has been questioned in there, and broken in there. Greg is just another in a long line of many. Luckily for Greg, all it took to get him talking was words. There's been plenty blood spilled in that room, and plenty of broken bones dished out, too.

The rest of the GCTF are sitting, waiting for what happens next. They all look up as Carter approaches. He looks them over. The task force was handpicked by him. *You want the gangs controlled,* he said to the chief, *then I need to pick the best.*

And he did. He picked those who were best suited for his needs and his plans here.

Nick Sanchez, Anthony Felton, and Delia Curtis. Darren Wong, back in the storeroom with Greg, still. Carter's choices raised eyebrows. All four of them had a list of issues an arm's length. Mostly with regards to police brutality.

I need people who are ready to get brutal. What we're gonna be doing is brutal. The people we're going up against are gonna be brutal.

Delia is lifting weights, doing bicep curls where she sits. She puts the dumbbell down when she sees Carter. Other than Carter, she's the strongest member of the task force. She's heavy-set, short-haired, and her knuckles are thick with scars. She gets her hands dirty. She lives to get her hands dirty.

Nick Sanchez drops the cigarette he's smoking and crushes it under a heel. He rocks back and forth in his chair, balancing it on its back legs. His hands are in his pockets, probably fondling the switchblade he carries with him at all times. Nick is so laid back he's practically horizontal, but he's a vicious fuck, and when it's go-time he's all business.

Anthony Felton sits behind a desk, his front all lit up from the glow of his computer. He laces his hands atop his shaved head. He watches Carter with interest, raising his eyebrows, lowering a hand and scratching at his chin through his goatee. "What's the word?" he says.

Carter grins. "Saddle up," he says. "We got a stash house."

They decide to take the van. They pile inside and drive Greg out toward the stash house, following his directions. They park down the road from where it is. Darren and Greg stay with the van to begin with, but the rest of them spread out. Carter and Delia head to the front of the house. Nick and Anthony go around the back, covering the rear.

It's late. The dark keeps them covered, but they're careful. Carter has trained them up himself. He used to be SWAT, before he joined the police and headed up his own task force. He's showed them how to raid the way he wants it done. He's trained them the same way he was trained.

Carter's breath mists in front of his face. It's a cold night. Thin, dirty snow clings to the lawn. It lines the sidewalks and fills the gutters. He looks at Delia. They're both wearing jackets over body armour. They stand still, resolute. Delia sees him looking at her. She knows what he's thinking. He's waiting for her to shiver. She winks at him. She's not going to break.

Carter grins and turns back to the road. The street is quiet. He looks to the other houses. Some of them have boarded-up windows. He knows this block. Of course he does. He knows all of Detroit. He's never had any trouble here, though. Never had to bust any heads in these streets. It's a quiet place with quiet people who mind their business. If they have disputes – disputes that lead to boarded-up windows, say – they keep them low-key. Deal with things among themselves. They never dream of dialling 911.

Like he says, they mind their business. They're not peering out the intact windows, watching what everyone else is doing. If they have any interest in the stash house, it's as customers. They don't watch the place – if they want something, they walk right up and knock on the door.

If they know what's good for them, they'll stay indoors tonight. It's late – real late. If they wanted a buzz, they should've got it earlier, and now they should be tucked up in bed.

Everyone in place, Darren kicks Greg out the van and sends him on his way to the stash house. Darren stays behind.

Carter watches as Greg approaches. He's shivering in the cold. They picked him up from his apartment earlier, and they didn't give him a chance to grab a coat. He wipes his running nose with the palm of his hand. He glances over toward where Carter and Delia are hiding out. Carter glares at him and shakes his head. Greg is quick to turn away.

Carter nods at Delia. They pull out their Smith & Wesson M&Ps, holding them low. Greg pauses at the door. He sniffs hard, then takes a deep breath. He knocks on the door.

Carter is ready. Behind him, Delia is ready. Carter leans forward, listening. It takes a while for the door to open. It's late, and the occupants aren't expecting visitors.

Finally, they answer. Greg speaks to them. His voice is low. He mumbles. The man at the door is louder. "Man, what do you *want*? It's late. Come on, spit it out."

Greg raises his voice. "Just, whatever you got, man. I'm hurting." Carter can see him scratching at his arm. He's trembling all over, either for effect or because of the cold, it's hard to tell.

There's silence. The man inside says, "Who the fuck are you? I ain't seen you before. How'd you know us?"

"I got told," Greg says. "Man, I got money." He pulls out bills, provided by the GCTF. "I can pay."

The man at the door doesn't respond straight away. Likely thinking. Staring at the money. Making a decision. "All right. Wait here."

As he turns to head inside the house, Carter moves in. Delia sticks close. Carter knocks Greg out of the way with his shoulder, sees the back of the man just a few paces down the hall. Carter runs up behind him, slams the handle of his gun down across the back of his head, dropping him to the ground. He presses on. Delia stays behind, to secure the fallen man.

At the back of the house, he hears a window shatter. Nick and Anthony coming in. Darren would have radioed, given them the go-ahead when he saw Carter and Delia move in.

Carter moves room to room. He enters the kitchen.

There's a man at the table, body twisted, head turned toward the sound of the breaking glass. He snaps back to attention as Carter enters. He's not expecting to see Carter. He's expecting his buddy from the door. He's mid-sentence when he realises he doesn't know this white man. "Did you hear–?"

Carter raises his gun and puts two bullets in his chest. The man rocks in the chair, blinking. His eyes gradually close. He slumps.

Nick and Anthony come through. The three of them secure the rest of the house. There's no one else here. Delia pushes the man from the door through into the kitchen. She wrenches his arms behind his back. Greg sheepishly follows. It's clear he doesn't want to be here. Carter thinks Delia would have told him to follow. "What you found?" she says.

"Decent haul in the bedroom," Nick says.

"Any guns?" Carter says.

"Couple of Glocks in the living room, and a Ruger in the bedside table," Anthony says.

Carter expected there would be weaponry. On the off-chance there hadn't been, they always carry unmarked handguns ready to drop at the scene, close to the people they've killed. "Anything on them?"

"Nothing on this one," Delia says.

Nick pats down the man at the kitchen table. "Clear."

"Put a Glock on him," Carter says. "Bring them both, in fact." He turns to the dealer still living.

"You want me to take him out to the van?" Delia says.

Carter grins. "Get clear," he says.

Delia doesn't need told twice. She steps to the side. The dealer watches her go, not understanding. Carter puts a bullet through his head. Greg cries out and covers his eyes.

"Take a good look at it, Greg," Carter says, stepping up to him and snatching his hands away, forcing him to see. "Take a look and be grateful."

Greg stares. Tears roll down his cheeks.

"You know why I shot him?" Carter says. His face is close to Greg's.

"No," Greg says, his voice choking off, barely able to get the word out.

"Because he saw you," Carter says. "You're fucking welcome."

Greg closes his eyes again. Carter backs away, leaving him to cry. He's pathetic. Carter grins to himself. He didn't kill the dealer just for Greg's benefit. He was going to kill the man anyway. He just wanted Greg to get a good look, and to feel some sense of responsibility and guilt. Carter wants Greg to feel bad. He *should* feel bad. The man's a mess. He's a joke. Standing there, crying and shaking like a child. Carter wouldn't be surprised if he saw piss start to dribble out the bottom of his pant leg.

Fuck him. He's barely a man.

Carter turns to his people. Nick is already returning. "You know what to do," he says, and Nick nods. They make space so he can work. He's going to fire off a few rounds, make it look like the dealers fired first, and then he'll plant the guns on them.

Before it gets loud, Carter turns to Anthony. "How many drugs?"

Anthony grins. "Enough to skim, and still plenty left over for it to look like they were expecting a busy week."

"Make it look good," Carter says. "Delia, call our friends in the JJC, let them know we've got a gift for them." He turns to Greg, still standing and shaking close to the dead body.

Nick is ready with the Glocks. Ready to get to work. Carter clicks his fingers to get Greg's attention. "There's gonna be some shooting," he says. "You better leave."

5

Lewin isn't at the truck when Tom arrives early in the morning. Tom waits, folding his arms and leaning against the front of the vehicle. On his way over, he didn't see anyone he had trouble with last night. They were hurt badly. There were broken bones. They've probably moved on fast, to get medical attention and to avoid getting into more trouble.

The morning air is crisp. Tom breathes in and out through his nose, and sees it misting in front of his face. The sun shines down, but there's little warmth coming off it.

It doesn't take long for Lewin to appear. He makes his way over from the diner. He's carrying a take-out bag, and a couple of coffees. He smiles when he sees Tom.

"Sorry about the wait," he says, then holds up the bag. "I brought breakfast."

They get into the truck. Breakfast consists of donuts. Lewin eats while driving. The donuts feel heavy in Tom's stomach, but he doesn't complain. The feeling will wear off soon enough – long before they reach Detroit.

"We're not going direct to Detroit," Lewin says, as if reading his mind. "I have to make a stop-off in Idaho first."

"What for?" Tom says.

"Delivery," Lewin says. "Not all of this is going to Detroit. Just most of it. We shouldn't be too long in Idaho, but it's gonna take us out the way a little."

"How long?"

"Few hours." Lewin looks at Tom like he's expecting a complaint, but Tom doesn't protest.

"I told you," Tom says. "There's nowhere I need to be." He yawns. "It's going to be dark when we reach Detroit."

Lewin nods.

"Makes sense," Tom says. "I wasn't expecting they'd try and hit us while it was still light, and setting off this early put us on track to get there before night."

"Idaho slipped my mind," Lewin says. "I guess I saw that you could handle yourself, help me out, and I got carried away telling you about everything else. Explaining the route just didn't occur to me."

Tom sits back. He looks out the window. Lewin has brought water from the diner, too. A couple of bottles in the bag with the donuts. Tom sips from a bottle. The water is cold. He looks toward the trees that line the road, and he thinks about the car he had to leave behind yesterday. He wonders if it's been picked up yet. Wonders if it's been stripped, its carcass left by the side of the road, a metal skeleton left to rust.

Tom settles himself in the chair. They have a long road ahead of them. A fair way to go, and longer yet until Detroit. He looks to Lewin. "Wake me if I'm needed," he says, then turns to the side and closes his eyes.

6

Calvin Styles is sixteen years old, and school does not interest him.

He supposes, as he prepares to enter young adulthood, that he should start giving serious consideration to what his future holds and his intentions for it. The problem is, he can't see that far ahead. There are other focusses upon his mind that take up his time and attention. At fourteen, his development was stunted, and he hasn't been able to pull himself back from that.

Not yet, at least.

Maybe not ever.

But he has to believe that things will get better, one day. At home, he puts on a brave face for his sister. He smiles for her as best he's able, and he makes conversation, though most of the time he wants to sit in silence, to be alone with his thoughts. Ruth isn't often home, though. She's usually either working, or studying. She's exhausted, and Calvin can tell. Everyone can tell. *She* puts on a true brave face. She forces through. She never loses patience, or shows how tired she is, save for the occasional overwhelming yawn, and falling asleep in front of the television on the rare events they sit down and try to watch something together.

Calvin thinks that, if anything, his future might lie in boxing. He enjoys it, and he's good at it. It's given him direction, and purpose – though when he joined, he did so *with* a direction and a purpose already in mind. The coach at the gym, Noah Reed, says that Calvin is one of the most naturally gifted athletes he's ever seen. If Calvin had joined the gym in order to succeed as a boxer, this would mean a lot to him. It would give him hope that one day he could make a career out of it. And perhaps he can, but that's not why he took it up. He started at the gym, just under two years ago, to learn how to fight. So he would know how to handle himself.

Calvin does not have plans for his distant future, but he *does* have plans for his near future. Potentially his present. When the moment presents itself, he likes to think he'll be prepared. He likes to think that the last two years of mental and physical preparation have gotten him ready for what he needs to do.

After that, he's not sure where life will take him. It could be the *end* of his life – both literally and figuratively. He could end up in prison, or on the run, or dead. For Ruth's sake, he hopes it's not the latter, though he knows any option will crush her.

He tries not to think about that. About what his plans mean for Ruth. He blocks those thoughts out. He loves his sister, and appreciates all she has given up and sacrificed for him, but he can't let that stop him.

He can't let anything stop him.

His final period of the day is Math. Calvin is good enough at it that he can coast by. He does his work and waits for the day to end. For the bell to ring, signalling that he can finally get out and do the things that are important.

It used to be that he enjoyed school. He always excelled at Phys Ed, but he was no slouch in his other subjects, either. He enjoyed Physics and Chemistry. He'd thought, at one time, that he might like to be an engineer. His parents had been very supportive of that idea.

Now, he's like a ghost, floating through the corridors. He barely speaks, if he can help it. He sees his friends, but he doesn't speak to them. Doesn't sit with them, or make plans with them. They don't appear to begrudge him. They look saddened, if anything. They look like they miss him. Calvin misses them, too, but he can't waste time.

People leave him alone. They don't try to cajole him out of his silence. They don't try to get him to be how he used to be. He went through something traumatic, and they all know it. Other people at the school have gone through similar things. Some of them go to therapy. They talk to councillors. They try to get better. They have sessions at lunchtime where they all sit together and talk about their feelings. Ruth has tried to get Calvin to go to these sessions. He told her he'd think about it. Eventually, she gave up on trying.

The bell rings and Calvin leaves. He doesn't head home to the small apartment where he lives with Ruth. She won't be back yet. Either working or studying – Calvin can't keep track of her schedule. He doesn't try. All he knows for sure is that she's rarely home.

Calvin does not ride the bus to or from school. He takes his bike. He rides it to the gym, his sport bag bouncing on his back as he pedals.

The gym is an old warehouse in downtown. Most of the

buildings in this area are abandoned. They have smashed windows and doors, and are usually occupied by homeless people and junkies. The gym is never bothered, though. People know Noah. They don't want to hassle him. They don't want to mess with his equipment. He used to box heavyweight. He's not as firm as he was in his prime, but he's still a big guy. He knows how to handle himself. He lives above the gym, too. He's his own security system.

In the summer, they keep the corrugated steel door of the gym open, but it is March and though it's mostly melting, there is still snow on the ground and the door is firmly closed. There is no heating inside. The only warmth comes from the work they put in. Calvin enters through the side door and gets changed and gets to work. He runs laps around the room to get his blood pumping.

There are only a handful of others in the gym. Someone is skipping. Someone is working a heavy bag. Two people – one male, one female – are sparring in the ring under Noah's supervision.

Noah watches him running. "How was school?" he calls.

"Fine," Calvin says. His breathing is still easy.

"That all you got for me?" Noah says, grinning. "*Fine*?" Noah is fifty-four. There are a couple of framed pictures of him in his prime dotted around the gym. Other than the slight weight gain, he hasn't changed much. He's lost his hair, though, and where he used to be clean shaven, he now sports a beard that is more white than black.

"As fine as it ever is," Calvin says.

When he's warm, he hits the weights. He puts on his gloves and works a bag. The sweat is dripping down him, now. He's more than warm. He's grateful for the lack of heating.

Calvin stays late. He always does. Still here, still training, long after everyone else has gone. Pounding the heavy bag until he can barely lift his arms. Running drills with Noah, or sparring with him in the ring. Tonight, he jumps rope. He wants it to get later, and darker. He has somewhere he needs to be.

"Putting a shift in tonight, huh?" Noah says. He's been in his office in the far corner of the room for the last hour, while things have quietened. He takes a seat on the edge of a weight bench and looks up at Calvin.

Calvin stops skipping. He's breathing hard. He has to clear his throat to speak. "Felt like it," he says.

"That's good," Noah says. "I like to see determination. You'll go far with that." He checks his watch. It's half-eight. "You've been here a *long* time. Came straight after school, right? You eaten?"

Calvin shakes his head.

"Your sister working late tonight?"

"I'm not sure. Could be."

"Go hit the shower. I'll whip something up."

"It's fine," Calvin says. "I –"

"It wasn't an offer," Noah says, getting back to his feet. "I was telling you what's gonna happen." He winks.

"Okay," Calvin says, and he appreciates it. He allows himself to become aware of the grumbling in his stomach.

"Come on up to the apartment when you're ready," Noah says.

Calvin showers and dresses. He doesn't slip into the clothes he was planning on putting on when he left the gym. They would make Noah ask questions. Instead, he slips back into the things he wore for school. Jeans and a plain white T-shirt, along with his jacket. He turns off the lights in the gym and locks the side door on his way out, then goes around the back and up the stairs to the rooms Noah has appropriated as his apartment.

The rooms used to be the offices for the warehouse. There's a lot of space. Noah has knocked through some of the walls to make it look like a loft apartment. Noah lives alone, though Calvin knows he often has ladies up here with him. Tonight is not one of those nights. It's just the two of them. Calvin takes a seat at the round table adjacent to the kitchen area. Noah carries two plates. He sets one down in front of Calvin then sits opposite him. Beans, sausages, and some salad.

"I need to get some groceries in," Noah says, laughing. "But enough to make do."

They eat in silence. Calvin devours the food, hungrier than he realised. Noah takes his time. "You need a ride home?" he says.

"I've got my bike," Calvin says.

"It'll fit in the trunk."

Calvin doesn't want a ride. There's somewhere he wants to be. "It's better I cycle," he says. "Exercise. Gotta keep moving."

"You've been moving for a good few hours now."

"A little longer won't hurt."

Noah chuckles. "Like a shark. Can't stop, won't stop. You be careful outside though, you hear? And if anyone hassles you, you come straight back here and tell me."

"They never hassle me."

"Yeah, but it's dark and it's late, and you can never judge what a junkie might do."

"I'll be careful," Calvin says.

When Calvin is ready to leave, Noah walks him out to his

bike. "Watch yourself, Calvin," he says. "And if your sister asks, you make sure she knows I *offered* you a ride."

"I'll tell her," Calvin says. He says goodbye and sets off. He waits until he's far enough away, and around a corner, sure that Noah can't see him, then hops off his bike and props it against a nearby wall. He reaches into his sport bag and pulls out dark clothes – black jeans, black T-shirt, and a black hooded sweater. He strips down and re-dresses in the shadows, his head on a swivel as he does so, making sure no one is approaching or trying to sneak up on him. No one does.

Changed, he gets back on his bike. He's not going straight home. He rides deeper downtown, out to where the neighbourhoods are rundown. They're not abandoned, but they look like they should be. Despite this, they're active. There is a market. Drug sellers and drug users. Sometimes, there are gunshots. There are beatings. Calvin has been here before. He's seen all of these things.

He goes to a corner where he recognises the dealers. He doesn't go up to them. Doesn't ride past them. Keeps himself out of sight, moving through the shadows, stepping carefully, knowing there could be someone lying on the ground here and not wanting to tread on them. He doesn't want to do anything that could draw attention. Instead, he makes his way down the side of a house near to the corner. One of the dealers is leaning into a car that has just rolled up, talking to them, taking an order. Calvin settles in, ducking low, and he watches.

7

Carter takes the elevator up to Javon Johnson's penthouse and, same as he does every time he comes here, he shakes his head.

When he first met Javon, he was low-level. It wasn't even that long ago, not really. Just a few years. One thing that struck Carter about Javon, though, was his ambition. He was determined not to be low-level forever. He was going to get out of the streets. Leave that to others. Carter saw promise in him. Saw opportunity for himself, too. Now, to find Javon living in a penthouse, expanding his reach into investments and construction, Carter isn't too surprised. And, if he plays his cards right, it won't be too long before he's living the same way.

Javon greets him off the elevator. He's dressed only in a short robe, his legs and feet bare. "How you doing?" He wears a gold chain, too. His hair is styled short, and his beard is neatly trimmed. It's the kind of haircare that only an overcharging stylist can provide. When Carter first met him, he had dreadlocks, and his beard was unkempt.

Carter stifles a yawn. "Tired," he says. "It's been a long day."

"You ever sleep, man?"

"Of course I do," Carter says. "Just not often." He reaches into his jacket pocket and brings out a package. Taken from the stash house earlier, before the street cops turned up and took over the scene. "I've got a gift."

Javon takes it without checking what it is. He tosses it to one side, onto a glass table where it slides down to the abstract sculpture decorating it. "You didn't need to come all the way here to drop this off yourself."

"I was passing by," Carter says. "My team's outside. We're on our way to celebrate."

"Yeah? Where you going?"

Carter grins. "One of your places."

Javon laughs. "You cheap sons of bitches." Javon comps Carter and his team.

Carter looks around. The penthouse dwarves his own apartment. Could probably fit it in here ten times over. "You alone tonight?"

Javon shakes his head. "I was entertaining a couple of shorties in the bedroom when you called to say you were coming up. I've got them on pause right now."

"They from one of your clubs?" Carter says. Javon owns a few strip clubs sprinkled throughout the city. He has some nightclubs, too. Legitimate businesses through which he can launder his money.

"You mean are they strippers?" Javon says. "No, they don't work for me. I got Tyrell to pick them up – I don't know where he found them. Tyrell's in the games room right now. Probably trying to beat his high score or some shit." He turns and calls out. "Yo, Tyrell! Carter's out here. Come say hello."

"I'm probably not gonna be here long," Carter says.

Javon shrugs.

Tyrell emerges from a room at the far end of the penthouse. It's dark in the room, and Tyrell emerges squinting into the light. He carries the smell of weed smoke with him. Javon picks up on it, too.

"You smoking in there?"

"Just a little," Tyrell says.

"How many times I gotta tell you? You wanna smoke, you take it out on the balcony. I don't want you stinking my home up. I bring people here, man. People who don't do that kind of shit."

Tyrell sucks his teeth. He nods at Carter.

Whereas the Javon now could be a totally different person to the Javon Carter first met all those years ago, Tyrell is exactly the same. He still wears his hair in cornrows that hang down in long braids at the back of his head. A silver grill gleams in his mouth. He wears baggy jeans and an oversized Pistons jersey. Javon used to dress similarly, though now – when he's not in a robe – he wears suits. He wears designer clothes. He wears the kind of things that cost three months' worth – or more – of Carter's cop salary.

Tyrell is Javon's right hand. He oversees the day-to-day operations out in the streets for the JJC – the Double J Crew. Double J, of course, standing for Javon Johnson. As he attempts to legitimise himself, Javon tries to keep his name out of the streets as much as possible. He can't move away from it completely, though. It got him where he is, and he worked hard to build up the JJC. Money continues to flow to him from it, and he's not going to cut off that flow any time soon. Not for a while, anyway. Not until his legitimate income surpasses what he's making illegally.

Tyrell looks Javon up and down, seeing what he's wearing. He blinks, like he can hardly believe it. "The hell's that?" he says.

"I had to let Carter in," Javon says. "I'm naked under this. You want me to come out the bedroom dick flopping?"

"I appreciate the robe," Carter says.

"You wear that often?" Tyrell says, not prepared to let it go. "I've never seen it before."

"You're not always here." Javon glares at Tyrell. He's annoyed. He doesn't try to hide it.

Tyrell picks up on the vibe. He raises his hands. "I'm just saying, is all. I've never seen nothing like that before – especially not on *you*. And I've known you a long damn time. I expect to see you in boxer shorts or something, man. A *robe*? Looks bougie, man."

"*Bougie*?" Javon straightens. His tone raises Carter's eyebrows. It looks like it sends a chill down Tyrell's spine. He knows he's crossed a line. Carter watches, to see how it plays out.

At first, Tyrell doesn't say or do anything. He just looks back at Javon, holding his stare. Eventually, he clears his throat and looks away, backing down.

"You need to remember who the fuck you're talking to," Javon says. "You think I've got soft, that it? Throwing around *bougie* like it ain't no big deal."

"I'm sorry," Tyrell says without looking up.

"*Louder*," Javon says. "Do I look soft to you, motherfucker?"

"No," Tyrell says. He raises his head now. "I'm *sorry*," he says. "I wasn't thinking."

Carter stands with his arms crossed, watching them both. To anyone else, the situation would be awkward. To

Carter, it's amusing. He doesn't care about their squabbling, or the tension it has produced. Tyrell might fear Javon, but Carter doesn't. He doesn't fear any of them. He fears no one.

Javon glares at Tyrell a moment longer, then nods his head toward the package. "Carter brought us a gift."

"Okay," Tyrell says. "Who'd it come from?"

Carter shrugs. "Some new players. No one major, not yet, and we might have just crushed them before they ever got a chance to get some real momentum going, but I figured it was a good idea to make you all aware."

Tyrell grunts. "Shame it wasn't the DLB."

Javon laughs. "Ain't we taken enough from those boys?"

"Not while they're still breathing," Tyrell says.

"I'm gonna get on my way," Carter says, taking a step back. "I don't wanna keep the team waiting too long. Enjoy the package, and enjoy the rest of your night."

Javon nods. "Same to you and your people." He motions toward the package. "You'll get your cut soon. Won't take us long to shift this."

"I don't doubt it," Carter says, almost at the elevator. He notices the tension between Javon and Tyrell has not fully dissipated yet. The two men are wary of each other. Their body language is stiff and standoffish. "I'll see you all soon."

8

Tom and Lewin are in Detroit.

It's late, and it's dark, and they're in a quiet part of the city. It's been a long drive. After the stop in Idaho, they had lunch at a diner nearby. Tom made sure to eat light. He didn't want to feel sluggish and heavy. He's been careful not to let his body grow tight while they've been travelling. He's stretched his arms and his legs to stop them from seizing up. He's balled his toes and his fists to keep the blood flowing.

Now, in Detroit, Tom feels sharp. He's on alert. He watches the road, and the mirrors. He looks around, his head and his eyes not staying still.

"You sure this is the right place?" Tom says. "This is a quiet area. *Too* quiet."

Lewin's jaw is clenched tight. It's clear he doesn't like it, either. "This is the way the satnav's taking me. We're just a few blocks away, apparently. Maybe it gets livelier after those few blocks."

"Could do," Tom says.

They pass a burning drum on the sidewalk, a group of homeless people gathered around it for warmth. They watch the truck as it passes them by, and Tom watches them in turn. As they go by, the homeless don't suddenly shuck off their overcoats and reveal themselves as jackers in disguise, brandishing heavy weaponry. They stay right where they are, by the fire, trying to keep warm.

Beyond them, between the silhouettes of two dark buildings, something catches Tom's eye. A blur of movement. He frowns. He keeps watching. They pass another gap between buildings, and another. The same blur, both times. It looks like a bike. A motorized dirt bike. The rider is hunched low on it, but two times Tom sees him looking this way, toward the truck.

It could be nothing. The truck's movement could have caught the rider's eye, much the same way the bike caught Tom's. He feels the hairs on the back of his neck stand up, though. He doesn't dismiss this outright.

Instead, he checks the mirrors. He hasn't seen any other vehicles on this road, save for the ones that are parked, but now he sees movement again. Behind them this time. It comes up fast, and close. Another motorized dirt bike. It gets so close Tom can't see it in the side mirror. It comes periodically back into view, drifting out from behind, or else from the truck turning a little and revealing the rider with its movements.

"What is it?" Lewin says. No doubt he's seen the way Tom is leaning forward, watching the mirror, and the spaces between the buildings. "Is someone following us?" He looks to his own side mirror.

"Could be," Tom says. "For now, just keep driving.

Couple of bikes. That's not going to be enough. If someone's coming at us, they'll need to be in something bigger."

"What should I do?" Lewin says. There's an edge of panic creeping into his voice.

"Just keep doing what you're doing," Tom says. "Don't speed up, don't slow down. Stay calm. Stay the course. Let me worry about everything else."

Lewin does as he's told. He focusses on the road, keeps his eyes off the mirrors.

Tom watches. The dirt bike Tom spied through the buildings has disappeared. It doesn't take long to see where it's gone. It's sped ahead, up near a crossroad. It waits as the truck passes, the rider's head turning with its passage, brazenly watching it go. He pulls back out once it's passed, joining up with the other dirt bike. They both pull back, so that Tom can see them both in the mirror. They've created some distance, but they're not going anywhere. They stick to the truck.

They travel down another block. The dirt bikes stay with them. They don't try anything. They just follow, for now.

Lewin begins to signal at the end of the block. Tom looks ahead. As they turn, they see that the road ahead is blocked.

"Oh, shit," Lewin says. He's breathing hard. He has to stop the truck. "Oh, *shit*. What do I do? What do we do?"

There's a crude barricade across the road made up of what look like thick wooden sawhorses. They couldn't stop the truck from forcing its way through, but this is not what has caused Lewin to stop. It's the Lincoln Navigator parked alongside it, all four of its doors open, its headlights on and shining onto the front of the truck. The men from inside the Navigator are all outside, waiting. They're armed. They carry small automatic guns – Tom spots a Sig Sauer Rattler, and a couple of Uzis. He can't see what the man at the passenger side rear is carrying, but he's sure it's just as lethal.

"Oh my God," Lewin says, swallowing. "I didn't realise it was as bad as this. Holy shit, they're gonna gun us down. We're dead. We're *dead*."

"Stay calm," Tom says. Behind them, the dirt bikes spread out, one on the driver's side and one on the passenger side. They idle on their bikes. They flash handguns.

"Tom, I'm sorry," Lewin says. "I didn't know it was gonna be this bad. I shouldn't have asked you to do this."

"Lewin," Tom says, his voice firm. "Be quiet."

Lewin clamps his mouth shut, but his hands continue to worry at the steering wheel, twisting at it like he's trying to roll up a newspaper.

Tom watches the Navigator. One of the men starts to come forward, holding up his Uzi. He takes his time, motioning for Lewin to open the driver's door so they can talk.

"I think we should give up," Lewin says. "It's all we can do."

"Not gonna happen," Tom says. "Move over. I'm gonna take the wheel."

Lewin looks at him. "What – what are you going to do?"

"I'm going to do what you hired me to do," Tom says. "I'm going to protect this truck. Move over."

9

Tom is banking on the gangbangers not opening fire when he starts driving. First of all, the truck isn't fast, but the cab lurching into motion will catch them by surprise and get by them fast *enough* – they won't be able to hit the people inside. Secondly, they *want* what's in the truck. They want the cargo. They're not going to risk opening up with automatic fire and damaging the load.

Sure enough, as Tom presses his foot down on the accelerator, he catches them off-guard. The man approaching them leaps back out of the way. The surprise gives Tom enough time to get the truck clear. He rams it through the makeshift barricade.

Lewin presses himself up against the door, holding on tight. "Holy shit," he says. "Oh, Christ!"

"I'm going to shake them," Tom says, "and then you can direct me to the store."

"*Shake* them?" Lewin says. "In *this*?"

Tom charges forward. He glances in the mirror. The dirt

bikes are following. The men are returning to the Navigator. They need to get themselves turned around. "I'm gonna shake them literally," Tom says, and he swings the wheel to the left, toward the dirt bike coming up on the driver's side. The truck doesn't connect, but the rider panics. He loses control. His bike goes down and both it and the rider slide across the road and bump up onto the sidewalk.

"We can't lose them in this," Tom says, "so I'm gonna have to hurt them."

Lewin stares at Tom wide eyed, looking at him like he's a stranger, as if he's seeing him for the very first time and wondering what he's doing here in the cab of his truck, driving it.

"Do you own this truck?" Tom says.

"It's provided by the company," Lewin says.

Tom spins the wheel, taking a corner. "Will they dock you if it gets damaged?"

"Yes."

"Then I'll do my best to keep it in one piece."

Tom speeds ahead. The road is not so quiet here. There are other vehicles around, but it's late and there aren't many of them. He blares the horn, swerving to get around them. Most of the cars react to the sound, and the sight. They slam on their brakes and quickly pull to the side to get out of the way.

In the mirror, Tom spots the Navigator catching up. It blares its horn too and flashes its lights. Tom thinks he hears a gunshot – fired up into the air to show they mean business and they want people out of their way.

The biker who fell has not returned. The biker who remains stays on their tail, but he's wary of getting too close. Tom gets the truck away from where the road is at its busiest.

He heads back toward where they first found the barricade, where the roads were quiet and the buildings looked abandoned. The Navigator and the bike stay close.

"Get my bag," Tom says.

"What?" Lewin doesn't understand.

"Get my bag – it's at your feet."

Lewin reaches down for it.

"There's a gun inside – take it out."

Lewin's eyes bulge. He doesn't reach into the bag.

"You don't need to use it," Tom says. "Just get it out."

Lewin does. Tom looks ahead. He sees a stretch of road ahead of them, lined by dark buildings on either side. He spots the burning drum they passed earlier, surrounded by homeless. He slows the truck. He doesn't want to get too close to them. Doesn't want to put them in danger. "Get ready to take the wheel."

Lewin holds the Beretta away from himself. He's terrified of the gun.

The truck slowing, the remaining biker sees an opportunity. He speeds up, coming down the side. Tom waits for him to get close. When he does, Tom slams the brakes. The truck does not instantly stop. It's too big and too heavy. It slides forward, tyres screeching. The biker overshoots, as Tom intended. He swings open the driver's door. The rider can't stop in time. He hits the door and flies back off the bike, landing hard on the road.

The Navigator has slammed its brakes to avoid plowing into the back of the truck. Tom pulls the door closed, slamming it. He doesn't get back behind the wheel. He keeps moving. "Take over," he tells Lewin, sliding past him and taking the Beretta. "Start moving – I'll catch up."

Lewin scrambles across to the driver's seat. Tom opens

the passenger door and drops to the ground. He holds the Beretta up and heads to the back of the truck. The Navigator is angled toward the driver's side – they can't see him coming.

The truck starts rolling forward. It's slow to get going – Tom knows this. He was expecting this. Banking on it. The truck passes him. The Navigator will be able to see him now. He doesn't give them a chance to react. The four men remain inside the vehicle. Tom opens fire upon it. He fires twice at the hood, just to spook them, and once into the centre of the windshield to make it hard for them to see, then concentrates his fire upon the wheels. One of his bullets bounces off the hood and cracks the windshield further. The passenger tyre pops first, then the driver's side. It's enough. Tom turns, runs, pumping his arms and legs as fast as he can, and catches up to the still-open passenger side door. He leaps up, grabbing hold of the door, and climbs inside. He slams it shut and watches the mirror. He sees the four men jumping out of the Navigator. A couple of them raise their weapons and fire off a few rounds in frustration and anger, but the other two don't bother. Tom sees one of them pull out a phone, press it to his ear.

The two men don't shoot for long. There's no point. The truck is leaving them behind.

Tom puts his Beretta back into his bag. He sits back, and sees Lewin looking at him.

"You're *insane*," Lewin says, and then he bursts out laughing. "You crazy son of a bitch!"

Tom holds out his hands. "I always see a job through," he says.

Lewin laughs hard.

"Let's not get carried away," Tom says. "We're not clear

yet. I saw one of them get on his phone. There could be another blockade set up somewhere around here."

Lewin stops laughing. He gets serious. "We're gonna have to take the long way around," he says, reconfiguring the route on his satnav. "Seven minutes, it says."

The two of them remain vigilant for the seven minutes, but no one else appears. There are no further blockades, and no one follows them. They reach the store. Just a few blocks away, and this part of the city has more life. The roads are busier, despite the time. The store is lit up like a beacon. Lewin manoeuvres around the back, to the loading bay. He reverses up to it. This area is well lit. There are security cameras. Tom doesn't expect any kind of ambush to occur here.

Lewin kills the engine and opens his door. "You just wait here," he says. "I'll go let them know I'm here."

"You don't need a hand unloading?" Tom says.

Lewin grins at him. "Shit," he says, "you've done more than enough already. Let me finish up here and then I'll get the rest of your money. Man, you earned it."

10

Calvin didn't see it all, but he's seen enough.

At the corner, he was getting ready to leave when he saw a car pull up. A Lincoln. A couple of the guys at the corner got inside. That wasn't all. The Lincoln was trailed by a couple of dirt bikes. They sat and idled while the two men got inside, and then situated themselves. The Lincoln didn't set off straight away. He saw movement inside. The rear windows were blacked out, but he could see how the men in front handed things back to the two men they'd just picked up. It was too far for Calvin to see what was handed over. And then the small convoy set off. Calvin was curious. He checked the time. It was getting late. Ruth might already be home, wondering where he was. But he had two choices – he could either go home, or he could follow. It might lead him to something of interest. Something worthwhile. It might even lead him to a face he's been trying to find.

So he followed.

He just had his bike, and it was hard to keep up, but he

always managed to keep them in sight. Other, slower traffic helped. Stop signs and traffic lights helped. It was better for Calvin to keep his distance, though. He couldn't get too close. A kid on a bike, following, they'd easily spot him. They'd get suspicious. They'd confront him.

That never happened, though. He was never able to get close enough for them to see. When they finally stopped, in an almost-abandoned, rundown neighbourhood, Calvin held back, concealing himself down between two buildings, same as he had back at the corner he was watching. The men in the Lincoln went around to the back of the vehicle and took things out of it, setting them up across the road like a makeshift barricade. Calvin frowned, watching with interest, wondering what was happening.

And then he started to panic. Was this a setup for an ambush? Was there about to be a battle, a shooting? He felt sick suddenly. He didn't want to see anything like that. He didn't want to see anyone get shot. All he could think about was his parents. About what had happened to them. He didn't want to see that happen to someone else.

The dirt bikes didn't hang around. They revved loudly, then raced off into the night, disappearing.

Calvin couldn't move without being seen. He stayed where he was, concealed in the dark, but feeling his breathing grow heavier and harsher. He wiped sweat from his brow, despite the night's cold.

And then he saw why the barricade was erected. He saw the truck appear. Saw the men from the Lincoln try to jack it. He saw the chase.

But it's the chase he didn't see all of. Again, on his bike, it was hard for him to keep up. He's not even sure why he tried to follow, but a part of him wanted to see how it all played out. To see what happened. If the men from the Lincoln were successful, if they stole from the truck, would they take it to the man he was looking for?

Calvin saw an opportunity for answers, and he pursued it.

The chase turned around on itself, and that's when Calvin was able to see its climax. The way the white man jumped down from the truck and shot out the Lincoln's front tyres, and then the truck was able to get away.

Calvin's breathing is heavy after pedalling so hard, trying to catch up. He's further down the road now, behind where the shooting occurred. He's close enough he can hear the men from the Lincoln, though. Most of them are cursing loudly. They stomp their feet and kick at a streetlight. One of them is on the phone. This is the one Calvin strains to hear. He doesn't catch the start of his side of the conversation, and he can't hear the person at the other end at all.

What he *does* hear, is this: "– had some guy with him, I dunno, but he was armed. Shot out our tyres. Dude could handle himself. Yeah, I don't think he was the driver. Well, when he jumped back into the truck he got in on the passenger side. I don't know. Yeah, yeah, maybe. What you want us to do, anyway? You wanna let this one go, or –" He falls silent for a moment, and Calvin thinks he can hear a raised voice coming from the other end. The man on the phone clears his throat. "No, no, you're right. Yeah. No, you're right. I get it. Is there anyone else close? Anyone that can catch them up? No, we're all outta commission – yeah, even the bikes. Shit, *especially* the bikes. Okay. Just a block away? Got you. We'll start running."

The speaker hangs up the phone and turns to the others – the ones still standing, at least. The ones who were inside the Lincoln. "Yo, listen up – we gotta *move*. Leave those two –" He motions toward the two bikers; the one who is close, and the vague direction of the other. "We'll have to come back for them. Let's *go*." He starts running, and the others don't question it. They follow.

Calvin deliberates. He *does* question things. He questions his next move. He looks toward the fallen biker. He lies very still. He's still breathing. Calvin can see the rise and fall of his chest. He's all the way out, though. Unconscious, and could be for a while.

Calvin bites his lip. He stares at the retreating backs of the four men, running as fast as they can down the block. He's still on his bike. He starts to follow.

11

Lewin pulls into the motel parking lot, blowing relieved air. The truck is empty. The cargo has reached its destination.

"Again, I can't thank you enough," he says.

"That's what the money was for," Tom says.

Lewin laughs. He peers out at the motel. "You're sure this will do?"

"I asked a guy at the store, and he said it was cheap, but safe. It'll do. I'm not planning on hanging around Detroit for long."

Lewin is not heading straight back. He's going to park up at a truck stop on the outskirts of the city for a couple of days. Rest up before he starts the long drive home. Otherwise, he said, he would have offered to give Tom a ride elsewhere.

"It'll be fine," Tom says. "A night's sleep and then I'm on my way."

"You thought about where you're going next?" Lewin says.

"Doesn't matter," Tom says.

"Sure," Lewin says, smiling.

"I'm gonna need a car to get there, though. That's job number one tomorrow."

"Money not a problem for you, Tom?"

"Sometimes it is," Tom says. "Not right now, though. I have what you gave me. That'll get me something decent enough to drive until the wheels fall off. That's all I need."

"It's a hell of a way to live."

"It is what it is. And I have savings. I could settle if I wanted. I just don't want to."

Lewin nods at this. It's a sentiment he can appreciate. It probably reminds him of his father again. "Then I guess this is goodbye." He holds out a hand.

They shake. "Until the next time you find me walking by the side of the road," Tom says.

"Until the next time I need to go somewhere dangerous," Lewin says.

"You've got my number," Tom says. "If I'm close, I'll come running. And hey – find out who's selling the info on your routes. You find that, you shouldn't be in that kind of trouble again."

Lewin salutes with two fingers. "I'll do my best."

Tom gets out of the truck and takes a step back as Lewin pulls forward to leave the parking lot. He flashes his signal lights in farewell. Tom raises a hand to wave. When Lewin is gone, Tom makes his way to the reception with its glowing neon 'vacancy' sign. Before he enters the small office, he pauses, something in his peripheral catching his attention. He looks toward the road, the opposite direction to where Lewin has just gone. There's a black van there. It's parked, but its engine is running and its lights are on. Tom can't see inside through the dark windows, but he can feel eyes. It could just be his imagination, but it rarely is.

He gets the keys to a room and leaves the reception. The van is still there, pulled to the side of the road. It's turned its lights and engine off now. Tom doesn't stare. He watches it out the corner of his eye as he crosses the parking lot and heads up the stairs to his room. The van is off to his right. As he unlocks the door, he takes a casual look around. He thinks he'll be able to see the van from inside.

When he's in, he locks the door but keeps the lights off for now. He goes to the far end of the nearest window and peers around the closed curtains. He can see the van. It remains in darkness for now, but he can't guarantee that it's empty.

Stepping away, he hits the light and looks the rest of the room over. A bed, and a television mounted on the wall. It's cheap and it's basic. Tom goes into the bathroom. He opens the window and looks out. There's a fire escape. It wasn't clear from the front of the building that this was here. This is good to know. Anyone that attempts to come up to the room will likely only come via the front, unless they know this motel already.

Tom closes the window and takes a seat at the foot of the bed, opening his backpack. He leaves the light on for now. If anyone is going to come, they'll do it when it's dark. If anyone is going to come, Tom will be ready for them. He pulls out his Beretta, pops the magazine, and reloads the magazine from one of the boxes of bullets in the bottom of the bag. His bag contains burner phones. At the tops of some of them, names written on pieces of paper are stuck on with tape. Cindy, Zeke, his father, a couple of others. He checks them all. No missed calls. No messages. No news is good news. The batteries on them are running low, though. He'll have to find some time to charge them back up. Tonight is not the night, however. Not with that van sitting outside.

If the van is a problem, he thinks about who could be inside. The gangbangers who attempted to jack Lewin's truck, most likely. He can't imagine why it would be anyone else, but he's been surprised before.

He keeps the Beretta out, placing it on the bedside table within easy reach. Reaching into his backpack, he brings out his KA-BAR. He slips its sheath onto his belt, then zips the bag closed again. He puts it next to the bathroom door, where he can grab it with ease on his way past.

He remains on the edge of the bed, but he positions himself so he's facing toward the door now, and closer to the gun. He takes deep breaths and waits for a realistic amount of time to pass before he turns off the light. If anyone is watching, he doesn't want them to be suspicious of his actions via his timings. He wants them to think everything is how they want it to be. That'll make them careless.

He turns off the light and returns to the window. He peers toward the van from the furthest side of the window, careful not to twitch the curtains. The van is still there. Tom watches it, and waits. Two hours, minimum, and then if nothing has happened, he'll set up a makeshift alert and then try to get some sleep. But until then, he stays on watch.

12

Carter grits his teeth and clenches his jaw to stifle a yawn. He doesn't want to look tired to his team. Tiredness is another form of weakness, and he will never allow himself to appear weak to them. When they see him, they need to see an unstoppable machine. A freight train. The fucking Terminator.

They're at one of Javon's strip clubs. The drinks and dances are comped. Carter and his people know the staff – including the dancers – roll their eyes when they come around. Not just because they're cops, though that probably plays a role too, but because they don't have to pay. And because they don't have to pay, they don't tip, either. Carter isn't sure why the staff care. It's not like what people spend in here keeps the door open and the lights on. These clubs run on Javon's money, laundering all of his dirty cash obtained through the JJC. They'll never close down unless Javon decides that it's time to close them down.

They're here to celebrate. Another successful raid. Another successful heist, depending on how it's looked at.

He sits in a cordoned-off area with Darren and Delia. Anthony and Nick are getting dances in a back room. Carter looks around the club. There are people in, but it's not the busiest that Carter has ever seen it. People look their way, look into the VIP area, and wonder who they are. It probably doesn't cross their mind that these people are cops. The Gang Control Task Force, to be precise. Or, maybe some of them do. They make the news often enough, bragging of the collars they have made and showing off the spoils they have recovered.

Well, *some* of the spoils.

Delia takes a drink from her bottle. She clears her throat. "Greg looked shaken," she says, to both of them. She has to raise her voice to be heard. The DJ plays J Dilla instrumentals for the girls dancing on the stage, swinging round the poles. When the task force first entered, he was playing drill music. Carter isn't a big fan of drill. He prefers the older stuff. J Dilla is more to his taste.

Carter shrugs with regards to Greg.

Darren laughs. "He'll be fine," he says. "Tougher than he looks. He'll drop a couple of yellowjackets, or whatever it is he's on these days, and he'll be right as rain first thing in the morning."

"He seen anything that intense before?" Delia says.

"Not around us," Darren says.

"He'll keep his mouth shut," Carter says. "If he doesn't..." He trails off. They all understand.

"Greg gets it," Darren says. "He's smarter than he looks, too. He's not gonna say shit."

"I'll hold you to that," Carter says. "He runs his mouth, you're gonna be the one to shut him up."

Darren holds up his hands, like *that won't be a problem*.

Anthony returns from his lap-dance in the back. He's wearing a satisfied grin, that kind that usually comes onto his face post a hand- or blowjob.

Darren sees it. "I know we get comped, but I hope you at least tipped her for that smile she put on your face."

Anthony laughs and drops into a seat, picking up a bottle from the table.

"You not seeing your girl tonight?" Carter says, looking at him across the table.

"Shit, she should be tucked up in bed right now," Anthony says. "She's no night owl. She goes to bed way too early for me."

"Dreaming sweet dreams of you, huh?" Delia says.

"Who else?" Anthony says, and laughs.

"You keep that girl sweet," Carter says. He's not laughing and joking like the rest of them. Anthony sees his face is serious, and he quickly gets serious himself. He takes a drink and nods his head. "She's important to us," Carter says. "Last thing we want is for you to piss her off."

"I know," Anthony says. "I know, I get it."

"I'm just saying, anything that happens here in the club, in that backroom, she can't find out about it. Never. You keep her on the line."

Anthony nods. He's not grinning anymore. His post-nut glow has dissipated. "You can count on me," he says.

Carter grunts. He finishes his beer and then gets to his feet. "I'm gonna call it a night. When Nick shows his face again, tell him I said goodbye. I'll see the rest of you in the morning."

They all say their goodbyes. Carter makes his way through the club, watching the women dancing on the stage as he goes. He could hang around, if he wanted. He could get a dance too, and head into the backroom where the girls are pliant for the GCTF, and anyone else who is a friend of Javon and the JJC. He doesn't, though. He leaves and heads home to his apartment. It's late, and it's dark, and it's cold, and it's already been a long day.

But it's not over for Carter. Much as he'd like to, he's not planning on sleeping just yet.

He drives through Detroit, focussing himself. Psyching himself up. His day is not over. He reminds himself of this, over and over. A mantra. It keeps his eyes wide. Keeps him wired. He watches the streets as he passes them. It's not so bad around here, where he lives. It's a cleaner, more affluent part of town. The crime rate here is low. Cops live here – not cops with families, but single men who live in one-bedroom apartments, like himself. Cops nonetheless.

He hates this city. He's been here too long. Carter isn't Detroit born and bred like the rest of the task force. He's from Florida. He's used to warmer climes. It's the cold that he hates most of all. It chills his blood. It seeps into his bones. It drains the life from him.

He was transferred here ten years ago. Ten years he's been in Detroit. He started out in SWAT. That was down in Florida, originally. Then he came up to Detroit, and spent another four years doing that. After he left SWAT, he was granted his own task force. The Gang Control Task Force. He was a shining beacon of hope for the city. The white knight in shining armour, coming to town to finally get these wild gangs under control.

Carter never had any interest in getting them under control. He just needed to see the way the land lay. To work out who was running things, and whom to throw his lot in with.

Enter the JJC.

Enter Javon Johnson.

Carter is sick of Detroit. He's sick of being a cop. He's sick of seeing gangbangers drive around in newer cars that his. Sick of seeing them living in homes and apartments bigger than his own. He's been sick of this all for a long, long time.

Enter Javon, and the means for Carter to do something about it.

Carter's been saving his money. Hiding it away, ready for when he's going to split town. Head back south, to somewhere hot. He already knows where he's going to go. In his kitchen, next to the refrigerator, there is a poster. A sun-kissed woman in a lime-green bikini, striking a pose on the beach, palm trees stabbing into the sky behind her. In the top right corner, in slanted yellow writing, the place: *Miami*.

That's his goal.

Carter hydrates. He only had the one beer. He wasn't even buzzed when he left the club. He goes through to his bedroom and takes a seat at the foot of his bed. From the bottom drawer of his bedside table, he takes out his works. He removes a needle. He keeps them in a nylon kit. Wrapping rubber tubing high around his left arm, he finds a vein. It doesn't take long. He's very vascular. He pumps steroids into his blood. He takes a deep breath and returns to the living room.

The room is spartan. There is a sofa he rarely sits in in front of a television he rarely watches. In the corner of the room hangs a heavy bag. Close to this there is a weight bench, and his weights. Carter takes off his T-shirt and stretches out his chest. He keeps on his jeans.

It's late, and he's tired, but he won't stop. He can't stop. He goes to the heavy bag first. He doesn't bother with gloves.

Strikes it with bare fists. The calluses on his knuckles are thick. He punches until sweat is running down his body. When he is done here, he will hit the weights. Then, and only then, will he allow himself a few hours of sleep.

He doesn't have to be here forever. He *won't* be here forever. He and Javon will help each other. Through Javon he will make his money. Then, when he can, he'll split. Miami beckons. He'll split, and he'll live the rest of his life in the sunshine, surrounded by bikini-clad women like the one on the poster. In the future, all of his workouts will be on the beach.

This is what drives him.

This is what keeps him going.

13

The van has remained stationary, but Tom continues to watch it.

He calls Lewin to check in. "Missing me already?" Lewin says when he answers.

"Has anyone followed you?" Tom says.

Lewin sounds alarmed. "Followed me? What do you mean?"

"A car or a van, anyone hanging around your truck that you don't like the looks of?"

Lewin doesn't answer, but Tom can hear him moving around, checking. He comes back on the line. "All I see are other trucks."

"Okay," Tom says. "That's good. Call me if that changes."

"Tom, what's going on? Are you all right?"

"I'm fine," Tom says. "It's nothing. I was just checking in, making sure you got out there okay."

"Well, okay. Your tone can be blunt though, buddy. You had me spooked there. Sounded like you were in trouble."

Tom sees movement at the van. It's coming from inside.

The front and rear doors are opening. "No," he says. "No trouble. Good night, Lewin."

He recognises a couple of the men. He saw them through the windshield of the Navigator as he shot out its front tyres. There are five men coming toward the motel. The driver's door didn't open. The driver could have stayed behind. Six men total. The five coming his way are armed, carrying their weapons low by their sides to keep them concealed for now.

Tom thinks about Lewin. About how he has not been followed, and yet these men are coming after him, making their way to his motel room. He considers this. They've probably realised the truck is empty now, and therefore worthless to them. Though for them to know Tom is here, they must have followed it for a while. Could be they *saw* the truck being emptied. And then they saw Tom being dropped off here. Recognised him as the shooter. The one who prevented their robbery. Decided to stick around rather than pursue the truck, looking for revenge.

Whatever the reason, Tom isn't hanging around. He leaves the window and grabs his Beretta. He tucks it down the back of his jeans as he heads toward the bathroom. He scoops up his backpack on the way past and hooks his arms through its straps.

Tom waits by the bathroom window, opening it wide, ready to slip out. While he's been watching the van, he's already resolved he's not going to engage. There's no point. There's nothing to be gained from it. He's already foiled their theft, and he's not planning on sticking around Detroit for much longer. This would be a fight for the sake of a fight.

Some people have told Tom that he's bloodthirsty. Some have said that he is addicted to war. Maybe they're right. He'd like to think they're not. This is a battle he's walking away from. Proof to them, and perhaps to himself, that war does not define him.

When he hears footsteps outside his door, he checks that no one has come to the fire escape at the back, and then he steps out onto it. He pushes the window closed behind him, then he climbs down the ladder and prepares to walk away.

He takes his time, passing around the motel. He pauses at the far corner and looks toward his room. He sees the five men. They test the handle, then they kick open the door and charge in, weapons raised.

Tom grins to himself, then starts to turn. He doesn't get all the way. Something over at the van catches his attention. Something that makes his blood run cold. Something that means he can't leave, not just yet.

14

Calvin has seen the five men leave the van and cross the road to the motel. He caught up to them late, so he doesn't know who's inside and what the problem is. He assumed the van was coming after the truck, but there's no sign of the truck here.

That doesn't matter, though. What matters is, he thinks he's found an opportunity. His search has been all about waiting for opportunities, and one may have just presented itself to him. Five men have crossed to the motel, but there were six men inside the van. The driver did not get out with the others. He's still inside. Sitting, watching, waiting. He has his window down. Calvin can see him. His jaw works, like he's chewing on something.

Calvin takes a deep breath. He's told himself, these last two years, that if an opportunity comes, he won't waste it. He can't get nervous or back down. He has to seize it. Steeling himself, he pulls the picture from his pocket and goes to the open window.

"Excuse me," he says.

The driver gives a start in his seat. His eyes bulge as he turns to Calvin. "Jesus Christ, kid! The fuck are you thinking, sneaking up on me like that?"

"I just need to ask you a question," Calvin says.

The driver waves a dismissive hand, looking back toward the motel. "Get outta here."

Calvin holds the picture tight. "It's just one question."

The driver shoots Calvin a look, but his attention is on the motel.

Calvin doesn't back down. "I just need you to look at this picture –"

"You're on my last nerve, boy," the driver says, glaring at Calvin now.

Calvin tries to hold up the picture. The driver ignores it, pushing the door open and stepping out. As he steps out, though, he finally sees the picture. Catches a glimpse of it. The glimpse turns into a double-take, and then he zeroes in. The man in the picture, snapped unaware as he speeds away in a stolen car. The picture has been zoomed in and cropped to show only the man's face. The driver blinks at the image. Calvin sees recognition. He feels a ping of hope in his chest.

But then the driver pulls out a handgun, and points it into Calvin's face. "I told you to get the fuck out of here," he says. "You shoulda done as I said."

Calvin is frozen to the spot. He stares down the barrel of the gun. His heart hammers in his chest. His throat constricts. It feels like he's choking. It's hard to breathe.

The driver nods toward the picture. "Where'd you get that?" he says.

Calvin can't answer. He can't speak. Can't move. Can't think.

One thought *does* come to Calvin. In this moment, he understands what a mistake he has made. He has made his way into this world, and he was not prepared for it. Not like he thought he was. Years of boxing training, he knows he can handle himself in a fight. A *fight*. A fair fight. One on one. Fists. No weapons. But that is not what it's like in this world. There is no such thing as *fair*. These people are not going to box with him. They'll put a bullet in him like it's nothing, and then they'll get on with their lives, forgetting all about him even as he lies dying, bleeding out in the gutter.

His fists cannot match up to a gun.

He's going to die here. He's going to die in the street, just like his parents did.

He thinks of Ruth. His eyes burn.

"A minute ago I couldn't shut you up," the driver says, his words cutting through the fog occupying the inside of Calvin's skull. "Where'd you get that picture? What is he to you?"

Still, Calvin cannot respond.

The driver shakes his head. "I ain't got time for you." He raises the gun, and for a moment Calvin thinks how the man is not going to shoot him. He's just going to beat him instead. He's going to bring the barrel of the gun down across his face and head, bloodying and scarring him. Except, maybe he *will* still shoot him. Once he's on the ground. Maybe he's going to beat answers out of Calvin, with regards to why he has this picture. The man clearly knows who the subject of the photo is. Calvin thought *he* would be the one capable of beating answers out of people. That's why he boxed. That's why he's trained so hard all of these years.

It's all been for nothing.

The driver doesn't get to strike Calvin. Doesn't get to

shoot him, either. Doesn't get to do anything. There's a blur to Calvin's left, and then it's in front of him, and then the driver is on the ground.

15

Tom saw the driver of the van pull a gun on the kid. Without thinking, he ran.

And now he throws himself into the driver, reaching out to force his gun – a Glock – high into the air in case it goes off during their collision. It does not. Tom drives him up into the side of the van. The driver nearly crumples to the ground with the impact. The wind has no doubt been knocked out of him. Tom doesn't give him a chance to fall or to recover. He twists his wrist, removing the gun from his hand, then grabs him by the back of the head and slams him repeatedly into the side of the van until he goes limp. Tom lets him fall.

Tom looks at the kid. He's frozen, eyes wide. Before Tom can speak to him, he hears noise behind, from back at the motel. At his room.

Tom glances back, sees the five men who went into his room exiting it now. They're looking his way. They've seen what has happened. They're running.

Tom looks back at the kid. He can see a bicycle nearby, propped against the wall. "That your bike?"

The kid's mouth works, but he can't speak. Instead, he nods.

"Throw it in the back of the van – let's go, *move*!"

With a start, the kid runs toward the bike. Tom looks into the van. The driver has left the keys in the ignition. He jumps behind the wheel and starts the engine. Behind, he hears the kid throw his bike into the back, then slam the doors shut. Tom sees him in the mirror, running down the side to get in.

Tom looks toward the five. They're on their way, raising their guns, preparing to fire. As the kid slams the door shut after him, Tom slams down on the accelerator and races down the road, skidding to the side as he takes the first right-hand turn he sees, getting them clear of the motel.

16

The kid's name is Calvin Styles.

Getting his name wasn't easy, but he eventually gave it up after Tom shared his own. Trying to find where he lives so Tom can take him home is proving more challenging.

"You live nearby?"

"Just let me out here," Calvin says. "I can make my own way."

"I'd like to do that, Calvin, and ordinarily I would, no problem. But you just had a gun pointed in your face. Your hands are still shaking."

Calvin balls his fists. "They'll stop. I'm fine."

"I'm sure they will. But the main thing is, the two of us are being chased right now. It might not seem like it, seeing as how I'm able to drive the limit and we're not having to duck and weave through the traffic, but we have stolen their van. They're not gonna be happy about that. And their driver won't be unconscious forever, and he got a good look at you. I drop you off here, it could be that those men back there will catch up to you. You think you can outrun them on your bike?"

"You took their van," Calvin says. "They're on foot. We've got a big head start on them. They're not going to catch us up."

"I thought that earlier tonight," Tom says. "But they still managed to find me."

"There was another van nearby. They called it in, followed you from there."

Tom looks at him.

Calvin realises what he's said. He lowers himself in the seat.

"You were there?" Tom says.

"I wasn't – I wasn't *with* them," Calvin says.

"I didn't think you were."

Calvin sighs. "I saw what happened. Most of it, anyway."

"And you decided to follow them following me?"

Calvin doesn't answer.

"What was it you were showing the driver of the van?" Tom says. "Why was he pointing a gun at you?"

"I don't know why he was pointing his gun. I guess I was pissing him off."

"It wasn't anything to do with the picture?"

"I – I don't know. I think he was going to do it anyway."

"Are you going to tell me what the picture *is*?"

Calvin doesn't respond, and this feels like answer enough.

"Why were you out there?" Tom says. "These are dangerous men, Calvin. Why were you following them? What were you trying to find out?"

"I was looking for someone, all right?" Calvin says,

raising his voice. "It's got nothing to do with you, man, so don't worry about it. Just forget it."

Calvin turns away, looking out the window. He folds his arms. Tom watches him out the corner of his eye. He checks the mirrors, too. No one is following them. He checks the fuel gauge. The van has plenty of gas.

"Listen," Tom says, "I can drive in circles all night, or you can tell me where to go. It's getting late. Don't you want to go home? Won't your parents be worried about you?"

Calvin stiffens at this. Tom notices.

"What is it?" he says. "Is that who you were trying to find? Your parents?"

Calvin wheels on him. "My parents are *dead*." He sits back, staring straight ahead now. "Just go straight," he says. "I'll direct you."

"I'm sorry to hear that," Tom says. He drives straight, as Calvin instructs. He thinks. Connects dots, though they may be loose. After a moment, he says, "Did those men back there have something to do with their deaths?"

"Not this right, but the next," Calvin says. He doesn't answer Tom's question.

Tom doesn't push it. If Calvin doesn't want to talk, he can't force him.

He hears a buzzing. Calvin shifts his weight and pulls out his phone. "Ah, shit," he mutters.

Tom glances over. He sees the name 'Ruth'. The call ends. Calvin is too slow to answer. On the screen, Tom sees that this is not the first time she has called. The screen says that Calvin has six missed calls. They could have happened back outside the motel, while they were busy, and Calvin would not have noticed. They could have happened at any point tonight, while he's been riding around on his bike, following dangerous men for reasons he refuses to elaborate upon.

"I need to call my sister back," Calvin says. "Just – just don't say anything, okay?"

"Sure," Tom says.

Calvin looks at him like he has his doubts, then he calls Ruth back. "Hey, Ruth – yeah, yeah, I know it's late. I just got held up with Noah. What? Yeah, if you call him he'll tell you I was there."

Tom can't hear everything that Ruth says. Her voice is not raised. Tom imagines she's probably worried more than anything else. Calvin points for Tom to make a left. Tom does. The phone is not pressed so tight to Calvin's face anymore, and Tom can hear Ruth's voice a little clearer.

"Are you in a car?" she says.

Calvin clears his throat. "Uh, yeah."

"Who's driving?"

Calvin looks at Tom. Tom looks back at him.

"Just – just a friend."

"What friend?" Ruth says. "I know your friends."

"It's Noah," Calvin says. It would be clear to anyone that he's lying.

"I know it's not Noah," Ruth says. "Who you in a car with right now, Calvin?"

"He's just – just – it's just some guy. Some white guy."

There's a pause. "And what's this white guy's name?"

"It's Tom."

"Tom who?"

"Tom Rollins. You're not gonna know him, Ruth. I don't think he's from around here."

"How the hell do *you* know him?" She's starting to sound

exasperated now, close to anger. "Damn it, put him on the phone, Calvin."

"He's driving."

"I don't care."

Calvin hesitates. "Listen, we'll be back in like, five minutes. I'll see you soon." He hangs up.

"She sounds worried," Tom says.

"I don't make a habit of riding around with strangers," Calvin says. "She's just – just alarmed is all."

"Do you make a habit of confronting armed men?"

Calvin doesn't respond to this.

"Who's Noah?" Tom says.

"He's my coach."

"Your coach?"

"I box," Calvin says.

"Oh yeah? How long have you been doing that for?"

"Few years."

"You had any fights yet?"

"Not yet. Noah said he didn't want to rush me. He says I've got promise."

"Yeah? Maybe I'll see you on PPV one day."

Calvin makes a noise. It could be a snort, it could be a laugh. He continues to give directions. It doesn't take long for them to reach the apartment block. Calvin's face drops as it comes into view.

"*Shit*," he says.

There's a woman standing out front. She's young, but looks about ten years older than Calvin. She's wearing a thick coat to keep herself warm while she's outside, and she stands with her arms folded.

"Your sister?" Tom says.

"Just drop me here," Calvin says.

Ruth has seen the van. She's cocked her head at it, has seen Calvin inside. She starts walking over.

"I don't think that'll make a difference," Tom says. He keeps the van rolling, stopping only as he pulls alongside Ruth.

Tom winds down the window. She looks him over, an eyebrow raised. Her curly hair is tied up on top of her head. She has high cheekbones and almond-shaped eyes. She's very attractive, but she doesn't look very happy right now. "Tom Rollins?" she says.

Tom offers his hand. "That's me."

She looks at the hand as if surprised by it, but then she takes it and they shake.

"You must be Ruth Styles."

"That's right," she says. "Why is my brother riding in a van with you?" She looks past Tom, toward Calvin.

"I won't lie to you," Tom says. "We found ourselves in some mutual trouble, and we were able to help each other out of it."

She frowns. "What do you mean by that?" But before he can answer, she looks back at Calvin. "What have you been doing? Where have you been? Calvin, we've *talked* about this."

Calvin is silent.

"Calvin, look at me," Ruth says. "This needs to stop. You're going to get yourself killed."

Tom frowns at this. Ruth is clearly upset. Something that her brother is up to, something that he's done, concerns her.

"Mr. Rollins, will you step out of the van and talk to me, please?" She takes a step back.

Tom gets out of the van. He looks around, checking to make sure no one has followed them. The road behind them is clear. Ruth moves to her right, away from the open window and her brother. "What happened?" she says. "Please, just...just tell me what happened. Don't cover for him."

"I don't fully know," Tom says. "I saw a man pointing a gun at your brother."

Ruth gasps. A hand goes to her mouth.

"I don't know why, and Calvin wouldn't tell. Far as I could see, Calvin was showing him a picture. Maybe the picture upset the guy, I don't know. I didn't see what it was."

"Calvin showed the man a picture, and the guy pointed a gun at him?" Ruth says. "Who was the guy? What was happening – where was this?"

Tom gives her a condensed version of how the man came to be stalking him at his motel.

Ruth blinks. "But what does this have to do with Calvin? Where does he come into it?"

"I don't know," Tom says. "I think he might have been following them on his bike. Do you know what the picture might have been?"

Ruth bites her lip. "I'm going to take my brother inside," she says. Tom notices she's avoided the question. He thinks she probably *does* know what the picture is, and potentially what her brother was up to putting himself in danger like that. "Thank you for helping him, Mr. Rollins. And for bringing him home."

"Call me Tom. Calvin mentioned that your parents are deceased. Are you his guardian? He live with you?"

She nods.

"How old are you?"

"I'm twenty-seven."

"And how old is Calvin? Sixteen?"

She nods. "That's right."

"Do you have any other siblings?"

"It's just the two of us. I'm aware of the age difference. Our parents thought I was going to be an only child. Calvin was an unexpected surprise. I'm not saying he was an accident – our parents tried for a second child. They tried so long, and failed so long, that they didn't think it would ever happen."

"It's very noble of you, to step up and be his guardian. You're only eleven years older than him."

"What else was I going to do? I wasn't going to let him go into a group home, or foster care, and hope he ended up with a good family."

"What do you do to support the two of you? It can't be easy."

She frowns at him. "Why are you asking so many questions?"

"I'm just curious. I'm not intending to pry."

She pauses a beat, then sighs and says, "I'm a cleaner. When I'm not cleaning, I'm studying."

"Oh, yeah? To do what?"

"To be a nurse."

"That's impressive."

"I'm tired all the time," Ruth says, looking back at him. "But we all have to do what we have to do."

Tom nods. "Listen, Ruth, I can see that you're upset. You're worried about your brother. Is he in trouble? Are the two of you in danger?"

Ruth looks at him. "No," she says. "We're not. Neither of us."

Tom tilts his head, but Ruth moves away.

"Calvin," she says through the open window. "Come on, let's go."

Calvin gets out of the van and goes to the back to retrieve his bike. He pushes it past Tom, not looking at him as he goes.

"Thank you again, Mr. Rollins – *Tom*," Ruth says. She hesitates, wrapping her arms around herself. Behind her, Calvin continues pushing his bike toward the apartment building. Ruth clears her throat. She nods at him. "Goodbye."

Tom nods back. Ruth turns and follows her brother.

Tom gets into the van. He doesn't pull away. Not yet. He watches the siblings until they're inside the building. He checks the mirrors, to make sure one last time that no one has followed him here. It's clear. He looks to the building again. Ruth and Calvin are gone.

Something itches at Tom. It prickles the back of his neck. Ruth and Calvin were vague in their answers. They wouldn't respond to him directly. They wouldn't tell him what they were involved in – why Calvin is putting himself in danger, and why Ruth reacted like this is a recurring issue. It perturbs Tom. It concerns him. Whether Ruth would admit it or not, Tom believes that they're in trouble. That they could be in danger, and perhaps imminently so, if Calvin continues down the same path.

There's nothing here for Tom, outside of their building. No one has followed the van. There's no reason for him to stick around. He starts driving, leaving the apartment block behind.

17

Javon keeps an office downtown, near the riverfront. He's alone right now, and he sits at the window, looking toward Windsor, Canada, through the beams of early morning light. He's never been to Canada. He's lived in Detroit all his life, yet he's never crossed the border. Never had any reason to. When he was young, *very* young – just a child – he used to think of Canada as a magical land that he could run away to. When he was being beaten by his father, and when his drunk mother left him to fend for himself when it was time to eat or to get himself to school, he would think about running away. Of fleeing these awful people and finding someone over the river, in that magical land of Canada, finding someone who would care for him. Who wouldn't beat him, and wouldn't let him go hungry. And his parents would never be able to find him – they were both felons, and they wouldn't be able to cross the border, or at least it would be very difficult for them, though it was unlikely they'd have even come looking.

Javon smirks, remembering this. It was so long ago. A

memory deeply buried and forgotten. It feels strange now, seeing how far he has come and where he is in his life, that escape was ever a dream that he held.

Because one day he stopped thinking about escape. He needed to accept reality. Escape was never going to happen. Canada was just a dream for a child. What Javon needed was strength. He found that strength through friends. Friends who were older than him, bigger than him, and who carried weapons. *They* became his family. His true family. Javon didn't need to escape anymore. He'd found what he was looking for.

And now, more than twenty years later, he's the head of that family. He renamed it after himself – the Double J Crew.

Outside of the office is a secretary, a middle-aged white woman who sits here every day flicking through magazines or filing her nails unless Javon is present. When he is, that means he has people coming. That means he has meetings. She knows to make herself look busy for these people coming – knows to pretend to be taking phone calls, or filing documents. Knows to keep her magazines and her nail file out of view.

Today is a day of meetings. Five different meetings with five different construction companies. Javon has been looking to get into construction for a long time. This will take him to the next level, he's sure of it. Another few years, he won't need to keep any interests in the streets. The JJC can disband at that point for all he cares. He'll have moved on to a new family – a wealthier family.

His secretary buzzes through, and the first meeting is underway.

It's always the same. They come in and they pitch him. Explain how they're the best at what they do, and for the best cost. Javon hears them out. He keeps notes. They leave, and shortly after his second meeting is underway.

It's during the second meeting that the secretary buzzes through unexpectedly. Javon holds up an apologetic finger. "One minute," he says. He gets on the intercom and keeps his voice low. "What is it?"

"Mr. Johnson, Tyrell Washington is here to see you."

Javon grits his teeth. Tyrell knows about these meetings. He knows that Javon is not to be disturbed. "Tell him to come back in a half-hour."

There's a pause, but then she comes back on the line. "I'm so sorry, Mr. Johnson, he says it's important. He's very insistent."

Javon sits back from the intercom. He looks at the two men sitting on the other side of his desk, waiting to continue their pitch. Javon gets to his feet. He's wearing a charcoal-grey suit. He knows that Tyrell will not be wearing a suit. "I'll be right back," he says. "This won't take long." He leaves the office, keeping the door tight to his body as he slides out so that the men won't see Tyrell and how he's dressed if they happen to look back.

Sure enough, Tyrell wears baggy, three-quarter sagging jeans, and an oversized white T-shirt with a faux-fur-lined hooded denim jacket over the top. He wears a navy-blue bandana, too. Javon glares at him. He keeps his voice low, but his fury is evident. "What is it?" he says, through gritted teeth.

Tyrell glances at the secretary, then tilts his head back for Javon to step aside with him, so they can speak in private.

Javon goes to him. "This better be *very* fucking important," he says.

"I wouldn't come here if I didn't think it was," Tyrell says.

Javon waits. He circles a hand in the air. "Then get on with it. I'm in the middle of a meeting."

Tyrell stares at him. A flicker of distaste passes over his mouth. He isn't appreciative of Javon's tone, it's clear. He coughs before he speaks. "You know how the DLB have been hitting up those delivery trucks?"

Javon snorts. He rolls his eyes. He doesn't care. So far, this doesn't sound important enough to have dragged him from a meeting. Again, he circles a hand in the air for Tyrell to get on with it.

Tyrell doesn't ignore the hand. He shoots it a look like he wants to stick a knife through it. "Last night they tried to raid a truck. They failed. Some guy was with the driver. He fought them off. They couldn't get the truck."

Javon frowns. "How is any of this important?" he says. The DLB do not matter to him. They've been embroiled in a war with them for the last couple of years, but the DLB are perpetually on the backfoot. They can't match up to the JJC. They don't have the bodies, or the firepower, and they don't have an alliance with the Gang Control Task Force, either. As far as he's concerned, it's just a matter of time before the DLB are wiped out completely. Right now, all they are is an annoying bug dancing across their windshield, soon to be smeared into nothing just as soon as the wiper blade can catch up to them.

Tyrell continues as if uninterrupted. "I've paid off some people to keep an eye on the DLB, to keep me updated on what they're doing."

"What kind of people?"

"Street people – junkies, the homeless. No one important, and it doesn't cost me much to do it. But they're a way for me to keep my ear to the ground."

"I'm glad to hear it," Javon says. "That's proactive. I'm impressed. *However* – what does any of this have to do with *me*?"

"I'm getting to that," Tyrell says. "I come in here blurting shit out, it's not gonna make any sense to you. It's just gonna create more questions. I'm giving you the answer to those questions *now*." He stares at Javon, as if waiting for an interruption. Javon stares back, but he doesn't speak. He waits for Tyrell to continue, and to hopefully get to the point. "These people I pay off, some of them saw what happened *after* the DLB failed their raid. They went after the guy who cut them off. Followed him to the motel he was staying in. *Now* is when things are going to get interesting for you. *Real* interesting."

"Then get to it."

"While they were moving in on this guy, a kid appeared from out of nowhere, and he starts flashing a picture at the driver who took them out to the motel. He's asking questions about the picture. One of my guys, he was on the other side of the street, passing by, but he *saw* the picture. He recognised it. It was *you*."

Javon cocks his head. He feels the floor come out from under him. "What do you mean, it was me?"

"This kid was waving around a picture of you, and he was asking questions."

"What kind of questions?"

"We don't know. But does it really matter? He has your fucking picture, out there in the streets, and he's waving it around in front of the DLB."

Javon stares off to the side, considering this. He grinds his jaw, hears his teeth scraping in his ears. He looks back at Tyrell. "What happened next? Where's the kid?"

"The guy from the motel, he gave the DLB the slip again. Took out the driver and stole their van. He and the kid got away in it."

"You know where they went?"

Tyrell shakes his head. "I've reached out to the GCTF, see if they can find some nearby footage, give us some information on this van and the kid, find out who he is."

Javon stares back at the door leading to his office. Thinks of the men on the other side, sitting, waiting for his return. Waiting to talk further business.

Their hands aren't completely clean, sure, but embezzlement and fraud is to be expected in business. Getting involved with the head of a street gang, however, might give them cold feet. It might give all his current and potential business partners cold feet. Everything he's been working to build could crumble around him.

He turns back to Tyrell and leans in close. "I don't need any skeletons from my past being brought out into the light," he says. "If it harms me, it harms all of the JJC. Find this fucking kid."

"And then?" Tyrell says.

"Bring him in. I wanna know where he got my picture, and why. And I wanna know where he got it from."

18

Tom has kept hold of the van he took from the gangbangers. He doesn't plan on having it much longer. No doubt its owners are looking for it. He'll get rid of it soon.

He drove it to the outskirts of Detroit and slept in the back, using his backpack as a pillow. He parked under a train track. A train rambling by woke him early this morning. It wasn't like he'd slept well. He'd been thinking of the siblings. Of Ruth and Calvin. Mostly, he'd been thinking about the things they said, to him and to each other – and especially of all the things they *didn't* say.

They're in danger, that much was clear. Though it was potentially an indirect danger, as opposed to one bearing down on them. Still, Tom doesn't like it.

He sits at the back of the van, both doors open, and brushes his teeth. Beside him, off to the right, is a large patch of scrubland. To the left is an abandoned warehouse, its windows all smashed. He went inside last night, to check it out, make sure there was no one inside for him to be concerned about. There was not. It was empty. Just a few rats scurrying at his approach. He looks across the scrubland now, lost in his thoughts. Another train rumbles by overhead. It reminds him of Chicago, and the last time he saw his brother.

Again, he thinks of Ruth and Calvin. He thinks of how Calvin spoke of his boxing. Of his coach being high on him. He thinks of Ruth, working and studying. He thinks of their dead parents.

There is no reason for him to stay in Detroit, but he knows that if he leaves, he will be thinking of the brother and sister. He won't be able to get them out of his thoughts.

He gets to his feet and paces a little, spitting out toothpaste. He limbers up, breathing deep, clearing his mind. Other than the train tracks above him, it's quiet here. He hasn't seen anyone else around. It's easy for him to think. To make decisions. To accept what he's going to do next.

There's nowhere else he needs to be. This is what brought him here in the first place – his lack of direction led him to take up Lewin's job offer, and that brought him to Detroit. It led him to Calvin, and to Ruth. To whatever trouble they might be in.

Hanging around for a couple more days won't hurt. He can keep his distance, but he can watch them, make sure that no one is following them. Make sure that they're okay, and that no one comes after them following on from Calvin's hassling of the gangbangers last night. It'll be worth knowing he doesn't continue down that path, too. Next time he starts waving a picture in an armed gangbanger's face, he might not have someone like Tom around to help him out.

For Tom, it's decided. He's not going anywhere. Not yet.

First, though, he needs a pair of wheels. And he needs to get rid of this van.

He climbs back behind the wheel and takes off the handbrake. Starting the engine, he turns the wheel and lets it roll left into the scrubland. It bumps and jostles him over the rough and uneven terrain. He drives it to where a smattering of dying bushes are at their thickest. He parks it up, throws away the keys, then bursts all four tyres with his KA-BAR.

A train passes overhead. Tom shoulders his backpack and goes in search of a car dealership.

19

Carter stands in the centre of the GCTF headquarters, the calm in the centre of a perpetual storm. He doesn't yawn, though he's tired. He breathes deep and stays alert. Right now, he's running on coffee and uppers. He can hear his blood pounding in his ears. He sucks his teeth and feels himself unwittingly growl in the back of his throat as he exhales. No one else seems to notice it. He puts it down to lack of sleep, and aching from his late-night workout.

"What you got?" he says, directing the question to Anthony.

Anthony doesn't respond straight away. He's at his desk, on his computer, fingers typing away. He looks up and takes a sip of coffee before he responds. "Most of the cameras around that area are smashed," he says. "Probably by the DLB. It's gonna take me a while to find the van and the two guys that Javon is interested in. I'm going through footage from before the event, and matching it up with footage from after. Any van that heads toward that area, I'm following up on their route after they pass through, see if there's any change in occupants."

"How long?" Carter says.

Anthony shrugs. "Long as it takes." He sees how Carter looks at him. "But I'm going as quick as I can."

On his way to HQ this morning, Carter received a call from Tyrell Washington, Javon Johnson's right-hand man. He explained the situation. Carter understood how important it was. Issues with Javon and the JJC could potentially be traced back to the GCTF. When he reached HQ, he informed the team. Anthony is their computer expert. He's been scrolling through the footage all morning.

Nick and Delia sit to one side. Delia flicks through a bodybuilding magazine. Nick leans back in his chair and smokes a cigarette, tipping the ash into his empty coffee cup with his right hand. His left arm hangs idly down his side, in his hand his switchblade, popping and closing the blade, over and over. They wait for Anthony to find something. Nick and Delia are not computer literate. That's not why they're on the team. Everyone has a part to play. Nick and Delia are Carter's attack dogs. Anthony is his tech expert. Nick is the interrogator. Carter is the glue that holds them all together. Carter is the leash that keeps them all under control, and playing nice.

Darren arrives late. He's wearing shades, and he grimaces with every step like it sends a lightning bolt through his skull.

Carter has seen him first, but Nick is first to say something. "Good morning, starshine," he says. "You look like you slept well."

Darren drops himself into the seat at his desk. "I

would've been here earlier," he says, "but I checked in on Greg."

"That *all* you did?" Delia says. "You look like you've been dipping into some of Greg's stronger stash."

Darren takes off his sunglasses. His eyes are red. He blinks against the harsh light inside HQ. "Greg's not getting into his stronger stash any time soon. Or ever again, for that matter."

"What do you mean?" Delia says.

"He's dead," Darren says. "I found him overdosed."

"Well, shit," Nick says. "What'd you do?"

"Made it clear I'd never fucking been there, for a start," Darren says. "And I also made sure there was nothing in his place that could be linked back to us."

"You find anything?" Delia says.

Darren shakes his head.

"Was the overdose accidental?" Delia says.

Darren shrugs. "Who can say?"

"What'd you do with his stash?" Nick says.

"Left enough behind," Darren says, "but the majority of it's in my trunk."

"So Greg's dead?" Anthony says, looking up. "Shit – y'know, I actually kind of liked him. For a junkie CI, he wasn't that bad."

Carter snaps his fingers to get their attention. He points at Anthony. "Get back to work," he says. "Greg's dead. Sure, it is what it is. We've got other CI's. We need any more, we'll find more. It's never hard." He's looking at Darren. "Why are your eyes red? You been crying?"

"This?" Darren points at his eyes. "Shit, no. This is from last night. After we left the club, I didn't go straight home. I went to see this chick I know. I ended up not getting anywhere near as much sleep as I should've done."

Carter grunts. He brings Darren up to speed on what they have Anthony looking for.

Darren nods along. "Y'know, it wouldn't be the worst idea for us to think about bringing down the Detroit Lifer Boyz once and for all."

"Motherfuckers are hard to find," Delia says, returning her attention to her magazine.

"Uh-huh, but actually tracking them down is gonna benefit us on all sides," Darren says.

"I'm listening," Carter says.

"Well, first of all, it's gonna help out our buddies in the JJC, right?" Darren says. "Second of all – the DLB have been targeting truck drivers. Legitimate businesses. We put an end to that, we get some good press out of it. Praise from our superiors. I know we've got carte blanche out here, but we can't take that for granted. We want it to stay that way, we've gotta be bringing in the kinds of collars that get us front page attention. We put an end to the DLB, we get all that and more."

"We're in need of a new target," Nick says, leaning back on his chair, "since we hit that stash house last night."

"I'm not against it," Carter says. "The DLB have always been a target. But like Delia said, they're hard to find. We've got one name attributed to them – their boss. Other than that, we don't know who any of them are. You find them, I'll more than happily bust some heads and lock the sons of bitches up. But it ain't gonna be easy. The JJC run this city, but the DLB are the underdogs. They've got the hearts and minds. People on the streets, they wanna believe in the DLB. They wanna support them. The DLB have done some shit that's afforded them mythic status – you remember when they shot up that cruiser?"

"Who could forget?" Nick says. "They never found the shooter."

"They never found a single member of the DLB," Carter says. "No one who would admit to it, anyway. We wanna find them, we're doing it completely off the record – to begin with – and you know what that entails. We're gonna bust some heads. And we keep it as *quiet* as we can. That's the only way we find them."

Delia closes her magazine and tosses it to the side. "No time like the present, huh?" She laces her fingers and pops her knuckles. "Well, come on, fellas – the boss man says we're gonna bust some heads. Don't leave me with blue-balls over here."

Carter grins. Before he can say anything, Anthony starts laughing. "Oh boy," he says, his fingers no longer tapping at his computer's keys. "Oh man. I think I've got something!"

Carter stares at him.

"White guy and a Black kid, right?" Anthony says.

Carter nods.

Anthony grins. "Then in that case, I *know* I've got something."

20

Tom managed to get an old Ford. It was supposed to be twelve hundred, but he talked it down to eight on account of its age and a crack in the passenger side mirror.

He's driven it through Detroit, growing accustomed to how it handles. He took it straight to the apartment block where he left Calvin with Ruth. He'd had a busy morning, and it was still early. Calvin shouldn't have left for school yet. Tom waited. He saw Calvin setting off on his bike. Tom followed, keeping his distance.

Tom kept waiting for Calvin to turn off suddenly. To disappear into the city, continuing his search. He didn't, though. Calvin went to school. Tom saw where he locked up his bike near the main entrance, and has parked on the other side of the road, keeping the bike in sight. He's been outside the school for a few hours now. Calvin has not slipped out.

Tom is aware that nothing could happen. That he could spend a few days sitting on his hands, waiting for something that never comes. It won't be a waste of time, though. If nothing happens, that's good. It sets his mind at ease. It means he can leave Detroit, and go wherever he might be needed next.

He settles back in the chair and thinks of Ruth. He wonders where she is right now – if she's working, or studying. Today, he keeps an eye on Calvin. Tomorrow, he'll make sure no one is following Ruth. He'll be able to watch over the apartment building when they're both inside, too.

After a few days, *then* he can be content that they're not in any immediate danger. *Then*, his mind will be at rest. His conscience will stop plaguing him. It will be time to find a new cause.

21

Carter is with Delia. Parked around the corner, a couple of blocks away, Nick is with Anthony. Darren is on his own. He's not hitting the corner with the rest of them. He's talking to CI's. The GCTF are compiling information. Hunting down facts. Finding out where members of the DLB might be hiding out.

Carter and Delia lie low in an abandoned building over the road from a busy corner. Carter watches the dealers working. He sees the corner boy that runs back and forth. He can't be older than twelve. He's doing all the work. Two dealers sit on a corner stoop, watching over everything. Down from them is a heavyset man guarding the stash.

They've fed the information Anthony found on the van and the kid who was flashing Javon's picture back to Tyrell. They haven't heard anything back yet. Carter entrusts the JJC to deal with it. Turns out, this could be an issue for the GCTF, too. The kid is a ghost from their past, one Carter wasn't ever expecting to see again.

He doesn't think about that right now. The JJC are

dealing with it. The GCTF scratch their backs, and the JJC scratches theirs in turn.

"What do we know about the DLB?" Carter says without turning.

Delia is on the floor, sitting with her back to the wall. She's ready to move once Carter gives the say-so. "That they're a pissant gang compared to what they used to be," Delia says. "They used to be a big deal until they went up against the JJC. Used to have a hangout, but it got burned out by the JJC, and since then they've kept on the move. Been near impossible to track them down since then."

"Remind me, who's running them?"

"Darius Walker, but we don't know if he's even still alive at this point. He hasn't been seen in a while."

Carter repeats the name in his head, recalling his file. He spent time in juvie for aggravated assault, possession with intent to sell, and sexual battery. A real class act. Carter remembers the picture of him from back then, still a teenager. Shaved head and intense, deathly eyes. A killer's eyes, even as a kid. The GCTF need to find a more up-to-date picture of him, and stick it on the noticeboard at HQ.

"When we going in?" Delia says. "My ass is getting numb and I'm bored."

Carter doesn't answer. He watches the corner. It's been busy all the while they've been here. "Who do you think these guys work for?"

"They ain't JJC, so I don't give a shit," Delia says.

Carter grunts. "All right, call Nick and Anthony. Let's go."

Carter pulls out his Smith & Wesson M&P while Delia makes the call. She follows Carter to the door, heading out of the building. "They're coming," she says, and then she's armed, too. They leave the building via the rear, the same way they came in. The front is boarded over.

Carter leads the way. He knows Delia will be following close behind. They reach the corner of the building and wait for Nick and Anthony to arrive.

"Who do you like?" Delia says.

"Big guy," Carter says. "The one guarding the stash."

Delia whistles low. "You like a challenge."

"It's all fat," Carter says. "He's not the tough guy they think he is."

Anthony screeches the car to a halt in front of the corner. Nick jumps out of the passenger seat, gun raised. "Everybody freeze! On the fucking ground, right now! I said right now!" Anthony gets out, gun pointing.

The corner turns into chaos. Carter sees the runner do exactly that – he bolts. People approaching the corner quickly scatter. The two guys on the stoop freeze, caught like deer in the headlights. They raise their hands.

"I said kiss the fucking ground!" Nick says, striding up to them, keeping his gun on them. He grabs the man on the left and throws him down onto his front, then does the same to the one on the right. He covers them while Anthony pats them down.

The big guy is backing up. He thinks they haven't seen him. He turns and starts to run. He leaves the stash behind, probably hopes that it won't be found and he'll be able to come back to it later.

Carter and Delia start running. The big guy never sees them coming. First thing he's aware of is the heavy steps gaining on him. He starts to turn. Carter slams into him from behind, sends him rolling. Carter rolls through with him, but he's faster to his feet. Delia doesn't give the big guy a chance. She's on his back, pinning him. She strikes him in the side of the neck with the handle of her gun. Avoids his head – doesn't want him dizzy.

Carter approaches. "Turn this fat sack of shit over."

Delia gets to her feet and kicks the man in the side until he rolls onto his back. He groans. Carter drops to a knee and sticks the Smith & Wesson into his mouth, chipping his teeth. His eyes go wide.

"This motherfucker look like he's resisting arrest to you?" Carter says.

"I see it," Delia says. "Looks like he's armed, too." She lifts her shirt, flashes a revolver tucked into her waistband so the big guy can see it. He understands. He doesn't comply, they'll shoot him dead and plant a gun.

"You feeling talkative?" Carter says.

The big guy looks up at him and nods.

Carter slides the gun out of his mouth. "Name."

"Nate."

"You DLB?"

"Uh-uh."

"You sure? I hear they're pretty secretive. Truth be told, I wouldn't expect you to admit to it if you were."

"I ain't DLB. This is Warrendale, man – I'm a –"

"A Warrior," Carter says. "Looks busy on the corner today, Nate. Warrendale Warriors must be going pretty good for themselves lately. Last I heard, times were hard."

"I dunno, man," Nate says. "It's been a good winter."

"Uh-huh. How familiar are you with the Detroit Lifer Boyz?"

"I – I, uh..."

He's hesitating. Carter isn't sure why. Hiding something, clearly. "You pally with them, Nate? I hear the DLB aren't really too pally with anyone, especially not right now that they're running against the JJC."

Nate swallows.

Carter nods at Delia. She stomps on Nate's balls. He cries out.

Carter hits him in the side of the head with his gun. Not enough to daze him, just enough to tear his eyebrow and get some blood. "You know something about the DLB," Carter says. "You're a shitty liar, Nate. It's all over your face. Now, are you gonna tell us right here, or do we need to drag your ass in and make a day of it?"

Nate doesn't answer.

Carter hauls him up to a sitting position. He grabs his left arm and twists it behind his back. Nate closes his eyes tight. Carter presses the cold of the gun into his cheek, to keep him aware that it's present.

"I don't know where they are," Nate says, opening his eyes, and Carter can sense a 'but' coming. "But I know...I know where Darius's moms is."

"Darius Walker?" Carter says.

Nate swallows and nods.

Carter looks at Delia. "We don't know that."

Delia shakes her head. "She's not been registered anywhere for the last five years. Figure he keeps her moving, or else she's in a house under someone else's name."

Carter twists Nate's arm higher. "How'd you know that?"

Nate battles to get his words out, his body and mind rejecting the revelation. He has to force it past his lips. "His moms and mine, they go to church together."

"That's real sweet. You know the address right now, off the top of your head, or you gotta call your mother?"

Nate hesitates. "I know it." He tells them the address.

Carter looks at Delia. "Got it?"

She nods. "I got it."

Carter wrenches up on Nate's arm. He feels it snap. Feels it reverberate through his own arms. He bites his lip at the sensation, enjoying it, basking in it.

Nate rolls to the side, screaming, struggling to bring his left arm back around to his front so he can clutch it to him. "What the fuck! What was that for?"

Carter leans close. "Next time I ask you a question, you fucking *answer* me." He straightens and turns, winking at Delia. She grins. They head back to the corner. Nick and Anthony are still covering the two guys lying flat. They've taken a couple of Glocks from them. Carter gets Anthony's attention, points out where the stash is hidden. Anthony goes to it. Carter waves a finger in the air, heading to the car Nick and Anthony arrived in. He opens the driver's door. Delia goes around to the front passenger side. "Guns and drugs are coming with us," he says, loud for the benefit of the corner boys. "Clear your asses out – there's gonna be a patrol coming by here every hour from here on out."

The two men on the ground glare at him. Carter blows them a kiss. He gets into the car. Nick and Anthony climb in the back. Carter drives off, spinning the wheels as they go.

22

When he leaves school, Calvin doesn't go back the way he came. Tom perks up at this. He's not heading home. Staying in the car, and keeping his distance, Tom follows.

Calvin leads him through the city. They're travelling for a while. They're not heading toward the motel, or where the chase with Lewin's truck occurred. Tom thinks this might be a good sign, that Calvin isn't out looking for trouble. A couple of times, Tom has to fall back to avoid getting too close. Calvin is careful. He looks around a lot. He checks his six. Clever. He won't recognise the Ford Tom is driving. He sees it once, but Tom doesn't want to give him the chance to see it a second time. Twice, and he might start getting suspicious.

Calvin disappears down an alleyway. Tom can't follow in the car. He sticks to the road, taking the long way around, hoping to catch a glimpse of him coming out the end of the alleyway. Tom can't see him straight away. He turns down a block and slows, taking his time. He watches the road and the sidewalks. At the end of the block, he catches sight of a bike emerge between two buildings. It promptly disappears around the corner. It's hard to tell, but Tom thinks it was Calvin. He doesn't speed up too much. He needs to keep a low profile. Suddenly coming down on him is the opposite of that.

As he reaches the end of the block, he can see for sure that it is Calvin pedalling away down the road.

The neighbourhood is rundown. It's quiet. Most of the buildings look empty. There are abandoned warehouses. It is clear that there is no business going on here and there hasn't been for a long time.

Calvin stops in front of one of the warehouses. He hops off his bike and rolls it the rest of the way. Tom looks at the building. There is a sign in front. It says it's a boxing gym. It makes sense now.

Once Calvin has gone inside, Tom circles the block, then reverses into an alleyway, the front of his car pointing toward the gym. He kills the engine and settles in. He could be here for a while. About two hours, at least. Maybe more.

He stays alert while he watches. The area is quiet, but it's not devoid of life. He sees a couple of people passing by, but no one notices him. They shamble along, going wherever they're going. Likely looking for a place to spend the encroaching night. A couple more hours and it'll be dark, and colder than it is now. He sees some people leave the gym. A couple of them exit together, and a short while later a man leaves on his own. They all have cars. They get inside and drive away.

A car rolls into view from the right of Tom's view, getting close to the gym. A Chevy with blacked-out windows. It parks close to where Calvin entered the building. Tom watches. It keeps its engine running, but it's not going anywhere. He can't see the people inside. They could be here to pick someone up. Tom waits. No one leaves the gym. Tom checks how long he's been sat here. Two and a half hours. He watches the car now, also keeping an eye on the door to the side of the building Calvin went through.

The Chevy's engine is turned off. Tom sees how the car lowers, and how its exhaust stops pumping out fumes. Nothing happens straight away. No one gets out. Ten more minutes pass. No one leaves the car, or the gym.

Then, all four doors of the Chevy open. Four men get out. They look around. Tom ducks low behind his wheel, but he's tucked back in the alley. They can't see him back here.

The four men converse briefly. They nod at each other. They wear jeans and thick jackets. Tom can't see if they're armed or not. They turn and head toward the gym.

Tom doesn't like the look of it. It could be nothing, but his gut tells him that it's something. He watches as the men go inside the building.

Tom gets out of the car. It could be nothing, it could be something. Either way, he needs to know for sure. He crosses to the gym, and follows the men inside.

23

Calvin stands beneath the shower, the hot water running over his aching limbs, washing the sweat from his body. The water feels good against his skin. He went hard today. He always goes hard. Today, though, he feels like a walking bruise.

He forces himself to turn off the faucet and pat himself dry. It hurts to raise his arms while he dries himself. He takes a seat on the bench in front of his locker and presses the towel into his face. He sighs, running the towel down his face.

Last night, he came close. He came close to a lot of things – he came close to getting shot, for a start. But he also came close to finding out who the man in the picture is. He's sure of it. The man who pulled the gun on him, he recognised the picture. There was no doubt. He knew who it was, and he wasn't happy to see it.

Calvin still has the picture with him. He always does. It's stuffed into his gym bag. Dried off, he dresses himself and pulls out the picture, leaning into his locker, staring at the man. His features so familiar now, yet the man himself a complete stranger.

Calvin hears footsteps enter the changing rooms. He frowns. Other than Noah, he was the only person left in the gym when he came to shower. Whoever he can hear now, it's not Noah. It's more than one person. He closes the locker door a little, peers around it. Four men. All strangers to him. All staring at him.

Calvin doesn't speak. There's no point. The way they're all looking at him, he's pretty sure they're going to make what they want clear very soon.

"Calvin Styles," one of them, the man at the front, says. It's not a question.

Calvin closes his locker door. He slips the picture into his pocket. He doesn't answer.

The man who said his name grins. "You should come take a walk with us."

The three at his shoulder are glowering at Calvin. It's clear that Calvin doesn't have a choice, but at the same time, he knows that complying would be a mistake. A big mistake. The kind of mistake he might never walk away from.

He manages to shake his head. "I don't think I'm gonna do that," he says. He takes a step back.

"Where d'you think you're going?" the speaker says.

Calvin grits his teeth. He takes another step back.

The speaker raises an eyebrow, and then he grins. He shrugs. "You wanna do this the hard way, that's fine by us. Look at me, kid – hey, look at me."

Calvin does.

"We ain't gonna kill you," he says, "but we can *hurt* you. You feel me?"

Calvin looks the four men over. Their jackets are thick,

and it's hard for him to gauge their weights. Three of them are taller than him, though, and at least two of them are heavier. The other two look like they work out – they look like they can *run*. Do they run as often as Calvin does? Do they work out as often as he does? Are they faster than him – can they keep up?

More than that, Calvin wonders if they can fight. If they catch up to him, then what? Can they handle themselves? Have they had any kind of fight training of their own? Of course, if they pull a gun like the man last night, that won't make a difference. His fists can't match up against their bullets.

"He's gonna run," one of them says, nudging the main speaker.

"Oh yeah," the speaker says, nodding. He's one of the lighter of the four. He's the one Calvin thinks he'd have the most trouble outrunning. "I can see it. He ain't listening to me. He's gonna run."

Calvin spins on his heel and he runs, racing out of the locker room. He hears them give chase. He bursts through the door into the gym, leaping over a set of dumbbells and a weight bench.

Noah is in the gym, still. He's mopping. He looks up with a start. "Calvin!" he says. "What're you –?" He doesn't finish. He sees the four men pursuing. He drops the mop and steps forward, getting between them and Calvin.

"Noah, run!" Calvin says.

Noah doesn't. Calvin slows and turns. Noah spreads his arms wide. "I don't know who you fellas are," he says. "But you all need to get out of my gym, right now."

One of the bigger of the four men strides toward Noah. He throws a punch, expecting to put the older man down with ease. Noah weaves, easily avoids it. He comes up with a lightning-fast body shot with his right, then follows through with a left across the man's jaw, putting him down.

The other three might be surprised by Noah's reflexes and his fists, but they don't let it slow them down. Two more jump in to take the place of the one Noah knocked down. They attack Noah from both sides, striking him in the head and the ribs. They're younger and faster than Noah. He struggles to cover up, outnumbered against them. They knock him down.

Calvin can't leave now. He's glued to the spot. He can't leave Noah on his own. Noah is more than a coach – he's a father figure who stepped up when Calvin needed one. If Calvin were to flee, to abandon him, would the three still standing follow? Or would they stay on Noah and hurt him, or maybe even worse?

The two who have knocked Noah down are kicking him. The speaker isn't. He's staring at Calvin. "How bad we gotta hurt him before you play nice and come with us?"

Calvin doesn't get a chance to answer.

24

Tom followed the four men into the building, but he kept a safe distance. As he crept inside, he could hear them talking to Calvin in the locker room. Tom stepped lightly, peering around the wall. It was the end of the group discussion. Calvin turned and ran. The four chased.

Tom retains his element of surprise. He hears them in the gym. Hears a new voice join them, quickly followed by a scuffle. More talking.

Tom steps into the gym. He sees one of the four on the ground with a swollen jaw, and an older man being kicked by two others. He sees the fourth man talking to Calvin.

Next to Tom, there is a rack of dumbbells. Close by, there is a weight bench for bench pressing. There are loose plates close to Tom's foot. He picks up a five-pound plate. He holds it like a discus in his right hand, but places his two middle fingers in the centre hole. He goes to the two kicking at the older man. "Hey," Tom says, getting their attention.

The one on the right looks up first. Tom drives the plate into his stomach, doubling him over. He drops to his knees, gasping for breath. The kicker on the left lunges for Tom. Tom throws his right arm back, slamming his elbow into the centre of his face, breaking his nose. He doesn't go down. Tom follows through, slapping the plate flat against the side of his head. This puts him down. He trips over the man already on the ground from earlier. This man is starting to stir. He's trying to push himself up. Tom kicks him in the midsection, lying him out flat.

Tom spins back to the one man still standing.

"Tom!" Calvin shouts.

Tom sees why. The man is reaching behind himself. He's pulling out a gun. Tom sees a flash of it. It looks like a Glock. He doesn't wait until the whole thing is in view. He throws the five-pound plate, aiming it for the centre of the man's mass. It connects with his chest. Tom thinks he hears a rib crack. The man coughs, dropping his gun, both hands going to his sternum. The plate hits the ground with a thud. The man stumbles back, trying to catch his breath. Calvin kicks his legs out from under him, aiming for the bends in his knees. When he lands flat on his back, Calvin mounts him. He hits him twice across the face, until he goes limp.

Tom crouches down next to the older man, looking him over, checking him for wounds. Blood trickles from the corner of his mouth, dying the white hair of his beard bright red. "I don't think anything's broken," Tom says. "Probably a lot of contusions, but no breaks."

"Oh shit, Noah," Calvin says, coming over and helping to lift the older man to his feet. "Are you okay?"

Noah coughs as they straighten him up. They guide him over to the weight bench and sit him down.

Calvin looks across at Tom. "What are you doing here?"

"I hung around," Tom says. "To see if you were in trouble." He nods toward the four fallen men. "Looks like you are."

"Calvin," Noah says. He's breathing hard. "Who are these men?"

"I – I don't know," Calvin says.

Tom watches Calvin. He thinks he's telling the truth – or at least a half truth. He probably has a good idea that these men have something to do with the people he got into trouble with last night, but that doesn't mean he knows who they are.

Noah looks up at Tom. "And who are *you*?"

"Just helping out," Tom says. "I heard you might have a title contender one day. I just wanted to make sure he gets that opportunity."

Noah wipes the blood from his mouth. "What kind of trouble have you gotten yourself into, Calvin?"

"I –" Calvin begins, but he stops himself. His shoulders slump. He looks at Tom. His face is solemn. "I don't know, Noah."

"Is it anything to do with your folks?"

"I don't know," Calvin says again. "But...maybe. Maybe it is."

"Where's Ruth?" Tom says.

"I'm not sure," Calvin says. "Either working or studying."

"You should call her," Tom says. "Make sure she's okay. Make sure that no one has gone after her the way they have after you."

Calvin's eyes widen at this. "But – but why would they? Why would they go after Ruth?"

"Why did they come after you?"

"*Shit*," Calvin says, pulling out his phone. He tries to call his sister. Tom can't hear it ringing. "She doesn't always have it on her," Calvin says. "And sometimes, if she's studying, she turns it off so she can concentrate."

"What did it do?" Tom says. "Did it ring out, or was the phone off?"

"Off," Calvin says.

"Then that probably means she's studying, right? Where does she study?"

"Either in the library, or at home."

"Which one's closer?"

"Home."

"Let's go," Tom says, already pulling out his car keys.

Calvin doesn't move straight away, though he's bouncing on his toes and clearly eager to go. "Noah," he says, "you should come with us."

Noah waves a hand. "I'm not going anywhere," he says. "I need to deal with these four." He motions to the men on the ground.

"Their car's just outside," Tom says. He points to the one whose chest he threw the plate into. "He was the driver – he should have the keys."

Noah nods. "Then I'm gonna take them for a drive and get them far away from my gym." He looks at Calvin. "If these are the kind of men I think they are, others they work with aren't gonna be pleased about what's happened here. I'm gonna call in some buddies of mine. We're gonna spend the night on watch. Make sure no one comes back looking for revenge, or thinking they're gonna burn this place out."

"We need to go," Tom says to Calvin.

Noah nods in agreement. "Go get your sister," he says. "Make sure she's all right."

Calvin turns now. He follows Tom. They run out of the gym, and to Tom's concealed Ford.

25

Carter takes Nick with him to visit Rosette Walker.

"Reckon we might get lucky and he's gonna be there?" Nick says. "Two of them sitting at the dinner table, gossiping over tea?"

Carter grunts. "It's never that easy," he says.

Nick laughs.

Carter parks the car in front of her home and looks up at it. A small wooden house, whitewashed, a porch with a wrought-iron bench on it, facing out toward the road. The curtains are open. The windows are clear.

"Watch the back while I knock," Carter says, getting out of the car.

Nick hurries on ahead and slides down the side of the house. Carter mounts the porch. He bangs on the door with the side of his fist. He looks around the street. Despite the cold, despite it getting dark, he sees an old man sitting on the porch of the house on the opposite side of the road. He's watching. Carter stares him down. The man averts his gaze.

Carter keeps staring. The man gets to his feet, clearing his throat, and shuffles into his house.

The door opens. Carter turns. A little old lady is looking back at him, squinting through her circular glasses. She's a foot shorter than he is. Her clothes hang off her like she's recently lost a lot of weight. Her hair is white. Carter figures her to be in her late seventies. Darius is mid-twenties. She must have had him late.

"Rosette Walker?" Carter says.

She doesn't answer. Carter sees how she stiffens at her own name. She can see who he is. A white man in this neighbourhood. She knows he's a cop.

Carter doesn't wait for her to finally speak. He nods into the house. "You alone in there?"

She nods at this.

"Then I'm sure you won't mind me stepping in," Carter says, and brushes past her.

"Who are you?" she says, following him, speaking up now. Her voice is strained, wispy.

"Carter Brown," Carter says without turning, looking the small house over, making sure it's as empty as she claims. "Gang Control Task Force."

The living room is sparse, a sofa and a chair, both with patterned blankets draped over them. The television is on, but it's muted. On the coffee table is an open magazine, and next to that, on a coaster, a cup of tea. There's a fireplace, though it doesn't look like a fire has been lit in a long time. Rosette is likely too old, and doesn't have the energy to go out and buy more logs, or to get down on her knees and light it up. On the mantelpiece there are framed pictures. Carter thinks Darius is in a couple of them, but they're from when he's young.

Carter listens to the house. It's still. There's no one else in it. He goes through to the kitchen. The key is already in the back door. He turns the key and pushes open the door. Leaning out, he sees Nick waiting by the corner.

"It's clear," Carter says.

Nick follows him in.

Rosette looks between the two of them, blinking like a mole in daylight.

"Take a seat, Ms. Walker," Carter says, stepping toward her. He doesn't touch her, but his advancing size is enough to back her up into the living room. She sits in the chair. Carter remains standing. Nick looks around, heading through to the bedroom.

"My partner there is going to search your room," Carter says. "He's going through all of your things. Is there anything you want to tell us?"

"About what?" Rosette says.

"Don't play dumb, Ms. Walker. It's getting late and we wanna get this over with as quick as possible. We're here about your son."

"I have three sons," Rosette says. "And a daughter."

"I don't give a shit about your daughter," Carter says. "And which of your fucking sons do you *think* I'm talking about?"

She doesn't respond to this. Through in the bedroom, they can hear Nick banging around, tearing out drawers and flinging open the wardrobe. They can hear him cutting into the mattress and through pillows with his switchblade.

Carter grabs a framed picture on the mantelpiece. He's confident the young boy in it is Darius. Even smiling, even young, he has cold eyes. He's sitting on Rosette's lap. She looks to be about the right age for Darius to be a child here.

"This is him, right?" Carter says, holding the picture in front of her face.

She looks at it, but she doesn't speak.

"Where's your baby boy, Ms. Walker?"

She clears her throat. "I don't know," she says.

"You don't, huh?" Carter lowers the frame. "Who pays for this house, Ms. Walker? Hell, let's not be so formal – you don't mind if I call you Rosette, do you? Course you don't. Who pays for this house, Rosette?"

She's silent.

"Cos it ain't you, is it? Shit, it's not even in your name. You know how much trouble we had finding you? If you were registered, we could have come along and had us a nice chat a long time before now, but instead it's almost like you're hiding. Now, who would want you hidden, Rosette? My guess is the only one of your four kids still in Detroit." Carter holds up the picture again. "And the only one of them regularly in trouble, who knows he can't have his mama getting hassled."

"I don't know where Darius is," she says.

"At least you finally acknowledge who we're talking about."

"You were right – who else would it be?" she says, looking up at him now, a slight sneer on her lips. "Since that boy was young, the likes of you have done nothing but hassle him."

"I'm sure that's *exactly* how it's always gone," Carter says, snorting. "It's never your little boy blue who's running around and getting himself in trouble, is it? No, it's the *cops*, right? The cops, just desperate to pick on some kid."

"I don't have to justify anything to you," Rosette says.

"You made your mind up about Darius a long time ago, and nothing will change that."

"Sweetheart, he runs a street gang. He's shot up cop cars. I'd hate to see what the saints look like in your world."

Nick returns from the bedroom. He's carrying a cell phone. "Found this," he says. "No lock on it. No names on the contacts, either. Just a bunch of numbers."

Carter holds his hand out for the phone. He flicks through. There are calls and messages, all from different numbers. It doesn't take him long to spot a pattern. He goes back as far as he can through the record. The first set of numbers – both messages and calls – is all the same. Then the next batch have a new number. Same again for the third batch. All the numbers, lumped together.

Carter holds up the phone to Rosette. "That how he keeps in touch?" he says. "Burner phones. A new one every couple of weeks by the looks of it."

Rosette stares at him, but she doesn't speak.

Carter drops the phone on the coffee table. It clatters next to her cup of tea, causing some to splash out over the rim. "Where is he? Don't make me ask again."

She takes a deep breath. "I don't know where my son is," she says. "He don't have an address. He *can't*. Because of *you*. The likes of *you*."

"He don't come visit?"

"He doesn't keep a schedule."

Carter can believe this. Darius is careful, always has been. It stands to reason that even visiting his own mother could be a threat to his freedom and safety. He probably keeps moving her around, too. Other than the framed pictures, there is not much in the way of personalisation in this house.

Carter squeezes the picture frame down by his side while he thinks. He's barely aware he's doing it. The sound of the glass cracking brings him back around. He looks down. He sees the crack running down the centre of the picture, through child-Darius's face. Carter smirks. He drops the picture on the table, then picks the phone back up. "We're keeping this."

"I don't need it," Rosette says. She grins. She wants to say something, but she's trying to stop herself. She looks smug. She can't hold back. "You think you'll catch him through it, but you're wrong. He'll never call it again."

Carter stares back at her. He returns her smug smirk. "Someone's watching this house right now, aren't they?"

Her smile falters. She realises the mistake she's made.

Carter turns to Nick. "Toss the rest of the house. See if you can find any more phones."

Nick nods. Carter heads outside. He steps out onto the porch. He stays casual. He looks up and down the street. To the windows opposite. He thinks about the man sitting out on his porch earlier, when Carter first approached the door. He could be on the DLB payroll. Could have already placed a call to let Darius know that cops are talking to his mother.

Carter pulls out his phone and calls Anthony. "Call the precinct," he says when Anthony answers. "Tell them to send a couple of uniforms out here to Rosette Walker's address. I want the place under twenty-four-hour surveillance."

"On it," Anthony says.

Carter hangs up. He looks over the street again. Looks into the windows of the houses. He doesn't see anyone looking back at him.

26

Calvin has tried to call his sister a few more times, but still no answer. He's given up.

"We don't know that she's in any trouble," Tom says, though he's pushing the speed limit. "Whoever these people are, they might have just come after you."

Calvin chews his lip. He stares straight ahead, probably figuring out how close they are to the apartment building, and wondering if Ruth is even there.

"Did they say what they wanted?" Tom says.

"No," Calvin says, having to clear his throat to form the word. "They just wanted me to come with them." He turns to Tom. "Have you been following me?"

Tom nods. "I wanted to make sure you hadn't gotten into bigger trouble than you realised last night. When somebody pulls a gun on you, and someone else gets involved, that's not necessarily the end of things. Especially considering we took their van."

"I guess I appreciate it, but, man, I mean – *why*? We're no one to you, neither of us. Anything that happens here, it doesn't have to mean anything to you. You could walk away right now if you wanted to."

Tom stares straight ahead, remembering the route to the building. He has to wait at a traffic light. When it turns green, he's quick off the mark, not wanting to lose any more time. "I guess I don't want to," he says.

He can feel Calvin studying the side of his face.

"I don't know you well, Calvin," Tom says, "but you seem like a good kid. And your sister clearly cares about you. Now, I don't know what's happened to either of you in the past, but I was able to read between the lines enough last night to know that it was something bad, and that that something bad may be having a ripple effect into your present life. You're looking for something, and whatever it is it put you in a position where you had a gun in your face. And I get the feeling that you're not going to stop, and you could put yourself in that position again, and next time there probably won't be someone like me there to get that gun *out* of your face. Knowing that, I couldn't walk away. I know my conscience, and it wouldn't let me. I could be three states away, and I'd be checking the news in Detroit daily. And maybe one of those days I'd find your picture, with a headline about you lying dead in a gutter. And maybe about your sister being caught up in the crossfire. Could you walk away from something like that?"

Calvin doesn't answer straight away. They're not far from the apartment building now. "I guess not," he says, as the building comes into view.

There's no time to scope the area, though it wouldn't make much difference. Tom doesn't know this place well. He's not familiar with the vehicles that park outside here, wouldn't know if any of them were out of place. He could ask

Calvin, but there's no knowing if this is the kind of thing Calvin pays any attention to – and besides, he's already racing ahead. Tom follows, catches up and keeps pace. He lets Calvin lead the way. Tom doesn't know which number their apartment is, or how many floors up it is.

The building is a high-rise. Calvin heads straight to the elevator. Tom dives in with him. Calvin hits the number for floor eight. While they rise, Calvin bounces on the spot. He's worried about his sister. He pulls out his phone to check if Ruth has tried to get back in touch, but she hasn't.

They reach floor eight. The door opens.

There are two men coming toward the elevator. They're dragging Ruth along between them, one of them with a hand clamped over her mouth. Her wrists are bound together with a plastic cable. She sees Tom and Calvin. So do the two men.

They push Ruth to the side, but Calvin and Tom are on them. The two men are armed, but they don't get a chance to pull their weapons. Tom grabs for the man on the right. He spins with him, throws him up against the wall. He plants a knee into his stomach, headbutts him in the centre of the face, then slams a forearm across his jaw. The man is limp. He starts to fall. Tom places a hand on the side of his head and pushes him away. Turning, he sees Calvin strike the other man with a left, a right, and then an uppercut. He hears the man's teeth rattle together in his head. Calvin steps back, shaking his fists, wincing.

Tom goes to Ruth, pulling out his KA-BAR. He cuts the plastic cable. "There's more of them," she says, eyes wide. She looks down the hall, toward an open door. Tom assumes it's where Ruth and Calvin live. "Three more – they've got guns. They're searching the apartment."

The three men from the apartment have heard the fight. They appear in the doorway. They see their two fallen comrades. They raise their guns.

Tom pushes the siblings into the elevator. He hits the button for the ground floor. Bullets fly down the corridor. Footsteps follow. The elevator doors close.

"They'll be taking the stairs," Tom says. "The elevator should beat them. When we get to the bottom, *run*."

"Run *where*?" Ruth says.

"Just follow us," Calvin says.

Ruth nods. Her eyes blaze. She leans against the wall, a hand to her chest while she struggles to catch her breath. She looks at Tom like she wants to ask him what he's doing here, same as Calvin did, but she knows this isn't the time. They need to stay focussed.

The elevator reaches the bottom. It dings. The door opens. They run.

They race toward the car. As Tom gets behind the wheel and fires up the engine, he looks toward the building. He sees the door thrown open. The three from upstairs burst out, guns raised. They scan the area. They see Calvin and Ruth diving into the car. They open fire. Tom turns the wheel, keeping the handbrake on. He spins the car, then releases the handbrake. They lurch forward, speeding away from the building and the three shooters.

27

Darius Walker isn't alone when he gets the news.

The DLB's latest hideout is in Poletown East. One of his boys has a cousin who lives here. Darius is down in the basement. He's been conducting his business from here for the last week and a half. At all hours, there are four of his men upstairs on guard duty, watching out north, south, east, and west.

The basement wasn't doing much when Darius took it over. Just storage. He's pushed everything that was down here into a corner, then set up a desk for him to work at. He doesn't do much paperwork, but the desk makes him feel official. He knows it makes him look important. He's on his burner phones most of the time, occasionally on a laptop. Mostly, he uses the surface to count money, not that the DLB has been bringing in anywhere near as much as he'd like since they got caught up with the JJC. The desk is angled so he has a clear view of the door that leads down into the basement from the kitchen above. Darius keeps a Glock within easy reach at all times. He sees anyone he doesn't like the look of, he's shooting first and asking questions later. His men know to knock hard, and to announce themselves loudly.

The person who's come to see him, at the worst possible time, is some guy called Nate. He runs with the Warrendale Warriors. He was brought in by a member of the DLB. Nate came up to a DLB corner, said he needed to speak to Darius, said it was real important. Said he wouldn't talk to anyone but Darius himself. Darius's man called him, let him know this.

"What's he say it's about?" Darius said.

"Personal stuff. He won't say anything else."

Darius frowned at this. Personal stuff? Darius doesn't have any kind of personal life to speak of. "Fuck it, pat him down and bring him in. He can have five minutes of my time."

When they arrive, they pound loud on the door. "Darius, I've got this boy Nate with me."

Darius is behind his desk. He places the Glock atop it, close at hand, within sight of everyone. "Bring him down."

Nate is pushed down the steps. He almost stumbles and falls. His right arm is in a cast. The plaster looks fresh. He holds it close to his body.

"Ay, *ay*," Darius says, pointing, "you check that cast?"

"I checked it," his man says. "Stuck a rod down it, had a good poke around. Nothing down there." He guides Nate in front of the desk. "You want me to stick around?"

Darius shakes his head. "Stay close, though. Stay where you can hear. I'll let you know when I'm done with him."

The man nods and leaves. Darius doesn't speak until he's gone. Nate stands before him, shuffling his feet. There's nowhere for him to sit.

"All right," Darius says, leaning back. "I know your name and who you run with, so don't waste my time with any of that shit. What is it you want? I was told you had personal information, but I don't know you, so I don't see what you can know *personally* about me."

Nate swallows. Darius hears the dry click in his throat. "Our – our moms... They go to church together."

Darius sits forward. "This to do with my mom?"

"I – I swear to God, I didn't want to tell them – they broke my arm –" He holds up the cast.

Darius holds up a hand to shut him up. "I don't care about your fucking arm. What's this got to do with my mom?"

"Cops came to our corner – someone recognised a couple of them, said he'd seen them on TV or in a paper or something. Said they're the Gang Control Task Force. They were looking for *you*."

Darius grits his teeth. He spits his words through them. "Ay man, I'm only gonna ask you one more time – what does this have to do with my mom?"

One of his men upstairs bangs on the door. "Yo, Darius – I'm coming in! This is important!"

Darius stares at Nate as the door opens. One of his men hurries down the stairs. "Cops have been by your mom's place," he says. "The guys we've got out there on watch, they just called in."

Darius feels himself beginning to shake. His eyes have never left Nate. Nate wilts under his glare. "What did they do?"

"They were in there a while," the man says. "Looks like they tore the place up. The two guys who got there first, they've left now, but not until a couple of uniforms turned up. They're watching the whole street."

"They inside, or outside?"

"Outside, in their cruiser."

Darius nods. To Nate, he says, "You told them where my mom lives."

"I'm sorry," Nate says. "I thought I'd be able to get to you before they got there, but they broke my arm. It was all fucked up, I had to go to the emergency room and –"

Darius raises the Glock and shoots. The bullet catches Nate in the left shoulder. The impact knocks him onto his back. Darius rises from behind his desk. He goes to where Nate lies. Nate presses the cast to his bullet wound. The blood soaks into the plaster, turning it red. He whimpers. He pleads. Darius doesn't hear him. He spits in his face, then raises the Glock and empties the magazine into him.

"Mother*fucker*," Darius says when he's out of bullets. He turns to the man close to him. He's watched the scene unfold, his face impassive.

"What do you want me to do?" he says.

"First, get rid of this bitch's body," Darius says. He returns to his desk and takes a seat. "Then just let me think. This ain't gonna stand. They don't go after my fucking *mom*. They think they can go after my mom?" He slams a hand down on the desk. He shakes his head, anger threatening to overwhelm him. "They went after my mom," he says, his voice quiet now, more to himself than to the other man present. "They wanna come at me like that, fine. They even know what they done? They playing with fire now, boy. I'm gonna burn them all."

28

Tom found a parking lot and used his KA-BAR to unscrew the plates on his Ford. He swapped them with another Ford, then drove to a motel on the outskirts of the city, close to Grosse Pointe. He pays for the room in cash and then sends the siblings inside while he moves the car around to the back of the building, away from the road. He takes his time walking back around to the front, looking the area over, getting the lay of the land. It's dark and he peers into every parked car he sees, doing his best not to make it obvious.

Inside the room, they've turned on the lights. Tom turns off the overhead bulb and turns on the lamp in the corner. Calvin stands by the window, peering out. Ruth sits on the edge of the bed. She looks shell-shocked. All the way here, she hasn't spoken a word. She's rubbed at her arms where the men were manhandling her.

The room looks like most other cheap motel rooms Tom has stayed in across America. A bed, a television at the foot of the bed, and an adjoining bathroom. There is a chair in the corner, under the window. Tom checks the bathroom, sees how wide the windows open, and looks at what is out back. The parking lot, where he has parked his car directly outside. He returns to the main room. Calvin is standing. He's looking back at Tom.

"What now?" Calvin says.

Tom looks at Ruth. "Are you okay?" he says. "Did they hurt you?"

She blinks, raising her eyes. She rubs her forearms and her wrists. "I'm – I'm fine," she says. "Who – who were they?"

"I don't know," Tom says, looking at Calvin. He turns his attention back to Ruth. "Did they say anything to you?"

She shakes her head. "They knocked on the door, but before I could answer they kicked it down. They tackled me to the ground. I had no idea what was happening. I thought – I thought –" Her voice chokes off. She composes herself. "I thought they were going to rape me. Instead, they bound my wrists and dragged me out of the room. I could see the other three looking around. And then the two of you turned up. Mr. Rollins, what are you doing here?"

"Call me Tom."

"*Tom*, what are you doing here?"

"I hung around," Tom says. "Listen, last night when we all first met, it was clear to me that the two of you were holding something back. Whatever it is, I need you to tell me now. It could hold some answers as to who's coming after you."

Ruth and Calvin look at each other.

Tom waits. He folds his arms.

Calvin takes a deep breath. He's deliberating. He's close to talking but still deciding if he wants to share. "Two years ago," he says, finally, "our parents were killed."

"You think that's what all of this is about?" Ruth says, looking at her brother. "But why? What have you done?"

"What happened to your parents?" Tom says.

Ruth sighs. "It was two years ago, like Calvin said. They were gunned down. A drive-by shooting." She swallows.

"The killer was never caught?" Tom says.

Ruth shakes her head. "We don't know who killed them, or why."

"Tell him what happened after the funeral," Calvin says. Ruth looks at him. Calvin shrugs. "It might be important."

"It was a couple of days after the funeral," Ruth says. "There was an investigation into the shooting, but nothing was coming up. I was calling the station, asking questions, asking how come they didn't have anyone for it. Where the shooting happened, it wasn't quiet. There were other people around. Someone must have seen something. And there were security cameras, too. But they claimed they didn't have any footage. I guess I was making a lot of noise. I was hassling them. Someone didn't like it. A man came to our door. A big guy, white. He told me not to pursue things further." She bites her lip. "He didn't...he didn't *do* anything, but the way he looked at me, the way he *spoke*, there was threat in it. The look in his eyes, it made my skin crawl. It made my blood run cold. He was...he was *terrifying*. And I couldn't just think about myself anymore. I needed to think about Calvin, too. To keep him safe. So I did as the man said. I stopped pushing for answers. And nothing happened – we didn't get in any trouble. We were left alone."

"This guy who came to your door," Tom says, "have you ever seen him since?"

"No," Ruth says.

"What was he wearing? Was he in a uniform?"

Ruth shakes her head. "Jeans and a jacket. Just everyday clothes."

"If someone turned up to warn you off, it sounds like someone wanted your parents dead. And it sounds like they didn't want any follow-up questions, either."

"I don't know what happened to our parents. I don't know why anyone would target them specifically, but no one else was hurt that day. At first, we always thought maybe they just got caught in the middle of something. Wrong place at the wrong time. Right up until that man came and told me to butt out. That was when it started to feel like it wasn't an accident."

"All right," Tom says, turning to Calvin. "What have you got? What have you done?"

Calvin doesn't speak straight away. He looks at his sister, his lips pursed. He reaches into his pocket and pulls out a folded piece of paper. He unfolds it. "I have a picture of the killer," he says. "The man who shot our parents."

Ruth's eyes go wide. "*What*?"

"I've been trying to find out who he is. I've been watching and following gangbangers, but I haven't seen him yet. I don't know who he is. I don't know his name, or what gang he's a part of, but I have his picture, and that's something. It's a start. I can find him with this."

"He could be dead," Tom says.

"Maybe," Calvin says. "But I've searched online through every gang-related killing of the last couple of years, and his face hasn't turned up. I know that doesn't mean he's *not* dead, but I need to know for sure. And I don't think he is."

"Why not?" Ruth says.

"Last night, the man who put the gun in my face, he recognised the picture. I could tell. And then these men coming after me, and after you, too? It has to do with the picture, right, and whoever the man is?"

Tom gets his first good look at the picture. It's zeroed in on the face of a Black man driving a car. "That's from the shooting?" Tom says.

Calvin nods.

"Who took the picture?"

"He's called Montel," Calvin says. "Montel Lindo, and he was *there*. He saw the shooting happen. He says he jumped between two buildings and managed to snap this picture on his phone as the killer drove away."

"How'd you find Montel Lindo?" Ruth says.

"Online," Calvin says. "I found a chatroom talking about Detroit crime. I didn't post anything for a long time. I just read what people were saying, until I got a handle on the place. Finally, I posted about what happened to our parents. I used a fake name, though. I didn't want anyone to know I was looking. I kept everything I posted as vague as I could. Montel reached out to me, privately. He told me he had the picture."

"Why didn't he take it to the cops?"

"He did," Calvin says. "When he tried to give it to them, he was taken into a room, and left alone there for a while. A couple of men finally came to see him. They took his phone, deleted the picture. They destroyed the phone. Told him to forget about it. Said if he didn't, they'd come pay him a visit at home. Thing was, the picture had backed up onto the Cloud. Montel was able to get it back. He's kept hold of it ever since, in case it ever became important. But he kept his mouth shut, until I came along."

"And now you've been showing it around," Tom says, "trying to find out who the killer is."

"I haven't been showing it around," Calvin says. "Last night was the first time I showed it to anyone, and you saw what happened. Listen, I've been patient. I've been careful. For two years, I've gotten ready. I joined a gym, I learned how to box. I've prepared myself to find this man." He holds up the picture.

"Oh my God, Calvin," Ruth says. "What – what do you think you're going to do?"

Calvin falters a little at the question. Tom can see what Calvin is planning on doing – he wants to kill the man. To kill the killer. But now that Ruth has asked him outright, he can't bring himself to say it. He knows how it will sound.

Ruth says it for him. "Do you think you're going to kill him?" she says. She waits a beat. "Well? Do you? And then what? What if he kills *you*? He's clearly in a gang – what if his buddies kill you? You're going to throw away your life over this. Do you think that's what Mom and Dad would want for you?"

"Mom and Dad are dead," Calvin says. "Because of *him*. I can't – I can't just let him go around like he never did anything wrong, like he never destroyed our lives."

The siblings stare at each other. They're not squaring up, but neither of them is backing down, either. For the first time in a long time, they're perhaps seeing each other how they truly are. Seeing the secrets that they have been keeping from one another.

Tom breaks the silence. He's been thinking. He's been looking at the picture. Looking at the man. He has an idea. "You say you don't know what gang he's a part of."

Calvin turns to him slowly. "No," he says.

"Let me make a call."

Ruth gets to her feet. "What kind of a call?"

"A favour," Tom says. "Someone who can help me find out who *he* is."

Ruth shakes her head. "No. Haven't you been listening? I'm not going to let my brother try to kill someone, even if it *is* the piece of shit who killed our parents."

"I'm not suggesting sending your brother out to hunt that man down. But what do you think happens next, Ruth? You can't go home. They know where you live. If you want your life back, you're going to have to trust me. The only way I can help you is if I know who we're up against. I need to know who the man in that picture is just as much as the two of you do." Tom pulls out his phone and steps toward the door. "This won't take long."

29

Carter looks over the strip club. It's one of Javon's many. Also one of the many that Carter himself is a private partner in. It's not open right now. It's early morning. Opening is more than a couple of hours off. It's quiet. A bartender is working through inventory, doing a stocktake. None of the dancers is present. The place is clean, though. It's well kept. Carter is pleased to see how it looks.

He goes to the office in the back. Javon is inside with Tyrell. Javon leans back in his chair with his feet up on the desk. Tyrell stands to one side, leaning against the wall, arms folded. They both look up as Carter enters.

"Two days in a row," Javon says, clapping his hands together. "Look at you, getting to see our pretty faces day after day."

"How did it go?" Carter says, getting straight to business. He takes a seat.

Javon turns slightly in his chair, looking toward Tyrell. He raises his eyebrows. "You wanna tell him?"

"They got away," Tyrell says. He pinches his lips together

and runs his tongue over the front of his teeth. “Some white guy turned up. Helped them out.”

“You got a name?” Carter says.

“Do *you*? That picture you sent us was blurry, but it looked like him.”

“So we still don’t know who he is.”

Tyrell shakes his head. “Funnily enough, no one talked long enough while he was busting skulls.”

Javon and Carter both look at Tyrell, watching him.

“We’re working on it,” Tyrell says, shifting his weight. “On finding out where they’ve gone, and who the white guy is.”

“Uh-*huh*,” Javon says, exchanging looks with Carter. “What you got for me?”

“We’re hitting up the DLB,” Carter says.

“You having any luck finding them?”

“We found his mom,” Carter says. “Darius Walker’s mom, that is.”

Javon raises an eyebrow. “Yeah? I doubt she gave him up.”

“She didn’t, but it’s a lead. I’ve got uniforms watching the street. If he tries to move her, we’ll have him.”

Tyrell whistles low.

“You got something to add?” Javon says.

“Just, going after his mom,” Tyrell says. “You tear up her house? Yeah? You don’t think you can hassle the man’s mother like that and think there ain’t gonna be repercussions?”

“Repercussions?” Carter says, turning in his chair. “You serious? The GCTF, we *are* the repercussions. What’s he gonna fucking do? He’s scurrying like a rat, hiding wherever he can.”

“Yeah, but this is his *mom*. Who he’s been hiding away

too, right? He wouldn't hide her if he didn't care. You gotta watch your back, man – you and all your people. You mess with the man's mother, he's gonna come after you."

Carter waves a dismissive hand. He's unconcerned. "Let him come," he says. "Him, and all of his crew. That's what we want, ain't it?"

Javon chuckles. He points a finger gun at Carter. "Exactly," he says. "That's *exactly* what we fucking want."

30

The intercom on Lainey Wylder's desk buzzes. The voice of her secretary, Katy Doerr, comes through. "Fred Boothe is here to see you, Ms. Wylder."

Lainey puts the paperwork she's been working through to one side. "Send him in," she says.

Katy opens the door ahead of Fred and steps into the office, holding the door wide. Katy has been Lainey's secretary for the last four years. She's young, not yet thirty. White. Her brown hair is tied back into a sensible ponytail. She wears a black skirt and a white blouse with a cardigan over the top. "Mr. Boothe," she says, nodding as he steps through.

Lainey has known Fred a long time, but it's been a while since they last spoke face to face. He's white, in his early fifties, short and stocky. His hair is thin on top. He has a thick moustache, but he keeps it neatly trimmed to keep it from getting between his lips. Without waiting for an invite, he takes a seat. His presence here concerns Lainey. Usually he sends updates via encoded email. For him to come in person, it must be serious. His face is solemn.

Katy lingers at the open door. "Do you need anything else, Ms. Wylder?"

"No, Katy," Lainey says, "and please hold my calls. No interruptions while Mr. Boothe is here."

Katy nods, then leaves the office and closes the door behind her.

Lainey turns to Fred. "It doesn't look like good news," she says.

"It's not," Fred says.

"Don't keep me waiting."

"Someone made a move on the kids," Fred says. "They're on the run right now. In hiding."

Lainey leans back in her chair. She feels her chest tighten. "Were they hurt?"

Fred shakes his head. "If they were, it doesn't seem like it was anything serious."

Fred is a private detective. He has been for the last twelve years. He used to be a homicide detective in Baltimore. He doesn't talk about his time in Baltimore. Lainey asked him once what brought him to Detroit. He said he has family here. A sister. Being in Detroit meant he got to spend more time with his nieces and nephews. He's worked with Lainey for the last five years, in private, and mostly off the books. Katy knows his name, but she doesn't know who he is or what he does.

For the last two years, Lainey has paid him to keep an eye on Ruth and Calvin Styles, the children of Etta and Colby Styles.

Even thinking their names brings a pang to her chest.

"Who attacked them?" Lainey says.

"Gangbangers," Fred says. "Don't know which crew specifically."

"When'd you find out?"

"Woke up this morning, I had a message on my phone from one of their neighbours. I've paid a couple of people on their floor to tell me if anything happens, if anyone comes to see them or is lurking outside their apartment. Anyway, I got a message telling me there'd been a fight out in the corridor, then a gunfight out in front of the building."

"Jesus," Lainey says.

"The kids got away unharmed by the looks of it, along with their benefactor."

Lainey checks the time. It's eleven a.m. "If you found out this morning, why didn't you come straight to me?"

"Because I've been trying to get answers. Answers to questions I knew you'd ask. Like who the guy with them is."

"So who is he?"

"I'm looking into that. I didn't get many answers. Not yet, anyway. The neighbour said they hadn't seen him before. White guy. Looked like he could handle himself. They thought maybe he could be one of Calvin's boxing buddies, except they said he didn't fight like a boxer."

"Do you know where they've gone?"

Fred shakes his head. "I'm working on it. Contacted some tech geeks I know, see if they can get into security footage, pick up on wherever the three of them might be."

"You think they're going to stick with this guy, whoever he is?"

Fred shrugs. "I don't know. But they haven't come home, and they probably don't have many other options. If he's offering them a helping hand, it makes sense that they'll take it."

Lainey nods along. "Well, whoever it is, somebody has

made a move on them. I need to get them to safety. I won't have their blood on my hands, too."

"This could play in your favour, right?" Fred says. "The people you're trying to nail, if they're involved in this, they could've just shown themselves up, right?"

"I don't know," Lainey says, her mind racing. "Maybe. But if they've sent in a gang, then that's probably their way of keeping out of it, trying to make sure nothing gets back to them. Right now, my priority is the kids. I need you to find them, Fred. When you do, bring them to me."

Fred nods. He starts to rise.

Lainey reaches for her phone. "While you're doing that, I'm going to make some calls. Set some things up. It's not enough to find them. We have to have somewhere safe to keep them."

Fred heads for the door. "I'll be in touch."

"Soon," Lainey says, dialling out, thinking, *Hopefully soon.*

31

Ruth and Calvin are back at the motel. Tom has made them promise not to leave. Especially Calvin. Ruth said she'll make sure he doesn't go anywhere. Tom left them with a number to contact him on, in case anyone turns up. He's been gone a few hours now, and he hasn't heard anything. He told them to make sure one of them is on lookout at all times. He gave them tips on the kind of thing to look out for.

It's late now. It's dark. Tom rides shotgun with Lewin. Lewin drives slow. They're waiting for an ambush. They're hoping for one.

"I appreciate this," Tom says.

"Don't mention it," Lewin says. "You helped me out, I'll return the favour, no problem."

"You paid for my help." Tom offered Lewin payment in turn, but Lewin refused.

"I did, and that's your money now. Use it in whatever way you see fit, but for this? Consider it a favour."

"Feel free to call it in any time."

Lewin chuckles. "I just might. And hell, that idea you gave us, I wouldn't be surprised if it lands me some kind of bonus. You know how many losses we've taken because of this rip-and-run shit? No, man, you're doing us *all* a favour."

Lewin had called his boss after Tom called him, asking for his help. He'd told him of Tom's plan. He didn't tell him how it would benefit Tom, as well as Ruth and Calvin. He didn't need to know that part. Lewin just told his boss how it would benefit them. *We tell everyone in the company I'm transporting something different. Tell one person electrical goods, another alcohol, another cigarettes – valuable stuff. The kind of thing we know this gang has targeted in the past. Then, when we get one of them on board, we'll find out what they think I'm carrying. We know that, we know who it is that's selling out our routes.*

Lewin's boss was more than happy to oblige. *Let's nail this son of a bitch.*

"After this, you split Detroit," Tom says.

Lewin nods. "And I won't be back for a while. Few months, at least. We'll make sure of it."

"Good." Tom keeps his eyes on the road ahead, and on the mirrors. It's like the night he first arrived in Detroit. Staying alert. Waiting for an ambush.

They pass through the neighbourhood where they were originally hit. There is no barricade here awaiting them. Tom hasn't spotted any motorised dirt bikes yet, either. No vehicles following them.

"What you gonna do if no one turns up?" Lewin says.

"Back to the drawing board," Tom says. "I can't expect you to hang around. They don't bite for this, I'll have to find a new bait."

They're not far from the destination Lewin told his boss to give. The same destination was given, regardless of what people were told Lewin was transporting. A Walmart. Tom can already see its distant glow lighting up the night.

And then they get lucky.

"This it?" Lewin says. He sees it, too.

It's not as elaborate as last time. There's no barricade. Just an SUV pulled to the side of the road, its hood up, ostensibly broken down. A man stands in the road, waving down the truck for assistance. Tom can't see inside the SUV. It's too dark, and it's parked in between streetlamps. It could be filled with armed men, but he has no way of knowing. He can't see whether the man waving them down is armed or not, either.

"Stop for him," Tom says. "Could be who we're looking for."

Lewin slows the truck. The man steps around to his door while Lewin lowers the window. Tom watches the SUV. He listens to the conversation beside him.

"Car trouble?" Lewin says.

"Don't know anything about engines, do you?" the man says.

"Can't say as I do," Lewin says.

"Shit," the man says. "Could you give me a lift down the road? There's a gas station. I'll be able to call a tow truck from there."

Tom whispers, "Yes."

"Sure," Lewin says. "Come round to the passenger side. Hop on in."

The man passes around the front of the truck. Tom watches him and the SUV. The man reaches behind himself, down the back of his jeans. He nods at the SUV. The back doors start to open.

Tom opens the passenger door. He waits. The man could just be motioning to family. The passenger rear door of the SUV opens widest first. A man steps out. He's carrying a shotgun. Tom kicks the passenger door into the face of the man approaching. It connects with a thud. Tom jumps out and finds what he was reaching back for – a Glock, concealed in his jeans. Tom takes it and fires twice at the SUV. The man with the shotgun dives back inside. The other doors close. Tom scoops up the dazed man and bundles him into the cab of the truck.

"Go, go!" he says.

Lewin does. Tom jumps up as the truck begins to roll, pulls the door shut behind him. Lewin speeds down to the end of the block. Tom watches the SUV in the mirror. The men are gathered around it, but they don't get in and attempt to follow. Tom pats down the man they've captured. He has the keys to the SUV. Tom checks the mirror again. The truck is already too far gone for the other gangbangers to shoot at.

Lewin takes a left at the end of the block. Shortly after, he takes a right. "All right, pull over," Tom says.

Lewin does. Tom drops the car keys for the SUV down a nearby storm drain. There's no one else around. Tom reaches back into the cab and drags out the man they've captured. He takes him to the back of the truck, opens it up, and rolls him inside. He climbs in after him and closes the door.

There are lights inside the back that Tom placed earlier, before he and Lewin set off. Two of them toward the front of the truck, and fixed to the ground. They're already turned on. Tom drags the man along the ground. He's stirring, groaning. Tom doesn't bother hitting him again. He wants him alert. Wants him able to answer questions.

There's a hook dangling from the ceiling. Tom takes plastic ties from his pocket and binds the man's wrists. He gets him to his feet and raises his arms on the hook. It holds him up. The hook is high. The man has to balance on the tips of his toes, his arms straining. He's fully awake now.

"Jesus Christ," he says. "The hell are you doing to me?"

Tom stands in front of him, arms folded. He keeps his stance loose. A moment later, Lewin starts driving. They're not in contact. Lewin has estimated how long it would take Tom to get set up. The man lurches on the hook as the truck moves.

"Fuck!" he says. "*Fuck*! My shoulders! Jesus, damn it, my goddamn shoulders!"

Tom remains upright. He rolls with the truck's movements. "Your shoulders are gonna be the least of your concerns," Tom says. He steps closer. "What's your name?"

"Fuck you," the man says, showing his teeth, grimacing in pain.

"You'd be amazed at how many times people tell me that's their name. They always come round, though. How much is it gonna have to take for you to spit out a name more palatable? Because the thing is, fuck you, your name is the least interesting thing I want to know."

The man looks back into Tom's eyes. He winces at the pain in his shoulders. "My name's Reggie."

Tom smiles. "See how easy that was, Reggie? This whole thing can be *very* easy. As easy as you want it to be." He waits a beat, allowing his smile to fade. "Who do you run with, Reggie?"

"DLB," Reggie says, his voice straining.

"DLB?" Tom says. "Talk to me like I'm not a local, because I'm not."

"Detroit Lifer Boyz."

"With a z?"

Reggie nods.

"Is it the DLB who usually jack these trucks? I've heard it's been a regular problem lately."

"It's us," Reggie says, his eyes closed tight against the pain in his shoulders and arms.

"Who tells you what the trucks are carrying?"

"I don't know, man! I just get told who and when to raid, and I do it!"

"What were you told was in the back of this truck?"

"Alcohol – expensive shit. Spirits, stuff like that."

Tom nods. He files that away for Lewin.

"Damn it, what do you want from me?" Reggie says.

"We're just getting started, Reggie," Tom says. He reaches into his back pocket and pulls out the picture of the killer Calvin is looking for. "Who is this?"

Reggie's eyes widen. His nostrils flare. It's clear he knows who the man is. It's clear, too, that he's not a fan.

"Who is he?" Tom says, pushing the picture closer to Reggie's face.

"Javon Johnson," Reggie says.

"Remember I'm not a local."

Reggie looks like he wants to spit. "He leads the JJC – the Double J Crew."

"You look like you don't like him. The DLB and the JJC, do they have problems?"

"Yeah, we got beef. Major fucking beef."

Tom thinks at least he has a name now. And the name of his gang. Gives them something to work off, and to look into.

He thinks, too, about the man who came to see Ruth after her parents were killed. Who warned her off. She said he was white. "Javon have any white friends?"

Reggie frowns at this, but he has an answer. "Yeah, he got white friends. Everyone knows the JJC and the law are tight."

"That so?"

"Yeah, it's so – I said it, didn't I?"

"A friend of mine showed this picture to a member of the DLB just a couple of nights ago, and your buddy stuck a gun in his face. What was that all about?"

"I heard about that – the kid wouldn't leave him alone and they had shit to deal with."

"Me."

"Yeah, exactly – *you*, motherfucker."

"Javon Johnson runs the JJC – who runs the DLB?"

Reggie isn't so quick to answer this.

"It you, Reggie?"

Reggie grimaces.

"Give me a name, and then we're done here. And make it a real one, Reggie. Because I either find out the name of your boss now, or I find it out later. And if I find it out later and it's a different name to what you tell me now, I'll come back and find you, Reggie. It ain't gonna be hard for me. I have your name now. I know your face."

"Darius Walker," Reggie says. "But you ain't gonna find him. No one can. So you can take his name. It won't do you any favours."

Tom nods. "That's good to know." He reaches up to the hook and brings Reggie down. Reggie cries out as the blood rushes back into his arms. He falls to the ground. Tom drags him toward the back of the truck. He throws open the door. They can see the road behind them. There are no cars following. It's another quiet neighbourhood. Lewin has stuck to quiet areas.

"The hell are you doing?" Reggie says.

Tom grabs him by the wrists and hauls him back to his feet. "This is where we say goodbye, Reggie," he says. "I hope we never meet again." He throws Reggie from the back of the truck.

32

Darius waits for his men to return. The DLB aren't as big as they used to be, and he's spread them thin tonight. He's had to, though. The thing with his mom, that's important. But the new delivery coming into the city? That's an opportunity he can't pass up. He can't afford to let any opportunity pass him by, especially not with the way things have been lately.

In his mind, though, his mother is the priority. And everything that has happened with her. *That's* where his mind is right now. Not on the jacking.

He's in a different house now, but a similar basement. This one, however, is empty. The house is abandoned, save for two of his men upstairs standing guard. There was a fire in this neighbourhood a couple of years ago, and it's never been rebuilt. The buildings here are blackened and charred and close to collapse. The one they're inside of is at the end of the block. It sustained the least damage.

There's a chair in the centre of the room. Darius sits in it while he waits. The electric does not work, so he's set up some battery-powered lamps. He gets a call. "Speak to me."

"We've got your mom," the voice responds. "She's all packed up and we're moving her now."

"Good," Darius says. "Message me when you've got her in the safe place – *message*, don't call. I might still be busy when you get there. What about the other thing? You know how that's going?"

"They're on their way to you now."

"Any noise?"

"None."

"Good." Darius hangs up. He gets to his feet and pops the tendons in his neck. He goes upstairs, speaks to his two men on guard. "They're on their way," he says. "Be ready for them."

He goes back down into the basement. He doesn't sit now. He remains standing. He paces, preparing himself. His blood is still hot. It's taken a long time to calm himself. It took a lot of deep breaths before he was able to think straight, and to organise this whole thing.

Time passes. When the cars arrive, he's still pacing. He hears them pull up. Peering out a basement window, he can see the cars in front of the house. He sees the two cops hauled from the trunks, wrists and ankles bound, bags over their heads. They're dragged into the house. Darius turns and waits.

The two cops are brought down into the basement with him. The two cops who were watching his mom's house. The cruiser will still be there, parked outside, waiting for someone to notice that the men are gone.

Chances are, the men will be found before the cruiser is.

Darius nods at his men. They remove the bags from the

heads of the two cops. They're gagged, too. As his men remove the gags, the cops blink into the lights now blinding them, trying to look around and gather themselves, work out where they are.

Darius stands before them both. Their gazes finally fall upon him. Darius looks into their eyes. They're scared. Aside from their heavy breathing, neither of them has made a sound yet.

They're both white. One of them has dark hair and the other is balding and moustached. The one with hair, it clings to his scalp and forehead with sweat. There's blood at the corner of his mouth and a bruise high on his right cheek. The balding man has a swollen left eye. There's a cut on his cheek and another across the bridge of his nose. Blood mats the hair of his moustache.

Darius clears his throat. "Which of you," he says, "is familiar with the Gang Control Task Force?"

The cop with hair gulps. The two of them exchange glances. The balding cop speaks. "We – we both know them," he says.

Darius nods. "Do you know them well?"

The balding cop tilts his head toward his partner. "He probably knows them better than I do, but –"

Darius pulls out his Glock and shoots the balding cop through the head.

The cop with hair cries out. His legs go limp. His limbs are still bound and he almost falls. Darius's men catch him. They sit him in the chair. The cop stares back at his dead partner. Stares at the blood pooling under his head. He turns back to Darius. He's hyperventilating.

"Calm down," Darius says, making his voice soft. "Easy, easy. You keep breathing like that, you're gonna pass out. If you pass out, what good are you to me? There, that's better. I need you to be able to talk. You can talk?"

The cop nods.

"Come on now, man. You know that ain't what I asked."

"I can – I can talk," the cop says.

"Good," Darius says. "You know the Gang Control Task Force?"

"Yeah."

"You know their members?"

The cop nods.

"You know them well?"

"I've drank with them, but it was a while ago now. They usually just hang out among themselves."

"You know their names? You know where they live?"

The cop hesitates. He glances back at his dead partner, and then he quickly nods.

"They have you and your buddy here watching my mom's house. That mean they trust you?"

"They didn't request us," the cop says. "They said they needed a couple of uniforms to watch the house and the street. Despatch knew we knew them, so they sent us. Figured they'd prefer friendly faces on one of their cases."

"Why were they watching my mom's house? Why were they bothering her?"

"They're looking for you," the cop says, unable to look into Darius's face.

Darius thinks about the jackings. "I done something to upset them? Coming after my mom, that's some personal shit."

"I – I don't know," the cop says. "No one tells me that kind of thing. I was just there to watch and let them know if anyone turned up." His eyes flicker side to side. He looks at the other cop again. The corpse. He's thinking about his own life. About staying alive. Knows he needs to keep talking. To show his worth. Needs to tell them things of use if he wants to keep breathing. He looks at Darius now, his features and voice earnest. "But they're – they're *gang control*, right? It makes sense that they'd come after you eventually. And plus, there's the JJC –"

"What about the JJC?" Darius says.

The cop swallows. He tries to speak but can't. It takes him a moment. He's breathing hard again. "They – they're – I mean, this is just a rumour. If anyone said it out loud, the GCTF would gut them."

"Tell me the fucking rumour," Darius says, his voice and his gaze both ice cold.

"The JJC and the GCTF, they're – they're *close*, you know what I mean? Closer than a gang and a task force should be."

Darius nods. They've long known that the JJC have friends in law enforcement. Now they know who it is. "What about the rest of the force? The JJC have allegiances there, too?"

"I don't know," the cop says. "Maybe pay-offs here and there, but it's not like the whole force is in their back pocket."

Darius claps a hand onto the cop's shoulder. He shakes him, congratulating him on a job well done. "Shit, you've been a big help, man. I appreciate it. We all appreciate it." Darius summons one of his men closer. He steps up, pulling out his phone. The Notes app is open. "The GCTF," Darius says. "Names and addresses. I wanna know who each member is, and what they do within the task force. And I want to know where they live."

The cop hesitates. His eyes cut toward Darius's hand, still on his shoulder. "Then what?"

"Then we let you go," Darius says.

The cop looks like he has doubts, but he has no other choice. He gives the information. Darius's man punches it all into his phone.

"That everything?" Darius says when the cop is finished. "Five of them? Four men, one woman?"

The cop nods.

Darius pats him softly on the cheek. "My man," he says. "That's a good little piggie." He takes a step back. He nods at a man standing behind the cop. The man steps forward. He cuts the cop's throat.

33

Lewin is leaving Detroit. He has the information he and his boss need. He drops Tom off back at the motel with Ruth and Calvin.

Ruth and Calvin are both waiting for him. Ruth gets to her feet. "What did you find out?"

"That you were following the wrong gang," Tom tells Calvin.

He closes the door and takes a seat and brings them up to date on everything he's learnt. Ruth's furrowed brow deepens as he speaks. When he's finished, she says, "He's working with the cops?"

"They have some kind of relationship," Tom says. He goes to the window and peers out, checking the area. He checked it when he and Lewin first pulled up. It was clear then, too, but it's always worth looking.

Calvin has sat down in the chair in the corner. He stares off into space. He's not in the room with them. "Javon Johnson," he says. He has the name. The name of his enemy. The man who killed his parents. The man he's been looking for. He's testing it out. Feeling it in his mouth for the first time.

Ruth stands with her arms wrapped around herself. She looks toward her brother. This new knowledge has not calmed her concerns. She turns back to Tom. "What now?" she says. "What can we do?"

Tom doesn't answer straight away. It's a delicate situation. Suddenly he's found himself with the siblings not just looking for a killer, but caught up in the middle of a gang war, and law enforcement is of no help to them. If anything, going to the law would put them in more danger. And he still doesn't know why their parents were killed.

He looks back at Ruth. "I need to think," he says.

34

It's a recent development, but Javon finds that he likes seeing Tyrell less and less.

"What do you want?" Javon says when he sees him approaching. They're in a club. The same one where they earlier spoke to Carter. Tyrell left soon after Carter did. Javon was not expecting to see him again tonight. He's been setting up. He has a big meeting. Promising investors. The club is a way to schmooze them. To put smiles on their faces. The happier they are, the bigger the investments.

What he doesn't need right now is Tyrell turning up and causing issues. Lately, all Tyrell brings to him are issues. And not just of the physical threats they face out in the streets. It's his bad attitude, too. He rarely cracks a smile anymore. He's always pouting. Always complaining. Javon remembers the other night when Tyrell called him *bougie*. Things haven't been right between them since then. Tyrell looks at him in a different way. Javon waits for him to spit out whatever his problem is this time.

Tyrell doesn't speak straight away. He leans against a

stage and looks over the table that Javon has been setting up. Tomorrow, it will hold a buffet. With all the women he's going to have an offer, he's not sure how interested in food these men are going to be. Their minds are likely to be on eating something else.

"You don't have someone else to set this up for you?" Tyrell says.

"It's just a couple of tables," Javon says. "I asked you what you want."

Tyrell shrugs. "I don't want nothing. I was just heading back to the crib, passing by, thought I'd come back in." He looks around the club. He whistles between his teeth. "Who thought we'd be here one day, huh?"

"The club ain't nothing new to us," Javon says. He leaves the table for now. He stands straight, folds his arms. "Even when we were penniless, we'd find our ways into a place like this."

"Uh-huh – but now you *own* a fucking place like this. Shit, you own a few places like this. You own *this* fucking place."

"Hard work and dedication," Javon says, feeling a flicker of a smile at the corner of his mouth.

"And a loyal team," Tyrell says. He's not smiling.

The two of them stare at each other in silence. Javon rolls his neck, popping it. He makes a harsh sound in the back of his throat, clearing it. "There something you wanna say, Tyrell? Because if there is, I'd rather you just came out and said it instead of drawing it out like this. I ain't got time for you to be a pouty little bitch."

Tyrell raises an eyebrow. "That right?" He laughs, but there's no humour in it. "A pouty little bitch, huh? That how you see me?"

"It's how you're acting. You wanna act like that, then yeah, sure, that's how I see you. That's exactly what's in front of me."

Tyrell leans against the stage, shaking his head. "Oh, man," he says. "We come up together –"

"We didn't come up together, Tyrell," Javon says. "It's the Double J Crew, not the J and T Crew."

Tyrell shakes his head again, like he knew he should have expected this from Javon, but he's in disbelief that he's finally saying it all out loud. "Uh-huh. Sure, you joined before me back when it was still just *The Crew*, but who was by your side when you decided to make it your own? That was me. The loyal lieutenant. Not everyone had your back when you made that move."

"Most of them did."

"Because I told them to," Tyrell says, straightening up now and jabbing a thumb back into his own chest. "I kept them by your side. Shit, I kept the whole crew together – without me, there'd be no JJC. I was there for you, man. I've always been there for you. And shit, it's not just me – Jamar, Kameron, Alonzo – do I need to go on? There's a whole list of people who you owe just as much as you owe to me."

"Owe?" Javon says. "What are you getting at, Tyrell? I don't pay you enough, that it? Hell, sometimes I think I pay you more than your worth."

Tyrell bristles. "It ain't the money."

"It ain't?" Javon barks a laugh. "Well, if it ain't the money, what the hell is it?"

"It's the goddamn *respect*," Tyrell says, animated, showing his teeth.

Javon arches an eyebrow. "Respect?

"I know you know what it means," Tyrell says. "You

demand it often enough. That's why you took over The Crew in the first place, right? But you ain't showing us any respect. All that we've been through, all that we've come up through – *together* – and now... Heh, now you've got all new friends, ain't that right? *White* friends. That's who the table's for. That's who all the girls are gonna be for. And for the rest of us, for the JJC, you just look down on us." Tyrell looks Javon over. He studies his suit. "You're starting to look mighty pale yourself these days, Javon."

Javon grits his teeth. He doesn't rise to the bait. He takes deep breaths. Keeps himself calm. "It's unfortunate that you feel that way, Tyrell."

Tyrell rolls his eyes. "See? You've changed. Time was, you wouldn't let me talk to you like that – time was, I wouldn't fucking *dream* of talking to you like that. *It's unfortunate you feel that way* – man, get the fuck outta here with that."

Javon feels his lips twisting. He battles to keep his face blank. He stares at Tyrell. Imagines his hands wrapped around his throat. Imagines cracking the side of his skull open on the edge of the stage next to him.

Soon, Javon won't need the JJC at all. He won't need to put up with complaints and headaches like this. The investors coming tomorrow, if they sign up, they can take him away from street-level bullshit. Then the JJC can revert back to The Crew for all he cares.

"You know what your problem is, Tyrell?" Javon says, feeling in control again.

Tyrell smirks. "I'm sure you're gonna tell me."

"You're *small*, Tyrell. Everything about you is *small*. You think small. You dream small. You *live* small. You've confined your life to a handful of blocks in one city. There's a whole country out there, man. A whole world. The time has long been and gone when you needed to expand your horizons. You know what I worry? I worry that it's too late for you. That you're *incapable* of dreaming any bigger. But lucky for you, you have *me*."

Tyrell does not respond.

"Because without me, you'd be dead by now. Either dead, or on the run, or hiding out in some rundown, abandoned tenement. You wouldn't be wearing designer gear. You wouldn't be driving sport cars. You wouldn't have that apartment, even though you spend most of your time in *mine*. You'd still be nothing more than a corner boy. You know that, don't you? I can see it in your eyes. You know everything I've done for you already. You know how I've saved your life. How's *that* for respect? I dragged you up from the gutters. You hitched your wagon and I brought you all the way to *here*. *Me* – I did that. Because you *can't*, you ain't got the ambition, and you know that. Without me, you're nothing. And you know *that*, too."

They stare at each other in silence again. Tyrell looks like he wants to hit him. He won't dare, though. He knows what will happen if he tries.

Javon steps closer, as if daring him to take a swing. Javon is smiling now. "You wanna talk about respect? The respect needs to be flowing one way, Tyrell. It needs to be flowing *to* me. Think yourself lucky that any of it flows *from* me. We clear on that? You work for *me*, motherfucker. You wanna keep living in these bright, sunshiny days that I have built for us, you'd do well to remember that." He gets close to Tyrell. He puts his face inches from his. Tyrell holds his eye, the corners of his mouth downturned. "Now get the fuck out of here," Javon says. "I've got shit to do."

35

It's early morning. The GCTF have been summoned. They head to the scene in two cars. Carter drives. He has Delia and Anthony with him. Nick and Darren follow close behind.

"Why've we been called?" Anthony says. Anthony arrived to HQ after they received the call. They were already heading out to the cars when he turned up. "I ain't clear on that. Why've we gotta go?"

"Cop killing," Delia says. She's sitting up front. Anthony is in the back. She turns to see him better. "Two dead."

"Holy shit," Anthony says. "What do we know?"

"Nothing yet," Delia says. "Carter was called direct. They said they didn't wanna put it over the radio, but we needed to come over *fast*."

Carter glances in the mirror, checks that Nick and Darren are still behind. They are. The cop who called him is friendly to the GCTF. Carter remembers what the cop told him over the phone. He repeats it for Anthony. "He said we're in trouble," Carter says. "He said he's gonna keep the scene quiet for us, but then he'll have to make it known. Once he does that, we're on our own."

"What the fuck?" Anthony says, leaning forward. "What is it? How's it reflecting bad on us?"

Carter shakes his head. He grips the steering wheel tight. "We'll know soon enough."

They reach the scene. It's cordoned off, but there's no crowd, no one trying to snatch a look. The bodies have been dumped in scrubland. There are four cruisers parked around the area. The uniformed cops all turn to the GCTF as they pull up. Carter gets out first. He leads the way. The others follow.

The cop who called Carter direct comes over to him. "Word's getting out," he says. "People are finding out. I could only keep it quiet for so long."

Carter nods. They make their way through the cordon and toward the bodies.

"Dog-walker found them," the cop says. "I was closest in the area. They ain't in uniform and they don't have ID, but I recognised them both straight away."

Carter sees the bodies. He knows them both, too. They were put on Rosette Walker's house. They're both stripped naked. One has been shot through the head. The other's throat has been cut. Words have been carved into their bodies, predominantly in their torsos, but also in their stomachs and arms, and up and down their legs. The same pair of acronyms, over and over – DLB, and GCTF.

"*Fuck*," Nick breathes at Carter's shoulder.

Carter stares at the bodies. At the initials carved into them. There isn't much blood where they've been carved. They were already dead when this was done.

"We're gonna get raked over the coals for this," Delia says. She's at Carter's other shoulder.

Carter nods. He steps back, motions his team to come closer. "They were on Rosette Walker," he says. "This is no coincidence." He calls to the cop who called him. "Where's their car?"

"Where they left it," the cop says.

"Outside Rosette Walker's?" Carter says.

The cop shrugs. "If that's where they were."

Carter turns to his team. "Listen, I'm gonna head down into the station, get my ass chewed out over this. Anthony and Darren, you two get over to Rosette's place. She ain't gonna be there, but check anyway. See if anyone around there saw anything – they're not gonna talk, but that doesn't matter. Rough them up, do whatever, I don't give a shit. Nick and Delia, hit the streets. Hit them *hard*. I want the DLB. I want Darius Walker."

The four get into the other car. Carter gets into his own and heads toward the precinct rather than wait to be called in. Get it over and done with. The precinct is further away than Rosette Walker's house. He pulls into the parking lot and waits five minutes to see if Anthony and Darren check in. They do.

"She's gone," Darren says.

Carter is not surprised.

"We've been through the house," Darren continues. "Most of her clothes are gone. Looks like she's either skipped town, or she's in hiding now. Maybe with her son. I'm guessing her boy's men moved her out when they grabbed the cops."

"Sounds like it," Carter says.

"You been inside yet?"

"Not yet."

"Steeling yourself?"

"I'm steely enough. Whatever they wanna throw at us, I can handle it."

"Good luck, boss man. We're gonna hit the rest of the street, see what we can find. We get finished here, we'll go catch up with Nick and Delia, shake some more branches."

"Find us something good," Carter says. He hangs up and looks at the building. He gets out of the car and heads inside. He's expecting to eat some shit. He grins to himself. Sure, he can plaster an apologetic look on his face and pretend he cares. He can give that impression. He's not going to be in this city forever. Soon enough, they'll be eating *his* shit.

36

Tom is driving. Ruth sits up front with him. Calvin is in the back. They're going to see Montel Lindo. Calvin got in touch with him, told him they were coming over. Montel was hesitant.

"Is this about the picture?" he said. "I – I don't want to get involved any further, man. I gave you the picture. What you do with it is up to you. I don't wanna get involved."

"We just need a little help from you," Calvin said, using his most reassuring tone as per Tom's instruction.

Eventually, Montel agreed to let them come around.

Tom has the radio on. Every local station is playing news. It's a big morning. The reports are alarmed. Two cops have been killed in an apparent gangland murder. They aren't giving many details right now.

"Jesus, that's awful," Ruth says.

Tom nods. He turns the radio off. There's nothing more to learn about the murders. It'll be a while before all information is released.

Tom hasn't slept much. He stayed on guard through the night. If he hadn't been on guard, he would have lain awake thinking anyway. His mind couldn't settle. Come the morning, he'd decided they'd go and see the guy Calvin got the picture from. There wasn't anyone else they could turn to. Tom needs to know whom they're up against. He knows who Javon Johnson is and what he looks like, but he doesn't know who the GCTF are. He needs to know their names. He needs to know their faces. Tom's phone, however, has no internet connection. The kind of cheap burner phones he buys tend not to. Calvin's phone is still at Noah's gym, in his locker. Ruth's is back at their apartment. Tom has equipped them both with a couple of his burners, in case they get separated.

When they reach Montel's home, Calvin goes up first. Tom and Ruth get out of the car but they remain beside it, standing where Montel can see them both. When he answers the door, he doesn't open it all the way. He opens it a crack, peering out. He and Calvin speak briefly. Montel leans past him to see Tom and Ruth. Calvin steps aside to give him a better view. They speak a little more. Tom imagines Calvin is having to explain who he is.

Eventually, Montel steps back into the house and pushes the door open wide. Calvin waves Tom and Ruth over.

Montel is waiting for them in the hallway. "So you wanna know who the task force are," he says. It's not a question.

"We need to," Tom says.

"What are you planning on doing with that information?" Montel says.

"I don't know yet," Tom says. "But if these people are with our enemies, then I need to know who they are. If someone is coming at us, I need to know what they look like."

"All right," Montel says. He holds up his hands. "I'm not sure I want to know more than that. Come with me." He leads them through to his room. His laptop is already fired up. "They're public figures," he says, dropping into his seat. "This won't take long to find them."

"You familiar with them yourself?" Tom says as Montel begins his search.

"I've never needed to be," Montel says. "The less I have to do with cops, the better."

"That since they smashed your phone?"

"Calvin told you about that? Well, that particular incident didn't help, but no, it predates that."

"Why'd you go see them in the first place?"

"Because I'd just watched a man gun down two people." Montel clicks through pages. "And then I heard that the murdered couple were parents, and I had the picture, so how could I just sit on it? You try and do the right thing... Hey, wait a minute. There's something else coming up about the GCTF." He clicks onto a different page and starts reading through.

"What is it?" Tom says. Ruth and Calvin are standing close, too, watching the screen.

"You hear about them two dead cops?" Montel says.

"We heard on the radio," Ruth says.

Montel frowns at the screen. "Word online is that there was maybe a message carved into their bodies," he says.

"What did it say?"

"It didn't *say* anything – just initials, over and over. DLB, and GCTF."

Tom and Ruth glance at each other. "Going from what Reggie told me, it sounds like the war could be heating up between the JJC and the DLB," Tom says. "If this was the

DLB who did these killings – and it wouldn't make sense for the JJC to do them – carving the task force's initials into the cops' bodies is a big message to send." He points at the laptop screen. "Bring up the team."

"Sounds like the Detroit Lifer Boyz are trying to solve a problem for you," Montel says, clicking back through pages.

"I don't want to trust our fates into the hands of the DLB," Tom says. "They've already come at us. They're not on our side."

An image appears. A big man, thick with muscle, staring into the camera with cold, steely eyes while he has his picture taken. There's a sharp intake of breath to Tom's left. He looks. It's Ruth. She swallows, staring at the picture, staring at the man.

"That's him," she says, unable to tear her eyes away. "That's the man who came to our door, who told us not to press the investigation."

"Shit, you sure?" Calvin says, leaning around Montel and Tom to see his sister.

"I'll never forget him," Ruth says.

"Carter Brown," Montel says, reading the information to the right of the picture. "He runs the task force. Says here he's ex-SWAT, too. This guy's hardcore."

Tom commits Carter Brown's face to memory. He tells Montel to go through the rest of them. He commits their names and faces to memory, along with Carter. Delia Curtis, Anthony Felton, Darren Wong, and Nick Sanchez.

"These are the two who broke my phone," Montel says, toggling the images back and forth between Darren and Nick. "Or, to be precise, Nick broke it while Darren giggled."

Tom looks between Ruth and Calvin. "You got all that? Names and faces?"

Ruth nods. Calvin says, “I’ve got it.”

“Good,” Tom says. “You see any of those people coming, run.”

37

Tom drives back to the motel near Grosse Pointe with Ruth and Calvin. They're silent in the car. They had the radio on after they first left Montel's, but there were no updates to the murder of the two cops – it hasn't been reported officially yet about the carvings in their bodies. The police department no doubt wants to keep that information quiet for as long as possible, especially when one of those sets of initials is aimed at their much-lauded Gang Control Task Force.

Ruth sits up front again. As they near the motel, she speaks up. "What are we supposed to do?" she says. Her voice is quiet. She sounds defeated. "They're cops. They warned us off. They warned Montel off. Who knows how many other people they might have threatened? And they're working with the gang who killed our parents. They must know what Javon and his men are doing, right? They must know that they've been coming after us. What can – what can we do? Who can we turn to? Who's going to help us?"

"I'm helping you," Tom says.

"And we're thankful, but you're just one man. Who's going to help *you*?"

"We're just going to have to help each other," Tom says, taking his eyes off the road long enough to look into hers. He turns back to driving. "Right now, the three of us, we're all we can rely upon."

"Have you ever had problems with cops before?"

Tom laughs. "Yes."

"How did you deal with them?"

"That depends on the kind of problem we had with each other."

Ruth is silent. Tom can feel her watching the side of his face, studying him. "We haven't had much of a chance to talk yet, Tom, but I think some time soon we're going to have to have a very in-depth conversation about your background."

"I'm an open book," Tom says, "so long as you ask the right questions."

They reach the motel. On the opposite side of the road, Tom spots someone sitting inside a car that wasn't parked there when they left. He doesn't look directly at the vehicle. Out his peripheral vision, it looks like there is one man inside. Older, balding, white. Tom pulls around the back of the motel and parks up.

Ruth sees the look on his face. "What's wrong?"

"Might be nothing," Tom says. "Just stick close to me, both of you. And act casual. Be natural. Don't act like there might be something wrong."

Calvin leans forward. "*Is* there something wrong?"

"Act natural, and I'll be able to tell you," Tom says.

They get out of the car and head around the front of the motel, toward their room. Tom looks straight ahead. Again, he looks toward the car with his peripheral vision. It's hard to tell, but he thinks the man behind the wheel is watching them. He thinks, too, that he might have slid down in his seat in a too-late attempt to be inconspicuous.

When they reach the door and Tom is unlocking it, Calvin crowds him. "Did you see anything?"

Tom pushes the door open. "Just wait here," he says. He checks the doorway, then peers into the room. It's clear. "Follow me." He checks under the bed and looks into the bathroom. He checks the windows. They're all locked still. They haven't been tampered with.

Ruth is last into the room. She closes the door behind her, watching Tom.

"Close the curtains," Tom says. "Close them all the way and then leave them alone. No one try to look out of them."

"Are you gonna tell us what you saw?" Calvin says.

As Ruth closes the curtains, Tom goes to the door. He peers out of the spy hole. He can just make out the occupied car at the very left edge of the fishbowl view. "There's a man in a car out there," he says. "Could be nothing, could be something. Calvin, keep an eye on the parking lot at the rear."

"On it," Calvin says.

Ruth steps close to Tom. "What do you see?"

"He's still in the car," Tom says. "It's hard to tell through this. I can't actually see him, but the doors haven't opened."

"Did he look like he was on the task force, or in the gang?"

"I don't know," Tom says. "I just glanced him as we were passing. But I don't think he's part of either – he looked older. Middle age. Like I say, this could be nothing, but it's better to be sure." He glances at Ruth. She's standing very close. He can feel the warmth of her body against his left arm. "If it *is* something, and he starts making his way over here, I'm going to need some space."

"Then you tell me in advance when he's coming this way," Ruth says, "and I'll give you some space. But for now I'm standing here, with you."

"Fair enough," Tom says, returning his eye to the spyhole. "If he's going to come up, he's not going to do it straight away. He'd want us to get settled first."

"Do you think he knows you saw him?"

"I don't know," Tom says. "I tried not to make it obvious."

Ruth turns and calls through to Calvin. "What's it like out there?"

"It's fine," Calvin calls back. "It's quiet. There's no one out there, just some cars."

"They empty?" Tom says.

"Yeah, they're empty."

Ten minutes pass. Twenty. No one moves. The car remains where it's parked.

"How long are you going to give it?" Ruth says. She's pacing the floor now.

"Until he leaves," Tom says. "And then I'm going to go out there and take a look around, make sure there's nothing and no one I've missed."

Another fifteen minutes pass. Tom is already armed. He left the motel armed when they went to see Montel. His KA-BAR is strapped to his belt and his Beretta is tucked down his jeans.

Finally, there's movement. The car door opens. The man steps around the front of it, checking that the road is clear to cross. He comes toward the motel. He comes toward the room.

"He's on his way," Tom says. "Go in the bathroom with Calvin. Both of you get into the tub and lie low."

He hears Ruth doing as she's told behind him. Hears them both moving around in the bathroom, getting into the bathtub. Tom pulls out his Beretta and raises it so it rests against the door next to his face. He watches the man as he draws near. The man is probably in his fifties. He's stocky. As his features come into focus, it's clear that he's been in some scrapes over his life. His nose has obviously been broken a few times. He wears a heavy jacket that could easily conceal a holster. He pauses, looks left and right, checking the front of the motel. He looks toward the road again, and then turns and comes toward the door.

Tom opens the door and grabs him by the front of his shirt, dragging him inside, then slams the door shut and presses him up against it, Beretta jabbed into the side of his neck.

"Whoa, shit, Jesus!" the man cries out, surprised. "Hold up, just calm down a minute!"

Tom pats him down. He reaches inside the jacket, and sure enough there is a shoulder holster. Tom pulls out a Colt Python. He tosses it back onto the bed, pats the man down the rest of the way, checking him for ankle holsters, or anything else concealed. There's nothing. He finds his wallet. He throws it onto the bed next to the gun. Tom straightens up. "Start talking."

"Gladly," the man says, hands raised. "You wanna get this thing outta my neck first?"

"No," Tom says. "Talk."

"Listen, I get that you're all worked up, but trust me here, I'm on your side."

Tom says nothing.

The man sighs. He looks at Tom and he grins a little. "I had a feeling you were gonna be hard work," he says. "A real hard ass. I looked into you, Rollins. Took me a while to find a clear enough picture of the white guy the siblings were running around with, but I found it. Ex-Army, ex-CIA black ops, huh? At least they found themselves a useful friend."

Tom keeps his face blank. He betrays nothing. "You know who I am. That's nice. Now, I'm only gonna ask you one time – who are *you*?"

"Fred Boothe," the man says. "Ex-Baltimore PD, current private dick."

"A private detective?" Tom says. "What are you doing here?"

"That's what I'm gonna explain," Fred says. "I'm on *your* side, my man. Or, more accurately, I'm on the side of Ruth and Calvin Styles. You wanna bring them out here?"

"Not yet," Tom says. "And they can hear you just fine. So speak."

"I was hired by Lainey Wylder."

Tom cocks his head. He doesn't know the name.

"She's the District Attorney. I've worked for her for a while now, but for the last two years she's told me to keep an eye on Ruth and Calvin. To make sure they're okay. That no one was watching them, following them, giving them any trouble."

"You missed Calvin looking for trouble."

"I didn't follow them at all hours. And I have other responsibilities. So long as no one was lurking outside their apartment or their building, or following them to school or work, then it looked like they were safe to me."

"Why's the D.A. got such a vested interest in their wellbeing?"

"She can tell them herself. Probably best they hear it from her. She wants to see them."

"How'd you find us?"

"I didn't serve in the force around here, but I've still got some contacts. A few guys in tech support I know I can trust. They went through security footage, found the direction your car was going in. Couldn't track it all the way, but it was clear you were heading up toward Grosse Pointe. I got a list of motels and hotels in the area. After that, it was a matter of tipping the front desks and flashing your pictures. This motel hit paydirt. So I've sat tight since, and hoped you'd come back."

Tom keeps the gun on Fred. "Ruth, Calvin, come through here." Tom waits until he can hear them nearby. "Check his wallet. Find his ID. Read it out to me."

Tom keeps his eyes locked on Fred's while Ruth goes through the wallet.

"I've got his driver's license," she says.

"His name?"

"It's who he says he is." She rummages a little further. "His private detective ID is here, too."

"Listen, do I look like I'm running around with the JJC?" Fred says.

"You look like you could be real friendly with the GCTF," Tom says.

"You know about them, huh?" Fred says. "Well, let me tell you this – I *ain't* friendly with them. Not by a long stretch. I'm here to help."

Tom takes the gun away from Fred's neck, though he keeps it raised for now. He steps back. Slowly, he lowers the gun.

Fred looks at Ruth and Calvin. "Lainey wants to see you

both. She wants to keep you safe. I get that you don't trust me. You're paranoid right now. It makes sense. But here's what we can do – I drive out there, lead the way, you follow in your own car. Keep hold of my gun, keep hold of my wallet. We'll stick to open spaces. I won't lead you anywhere shady. I won't take you down any side roads or back streets. It's a straightforward drive."

Tom looks at Ruth and Calvin. "It's your call," Tom says.

"We should probably go," Ruth says. "The District Attorney, she can probably help us, right? We don't have anyone else."

"I can call her and we can be on our way," Fred says. "Since all this shit kicked off, she's been worried. I know she's gonna feel a lot better knowing that she can speak to you."

"They're not going without me," Tom says.

"Yeah," Calvin says.

Ruth nods her agreement.

Fred holds up his hands. "More the merrier. I don't give a shit."

"And we're not following you blindly," Tom says. "You call her now. I want to know where we're going in advance."

38

Lainey gets a call from Fred. She's alone in her office. She answers it fast. "Do you have good news?"

"Yeah, I've got good news," Fred says. "I've found the kids, and their protector. With them right now, in fact. They're willing to come see you, but they've got trust issues."

"That's understandable," Lainey says. "I assume you're doing your best to reassure them?"

"You know me, Lainey. I'm a friendly guy. An open book. I don't blame them for being careful. They're willing to meet, but they want to know where we're going in advance."

Lainey checks the time. She looks out of her window. "It's going to be dark soon," she says. "We can meet in an hour. Somewhere secluded."

"You got a place in mind?"

"Let me think on it. We need to be sure it'll be safe. I'll message you the details." She hangs up and thinks for a moment, considering locations. She's been to a few clandestine meet-ups in her time. They want somewhere safe and secure. Somewhere that's not going to spook them on the drive up to it. She has somewhere in mind. She sends Fred the address.

Getting to her feet, she gathers up her things. She told Fred they'd meet in an hour, and it will take her twenty minutes to get where they're going, but she knows there'll be traffic, at least at first. And she wants to get there early. To make sure it's clear, in case they need to quickly redirect.

She pulls on her coat, turns off the lights and leaves her office. Katy looks up at her as the door opens. She sees Lainey wearing her coat. Katy frowns.

"I need to head out," Lainey says. "I won't be coming back today."

"Oh," Katy says, surprised. She checks the time. Sees that it's still early. "Is there – is anything wrong?"

"No, no. Just a – a personal issue."

Katy is frowning. Probably wondering what kind of personal issue Lainey might have. She looks suspicious. She seems to realise what her face is doing. She shakes it loose and smiles. "Of course. I hope everything's all right. If anyone calls –"

"Just take a message," Lainey says. "Tell them I'll be in office tomorrow. I'll get back to them then."

Lainey doesn't wait for a response. She starts walking. Her heart is pounding. Ruth and Calvin have been found. This is important to her. She can't fix what happened two years ago, but she can at least try to make things right now.

She hopes that what she can offer is enough.

39

Javon's potential business partners are enjoying themselves.

It might be dark outside, but it's not late in the day. They're throwing themselves into the occasion with enthusiasm. Most of them are already drunk. A few have treated themselves to the lines of coke laid out for them, and as the evening and night wears on, Javon has no doubt that more and more of them will partake. After all, everything here for them is free. He's footing the bill.

"Just have a good time," he told them when they arrived. "I'll deal with everything."

The girls, too, are free. The music is pounding and some of the girls are up on the stages throughout the club, going through their routines. Most of them, though, are on the floor. With the suited men. Offering private dances, or else just giving them company while they drink and eat and talk and laugh.

Everything has a cost, though. These men, right now,

they're blissfully ignorant, but in time they will understand what this night has cost them.

Of course, that's only if they make things difficult.

If they do what Javon hopes they will, if they partner up with him and invest in his projects, if they're all willing to make each other a lot of money, then there will be no problems. They can all continue smiling and laughing together.

If they *don't*, then Javon will have to get dirty. He has no problem with getting dirty.

Some of Javon's men are also present. They stick to the sidelines, keeping out of the way. He picked the ones who look best in suits. The ones who aren't likely to draw much attention to themselves. The ones who can behave best, who can smile at these rich, fat white men in their own ill-fitting suits, no matter how sweaty and obnoxious they get as the night rolls on.

"Just keep smiling," Javon told them. "They can't say or do a damn thing to upset you tonight, you got that? I want these motherfuckers *happy*. And I want all of you to capture *exactly* how happy they are."

Javon talked to the girls, too. "I don't care how gross these men might appear to you. I don't care how much they might dry you up. Anything they want, you give it to them. You got me? You go all the fucking way if that's what they want. They want you to stick a bottle up their ass while they suck your toes, you do it. The more incriminating the better."

As it gets later, and wilder, Javon's men will start filming. Right now, they wait. They stick to the shadows. When the time is right, Javon will give them the nod. Everything on the club floor is open to them – capture it all. Already, he has men behind two-way mirrors in the backrooms, capturing what is happening there. Javon is sure the footage will only become more colourful as the night progresses.

Most of these men are married. They're respectable businessmen. Footage of them tangled with strippers and drunkenly snorting copious amounts of drugs will not go down well with their public image.

If they don't give Javon what he wants, if they don't play nice, he has no problem with resorting to blackmail.

Javon mingled when the party first started. He made small-talk, helped set the men's minds at ease, invited them to partake of everything on offer. As the businessmen have loosened up, he's retreated from the floor. He stands off to the side now, watching it all. The men are getting louder, but they're not wild enough. Not yet. The club floor is still tame, compared to how he expects it to become.

Tyrell comes and stands beside him, watching over it all. Javon glances at him, looks him up and down. He's wearing baggy jeans and an oversized jacket, hands in both pockets. Javon rolls his eyes, turning away. "Didn't you get the memo? You should be in a suit."

"I didn't know I was invited," Tyrell says.

"It's a surprise to see you, I've gotta say." It's not too much of a surprise, truthfully. Tyrell always comes back. He doesn't apologise, but he always comes back. "What are you doing here?"

"Just came to see how it's going." Tyrell doesn't look at Javon. He watches the men, and the naked and half-naked girls who serve and straddle them. "They're drunk."

"They're going to get a lot drunker," Javon says.

"You spiked the drinks?"

"Keep your voice down," Javon says. "And no. There's no need. There're drugs already on offer, and it's all free."

"They're animals," Tyrell says, watching them with disgust. "Pigs."

"They're also *very* fucking rich. That's all that matters to us."

"It's all that matters to *you*."

Javon sighs. "We gonna go through this again? Don't try and pretend to me like you don't give a shit about making money."

Tyrell doesn't respond. He clears his throat purposefully. "The kid we went after," he says, changing the subject, "and his sister, and the guy with them – that all don't concern you?"

Javon shrugs. "Not particularly. It'll be dealt with. Our people are out there looking for them, and so is Carter and *his* people. They'll be found. They can't hide forever."

"Carter and his people got their *own* problems right now. You heard what the DLB did to two cops?"

"Of course I heard about it," Javon says.

"I fucking warned him about this. I told Carter, to his goddamn face, that it would be a problem. He didn't listen – same way *you* don't listen to me no more. We've got this kid and his sister, and that's a big problem for *you* especially, and they've got this guy helping them, *and* we've got the DLB causing problems, and you're here at some fucking party for a bunch of rich assholes."

Javon stays calm. "Without these rich assholes, how can we ever become rich assholes ourselves?"

Tyrell makes a noise, clucking his tongue against his teeth. "You know what your problem is, man?"

Javon snorts. "I'm sure you're gonna tell me."

"You're looking too far ahead, when you need to be focusing on the *right now*. None of this – *none of this* –" he motions toward the party, "matters if we don't deal with what's affecting us in the present."

Javon turns and stares at Tyrell until Tyrell finally faces him. Javon leans in close, eyes locked. "Then why don't you go out there and *do* something about all of these problems?"

Tyrell bristles.

"The street-level shit is *your* responsibility," Javon says. "I'm done with this conversation." Without another word, without waiting for a response, he turns and makes his way over to the gathering, shaking grateful hands and inserting himself into conversations. He checks in with people, sees how they're doing, if they're having a good time, if they need anything else. One of his girls, wearing only heels and a thong, comes to his side and he wraps an arm around her waist. He sees how the men he's talking to stare lasciviously at her, not making any attempt to hide where their eyes settle upon her chest.

Javon glances back to where he stood with Tyrell. Tyrell is still there. Still standing, both hands in pockets. He's staring back at Javon. Javon holds his eyes just a moment longer, and thinks on how Tyrell is becoming a problem for him. He's becoming an issue. Javon might need to replace him. There are any number of people within the JJC ready to step up and take Tyrell's place. Javon remembers the names Tyrell mentioned yesterday: Jamar, Kameron, and Alonzo. He thinks on them. Any one of them would gladly ascend to his right hand and take Tyrell's place. Javon smirks to himself. Tyrell wanted to talk about loyalty. Javon can show him how easily loyalty can be bought by finding his replacement.

Javon turns his back on Tyrell, and turns his attention fully to the party.

40

Fred leads the way. True to his word, he doesn't try anything stupid. He sticks to open roads and obvious roads, at no time trying to lure them down a shady street or easily entrapped alleyway.

"Should we trust him?" Ruth says. She's riding shotgun. Calvin leans forward from the back, watching the car ahead of them. On the seat beside him, they have Fred's Colt Python and his wallet.

"He's been on the level so far," Tom says. "But we'll wait and see. I'm reticent to trust anyone too fully straight off the bat."

"He said he works for the District Attorney," Calvin says. "What's that got to do with us? Do you think it has anything to do with our parents' shooting?"

"We'll know soon enough," Tom says.

They head to a quiet part of the city, and stop the cars at a wasteland.

"I know this place," Ruth says, looking around. "There

used to be houses here. They were demolished a few years ago. Nothing's been built on this ground since."

"It's secluded," Tom says. "Quiet." It's open, too, which means Tom has a clear view of the surrounding area, which is well lit by streetlamps, both near and distant. The light from them means he can see the outline of the woman standing in the field, her coat wrapped tight around herself against the cold, her hands deep in her pockets. Her own car, a Mercedes, is parked nearby. Fred has stopped his car behind it. Tom has parked behind him, but has left enough space to quickly turn out in case they need to flee.

"Wait here," Tom says. "I'll go over and make sure things are as they say. I'll get a better view of the area too, make sure no one's trying to get the drop on us."

Tom gets out of the car and waits for Fred to come over. "Do I get my things back yet?" Fred says.

"Not yet," Tom says.

Fred grins. "*You* armed?"

"You better believe it. Lead the way."

Fred turns and starts heading toward the shadowed shape standing in the field, waiting for them. Tom follows, but he holds back, keeps a safe distance, his hand close to his Beretta. He looks around, across the fields. He looks back, toward the cars, making sure no one is creeping up on Ruth and Calvin. The area is clear. The only sounds he can hear are distant – cars, and the faint churning of a factory. They get close and he sees the woman. She looks Tom over. She looks beyond him, to the car, where Ruth and Calvin sit. She's a tall woman. She stands erect, her spine straight. Authority emanates from her. She's a woman who is used to being listened to, because she's had to fight to be heard. "Ruth and Calvin Styles," she says, fixing Tom with a level stare. "Why haven't you brought them over?"

"Lainey, this is Tom Rollins. He's –" Fred says.

"I know who he is," Lainey says. "I read what you sent me on him. We appreciate what you've done, Mr. Rollins, but right now, I'm the person in the best position to help Ruth and Calvin."

"I'm sure you are," Tom says, "but I don't know who you are, and neither do they."

"I'm the District Attorney –"

"So we've been told, but anyone could tell us that."

"I'm a public figure. It's easily checked."

"We've been without internet. I'm going to need to see ID."

She doesn't protest. She reaches into her handbag and brings out her ID. She holds it out. Fred takes it from her and hands it to Tom. Tom turns toward the light. He hasn't seen ID for a District Attorney before, but it looks legit. The image is of the woman before him, and it has her name as Lainey Wylder. Tom hands the ID back to Fred.

"All right," Tom says. He motions to the car, to Ruth and Calvin. They get out and start making their way over. As they do, Tom hears Lainey's breath catch. When he looks at her, her face is still. Something about seeing the siblings, however, brought out an involuntary noise from her. A gasp, quickly swallowed down, choked off, not wanting it to be heard.

Ruth and Calvin stop next to Tom. They look at Lainey. Ruth cocks her head. "I recognise you," she says. "I've seen you before."

Lainey's mouth is turned down at the corners. Her expression is solemn.

"You were at our parents' funeral," Ruth says.

Lainey nods.

"I wondered who you were. There was a man with you. He was clearly a bodyguard, but he was pretending he wasn't. I didn't recognise you, but there were a lot of people there I didn't know. Mom and Dad had a lot of friends. There were a lot of people they knew from their jobs. I figured you must have been from their work."

Lainey has to cough before she can speak. She takes a deep breath. "I assume your parents never told you about me. I thought they wouldn't. To keep you both safe. To shield you from what was happening, what we were doing."

"What *were* you doing?" Calvin says.

"For the last few years, my team and I have been investigating accusations of corruption and brutality from within the Gang Control Task Force," Lainey says. She looks around, like she's suddenly worried about someone sneaking up on them. "It was difficult to get anything on them. Every time we thought we had something, the evidence would either disappear, or people who were willing to testify would suddenly clam up. But then your father saw something, and he was willing to testify, and no one could quiet him."

"What did he see?" Ruth says.

"There'd been a shootout," Lainey says. "The GCTF and a gang they were hunting. Your father was there, he and about half a dozen other paramedics. While he was tending to someone wounded in the shootout, he saw the GCTF kill another member of the gang in cold blood. He saw and overheard them extorting the man for information as to the whereabouts of a drug stash. Once he answered, they shot him dead, then planted a gun on his body. Your father saw all of that, and he was willing to talk to us. He was willing to testify to what he had seen. Not only did the GCTF kill that man in cold blood, the drug stash was never turned in. Two years later, it's probably long gone, up some noses and in bloodstreams."

"We don't care about the drugs," Ruth says, her voice hard, choked with reawakened grief.

"No, no, of course not, I'm sorry," Lainey says. "I wanted to put your father under protection, to keep him safe, but he didn't want to disrupt your lives – yours and your brother's, and your mother's. I didn't like it, but I couldn't force it. And at the time, your father had only spoken to me and a couple of others, people I trust. No one else knew about him, or what he was willing to do. But then he and your mother were shot down. Made to look like they were caught up in a drive-by. I've never believed that's how it happened. They were targeted, and I believe the GCTF hired the shooter."

Calvin takes the picture of Javon from his pocket. He unfolds it and holds it up for Lainey to see. Tom can see that Calvin's arm is shaking. He can't speak. He's too angry at all he has heard.

"Javon Johnson," Tom says. "Leader of the JJC. They have connections to the GCTF. They're in business together."

Lainey studies the picture. "I've heard of him," she says. "And we've heard rumours of the GCTF's connection to at least one gang in the city." She looks away from the picture. She looks at Ruth and Calvin. "I know there's nothing I can say, but I want you both to know that I understand what happened to your parents is my fault. I've lived with that guilt every day for the last two years. It eats at me. I'll never forget them. I'm so, so sorry for all that I've put you through."

Ruth and Calvin say nothing.

"I've had Fred here watching out for you both. The GCTF weren't watching you. They seemed to be leaving well enough alone. It seemed like you were safe. If it had ever appeared otherwise, I would have had Fred bring you both in sooner. I can protect you. The way I should have insisted to your parents. I have a safe house set up, and bodyguards. We can hide you out there until this is resolved."

"Until it's resolved?" Tom says. "That could take years."

"With recent goings-on, I believe that things will happen faster than we anticipate," Lainey says. "Have you heard about the two policemen who were murdered this morning?"

Tom nods. "And we heard it was the Detroit Lifer Boyz calling out the GCTF."

Lainey raises her eyebrows. "You heard about that, did you? My understanding was that information had not been released to the public."

"We've got our ways," Tom says.

"That where you were before you came back to the motel?" Fred says. "You've never told me where you'd gone."

"Because it wasn't any of your business," Tom says. He turns his attention back to Lainey. "What makes you think that a couple of dead cops is going to speed things up?"

"The DLB and the JJC are already at war, we know that," Lainey says. "If the DLB are going after the GCTF now, that means things are about to escalate. I believe it's only a matter of time before the GCTF expose themselves. They'll show their hands, give away their allegiances and their crookedness."

"Even if things work out like that, and you get to build your case, that could *still* take years before you ever get them in court. There's nothing to say they're going to be imprisoned in the meantime, either."

"What else can we do?" Lainey says. "This is our best option. I know it's not ideal but I'm failing to see the problem."

"The problem is that you're about to take years out of their lives," Tom says. "Calvin has the potential for a promising boxing career, and Ruth is in training to become a nurse. You hide them away for a couple of years or more, and they've both got to start over. Instead of graduating high school, Calvin's gonna have to find another way to get his GED. Instead of heading into work, Ruth's gonna have to re-enrol in college."

"The alternative is they get buried next to their parents," Lainey says.

"I think she's right, Tom," Ruth says, placing a hand on Tom's arm. "I don't like it either, but they've already come for us, for both of us. I thought – I thought they *had* me, before you and Calvin turned up." She leans closer, lowers her voice. "And I have to think about keeping Calvin safe. Yes, it's going to set us back a few years, but if we don't take her up on this, then Calvin's going to get himself killed."

"What are you saying?" Calvin says, frowning. He probably heard his name.

"It's your decision," Tom says.

"Will you come with us?" Ruth says.

"There's going to be a bodyguard present," Lainey says.

"I've vetted him myself," Fred says. "And while you're there, I'll be out on the streets, gathering information on the GCTF and their friends. I promise we won't keep you in that house any longer than you need to be."

"I appreciate that," Ruth says, "but I think we'd both

appreciate it more if Tom were there. That is, if that's all right with him."

"Tom's been with us when he didn't have to be," Calvin says. "He's probably got a target on his back now, too."

Lainey and Fred look at each other.

"It's your call," Fred says.

"Fine," Lainey says. "If it'll make you feel better, take Mr. Rollins here with you. I'll call ahead, let James know that he'll be accompanying you."

"Tom here hasn't said yet if he's going with them," Fred says.

Tom looks at Ruth and Calvin. He looks at Lainey and Fred. "I'll go," he says. He made a promise to the siblings. He swore he'd keep them safe. He swore he'd get them through this. He can't just pass them off onto someone else.

"Then give me back my gun and ID," Fred says, "and I'll take you out there."

41

Carter is raw.

Sure enough, the chief chewed him out. He wanted answers. Wanted to know why two of his men turned up dead, with acronyms carved into their bodies. He wanted to know what kind of message it was supposed to be sending.

Carter was able to play it mostly dumb. "It's an occupational hazard," he said. "Every day your men put on their uniforms, they run the risk of something like this happening. It's the same for us in the task force. And listen, we were always gonna ruffle some feathers. That's always been our purpose, right? We upset a gang – it's hardly surprising. It's just unfortunate how this has played out."

The chief wasn't satisfied, but Carter didn't expect him to be. He kept chewing. Red in the face, spittle flying from his lips, he was screaming. Carter sat very still, a sounding board for him to get it all out of his system.

The chief eventually wore himself out. His voice was raspy by the time he was done. "You bring these assholes down," he said, jabbing a finger into the top of his desk for emphasis. "They've killed two of ours – you wipe those motherfuckers out."

Carter nodded. "I intend to," he said.

He's heading back to his apartment now. He contacted the rest of his team, but they had nothing important to tell him. He pulls his car to a stop in front of his building and gets out. His blood is high. His fists open and close, squeezing tight. They itch for the punching bag. He'll be envisioning the face of the chief, he knows. Decimate it, knuckles on leather.

A workout will help it. Will make him feel better. Will bring everything back into focus. Right now, he can't even suck down a deep breath. It gets caught in his chest. His teeth are grinding. There's a growl in the back of his throat. When people see him coming, they scatter to get out of his way.

No one talks to him like that. No one shouts and screams and demeans him, no matter what has happened. Out on the streets, someone talks to him like that, he smashes their teeth under his boot. He shatters their jaw with his fists.

For now, Carter needs to take it. This place won't be his life forever. Before long, he'll be out of here. He just needs to remember that. Keep his cool, and remember that freedom is just over the horizon.

Carter pauses outside the door to his apartment. He looks at the handle. Something about it doesn't look right. He doesn't brush it off. He looks up and down the hallway, making sure it's clear, then gets down on a knee and checks closer. There are scrapes in the metal around the keyhole. Carter has never noticed these before. Someone could have picked his lock. Someone could be inside his apartment right now.

Carter straightens up. He reaches back and pulls out his Smith & Wesson M&P, holding it in his right hand while with his left he takes out his keys. He keeps the gun high as he unlocks the door. He pushes it open slowly.

Inside is in darkness. He steps through cautiously. Leaves the lights off. He looks around. There's no one to see in the kitchen and living room. Holding his breath, he listens. Everything is still. He focuses on the sofa. Someone could be behind it, ducking low. Carter steps further into the room. He's left the door open behind him. The light from out in the hall is the only light cast in his apartment. He keeps his steps careful, one foot over the other. He keeps the gun raised. His eyes scan left to right, across the living room, watching the sofa, checking the closed door leading through to his bedroom.

A floorboard creaks. It comes from his room. It could be nothing. Just a settling board. It could be someone in there waiting for him.

Carter pauses. Nothing more happens. No one jumps out. He's close enough to the sofa now that he can see over the top of it. There's no one ducking down on the other side. The living room is clear.

He turns his attention to the closed door. His bedroom. He hears laughter out in the hallway behind him. A woman's laugh. It doesn't come any closer. It's heading down the stairs. No one passes by his apartment. No one is lurking out in the corridor, staying close to his door.

Again, moving the search into his bedroom, Carter takes his time. Keeps the gun high. Opens the door wide. It's darker beyond – it's dark already outside, but the curtains are closed and prevent any other light from getting in. The light from the hallway doesn't penetrate this far.

Another board creaks. It comes from his bed. Carter zeroes in on it. He sees movement underneath. He points the gun. From behind the door, a pair of hands grab his wrist and throw his arm up. Carter fires involuntarily. A bullet hits the ceiling. He hears someone in the apartment above shriek.

The body emerges from behind the door. It's followed by another man. A third scrambles out from under the bed. Carter grits his teeth. He kicks hard, bringing his boot up between the legs of the man holding his arm. His grip slackens. Carter can see that the other two men are pulling out their guns. Carter spins the man he's just kicked, grabs him, holds him close. A human shield. He fires at the man who emerged from under the bed. He's still getting to his feet. Struggling to bring out his weapon. Carter fires twice, catching him in the chest and shoulder. The other man from behind the door has his gun up. He fires. The bullet catches the doorframe next to Carter's head. Carter falls back out of the room. He pushes his shield forward. As he stumbles, falling toward the open doorway, Carter shoots him three times in the back.

The man still in the room does not emerge. He stays where he is.

"You're trapped in there," Carter says. "Soon as you step out, I've got you."

"Then maybe I'll just wait for you to come to me," the man responds.

"You really think you're in a position to do that?" Carter says. "After all these gunshots, and a bullet went through the ceiling? You think the cops aren't on their way here right now, coming to get you?"

The man doesn't respond to this.

"You DLB?" Carter says.

"We're gonna get you, cocksucker," the man says, spitting the words. There's an aggravated tone to his voice, more than just being caught up in a gunfight and seeing two of his friends dead. He's bracing himself. What Carter said made sense to him. He knows he can't wait. He's about to charge.

"You're gonna try," Carter says.

The man runs out, screaming, firing wildly. Carter is ready for him. He's pressed up tight against the wall, making himself as narrow a target as possible. He fires back. He has more luck. The man drops, winged. Carter hurries to him, puts two bullets through his face.

He falls back against the wall, breathing hard. He looks to the open door, out into the hallway. There could be more DLB nearby. Could be more of them in the building. Carter makes his way out of the apartment. He's not going to wait around for the uniforms to show up, either. He can tell them what happened once he's elsewhere, somewhere safe. This little shootout might lead to another raking over the coals for him with the chief, demanding more answers.

If it does, Carter can handle it. He can handle anything.

He hurries out of the apartment, keeping his gun in his hand, careful as he makes his way down the stairs and through the lobby. There's no one else around. The other occupants of the building are likely indoors after hearing the gunshots, finding places to lie low and cover themselves.

Out on the street, Carter keeps his gun out. He sees a small crowd gathered, looking up at the building. He recognises some of them as neighbours he never talks to. He turns away before they can see him. He goes to his car and quickly checks it over, makes sure it hasn't been broken into, and that nothing has been planted on it. When he's confident it's clear, he gets inside and starts it up. He puts the gun on the passenger seat beside him, where he can easily grab it. He starts driving, watching his mirrors, checking to see if anyone is following. He hears sirens coming toward the building, so he drives in the opposite direction.

He pulls out his phone and thumbs through his contacts. Delia's name comes up first. He calls her. "Contact everyone," he says, hearing as he speaks how calm he sounds, as if he hasn't just been attacked and in turn killed three men. "Tell them to grab some overnight bags and come down to HQ."

"Why, what's happened?" Delia says.

"The DLB just took a shot at me," Carter says. "We need to stick together."

42

Lainey doesn't accompany them to the safe house, but Fred does. Much like when he took them to Lainey, he leads the way and they follow. Except this time, Fred has his gun and his wallet back.

It's a quiet suburb on the outskirts of the city. Fred pulls up at the side of the road in front of the house, but he motions for Tom to pull onto the driveway. Tom does. He looks up and down the rest of the street. It's dark and it's starting to get late. There isn't any life to see, beyond porch lights and the lights that poke out through drawn curtains and closed blinds. The house Fred has led them to is mostly in darkness, but looking at the front door Tom can see a light from a lamp in the hallway beyond.

"If we're going to be here a while," Calvin says, looking the house over, "what are we supposed to do about clothes?"

"I'm sure they'll supply us with some stuff," Ruth says.

Tom kills the engine but doesn't get out of the car. Following his lead, Ruth and Calvin stay put, too. Tom looks back toward Fred. He's coming their way. Tom opens the door so they can speak.

"You coming in?" Fred says.

Tom looks again to the street. There aren't many vehicles parked on the road. Most of them are on driveways. He commits the ones on the road to memory. "Quiet here," Tom says, getting out of the car.

"Wouldn't make much sense to put a safe house somewhere loud," Fred says.

"How many people know about this?"

"Me, the bodyguard inside, and Lainey."

"That it?"

Fred nods. "We're keeping this small. We're not taking any chances."

Fred leads the way to the door. He knocks. Tom can't hear any movement inside. He watches the spyhole, though. He can see a little light shining through it from the lamp. The light darkens momentarily, and Tom knows someone is looking out at them.

The door opens. A muscular Black man stands inside the house. He and Fred know each other. They exchange handshakes and brief pleasantries. Fred tells him who each of them are.

"James Strand," the man says, offering a hand to Tom.

"Tom Rollins." They shake. James shakes hands with Ruth and Calvin, then invites them inside. He gives them a tour of the house. It doesn't take long. It's not a big house. One floor. Living room, kitchen, two bathrooms, three bedrooms.

"I understand, Tom Rollins," James says, taking Tom aside in the kitchen, "that you're going to be helping me do my job."

Tom nods.

"I hear you're ex-Army, too. Ex-CIA."

Tom nods again. "You?"

"Marine," James says.

"How long ago did you give that up?"

"Seven years now. You?"

"About four."

"I'm sure we'll be able to cooperate well, so long as neither of us decides to turn this into some kind of pissing contest."

"My piss goes in the bowl," Tom says. "Unless I'm in the wild, then all bets are off."

James grins. He calls to Ruth and Calvin. "I've ordered pizza," he says. "I figured you all might be hungry. I wasn't sure what everyone liked so I got a couple of plain, and a couple of pepperoni. They should get here in the next half-hour."

"Wish I could hang around and partake in the pizza party," Fred says, "but I need to go. If things are coming to a head in the city, I need to be there for it." He shakes hands with James, then holds his hand out to Tom. "I won't hold a grudge for you sticking a gun in my neck," he says. "Even though I can feel the bruising."

Tom grins. "I'm glad to hear it. I'd think less of you otherwise."

Fred laughs. To Ruth and Calvin he says, "You two stay safe. I promise you both we'll do all we can."

The siblings don't respond. Fred leaves. Ruth puts her arm around Calvin's shoulder. She squeezes him. Tom watches them both. Ruth is only eleven years older than her brother, but she looks like she could pass for his mother. A very young mother, no doubt, but she's had two years of caring for him in order to look the part.

"I'm not hungry," Calvin says. He peels away from his sister and goes to one of the rooms, closing the door behind him. Ruth watches him go. She wraps her arms around herself. Ruth looks at Tom. James senses that they want to speak and he leaves the kitchen, goes through to the living room. Tom assumes he'll look the street over. Check the cars. It's what Tom would do.

"This is going to be hard on Calvin," Ruth says.

"It's going to be hard on both of you," Tom says.

"I can handle it," she says. "I'm just worried that maybe he can't." She looks at the closed door. "We're going to have to keep an eye on him. To make sure he doesn't try to sneak away, go back to the city after Javon."

Tom grunts. He had already considered this.

Ruth rubs her arms like she's cold. She looks around this new kitchen in this strange new house. She looks lost. She looks like she wishes she were home. Tom places a hand on her shoulder. He doesn't have anything to say. For now, this is the only comfort he can give.

43

The GCTF are in HQ. They're all present, except for Anthony. The GCTF are on lockdown, but Carter granted Anthony permission to go out. He's gone to see his girlfriend. They're not on a date. She called. Said it's important that they meet. They know she wouldn't throw that word around lightly. The rest of the GCTF await his return.

It's getting late but none of them sleep. The room is lit by dim lamps. They don't have on the overheads. Carter sits at his desk, staring into the darkness where there are no lamps, watching the door. The windows are boarded over. He's on high alert, but he's also thinking. Thinking about how the DLB found him. He thinks it probably has something to do with the two dead cops this morning. *That* was the message. The DLB are coming for the GCTF. They've made their first move, but they fucked up. Carter is determined that it is the only move they'll make. They came after him in his home – he's going to tear their throats out.

Most uniforms don't know where GCTF HQ is. It's kept

secret, for obvious reasons. The DLB shouldn't know about this place. They should be safe here. Despite this knowledge, Carter keeps his eyes on the door. He told Anthony to keep him updated via message. If he walks in without announcing himself first, he's likely to take a bullet to the chest.

Delia sits at her desk, leaning back in her chair with her feet up. She's flicking through a magazine, but she's barely reading it. Her face is bored. Close to her, at his own desk, Nick is cleaning his gun. He's already polished his switchblade. On the ground, Darren lies flat, resting his head on his overnight bag. He's holding his phone up in front of his face, the glow from it lighting his face. From the rapid movement of his thumbs, Carter guesses he's playing a game.

Carter glances at his own phone. Anthony is on his way back. He says he's ten minutes out. "Anthony's inbound," he says.

The others stir at this. Delia puts down her magazine. Darren puts down his phone and gets to his feet, twisting his body to stretch it out. Nick finishes cleaning his gun and puts it back together.

The ten minutes pass. Carter's phone rings. It's Anthony. "I'm coming in," he says. "Don't fucking shoot me."

"I make no promises," Carter says, and hangs up.

They hear Anthony unlock the door. He steps inside, hands raised. He turns and relocks the door.

"What have you got for us?" Carter says. "She made it sound big."

"It's pretty big," Anthony says, coming closer. He's solemn. "You're not going to like it."

"Then spit it out," Carter says.

"Katy says Lainey and her private detective have found the kid and his sister." Anthony's girlfriend is Katy Doerr, secretary to District Attorney Lainey Wylder. Anything Katy hears coming out of the office pertaining to the GCTF, she passes it on to Anthony. When she contacted him tonight, she told him it couldn't wait.

"Shit, what?" Darren says.

"When?" Delia says.

Carter doesn't speak. He worried this might be the case.

"Today," Anthony says. "Katy says Lainey split from her office in a hurry, cagey about where she was going. Katy said she waited until after hours, when everyone else had gone, then used her key to unlock the D.A.'s door and go inside, check the bugs she's planted. She picked up the conversation."

"What's she done with them?" Carter says.

"She doesn't know," Anthony says, "but she reckons she's probably moved them to a safe house. She's said before she always wished that's what she'd done with Colby and Etta, forced them into a safe house."

"Does she know where it is?"

Anthony shakes his head. "Lainey plays these things close to her chest, even with Katy. She says the only person who'll probably know is that private detective, Fred Boothe."

"Does she know where he is?"

"No, but she can find out."

Carter runs a hand back through his hair. "This is the last fucking thing we need right now."

"If the JJC didn't mess up –" Darren says.

"Yeah, well, they did," Carter says. "Mistakes happen. If it wasn't for this guy coming out the woodwork and helping them, they'd have dealt with things there and then." He looks at Anthony. "We need to resolve this ASAP. We don't need the District Attorney breathing down our fucking necks while we've got the DLB coming for our heads. Call Katy. Tell her we need everything she can give us."

"It's not gonna be much," Anthony says. "She told me everything she knew."

"Then she's going to have to find out more," Carter says, his voice firm. "She can find out where Fred Boothe is, can't she? Start with that. If she can't tell us where the safe house is, *he* can."

Anthony nods. "I'll call her now."

"What can the rest of us do?" Darren says.

Carter settles back in his chair. "There's nothing we can do. We've gotta wait until Katy gets back to us." He runs a hand down his face. "Get some sleep."

44

A few days have passed in the safe house. Time has crawled. During the day, they each find ways to pass the hours. Tom and James take turns on watch, monitoring the street. At night, they do the same, sleeping in shifts.

"What would you have done if I wasn't here?" Tom asked him last night.

"I wouldn't have slept," James said, his face so straight that Tom couldn't tell if he was joking or not.

Ruth is in the kitchen. Fred came by on their first day. He'd been by the apartment and picked some stuff up for them. He brought along her study books.

"You make sure no one followed you here?" Tom said when he arrived.

"Of course," Fred said. "I'm not an amateur. I picked these up six hours ago. I didn't come straight here."

Ruth works at her books now. They all find ways to stay sharp. Tom works out. James does the same. They all watch the news, checking for any further updates regarding the

JJC, the DLB, and the GCTF. Thus far, there's been nothing. Just more background on the lives of the two murdered policemen.

Calvin, though, has not left his room, save to go to the bathroom and to get food.

Tom passes through the kitchen on his way to the garage. He's going to work out. Calisthenics. Ruth looks up from her books as he passes. "Hey, Tom?" she says.

"Yeah?"

"We haven't had a chance to talk about this yet," she says, "but I've heard them say that you used to be in the CIA."

Tom nods.

"That's impressive, right?"

"Guess that depends on who you ask."

"You didn't like it?"

"It wasn't my favourite time. I learned from it, though. If you can gain new skills in a profession, then it's never a complete waste."

Ruth smiles. "That's one way to look at it, I suppose." She pauses. Her face turns serious. "Can I ask you a favour?"

Tom takes a seat opposite her. "Sure."

She hesitates. "It's Calvin," she says. "He hasn't left that room since we got here. I've tried talking to him, but he's not exactly conversational right now. He just grunts. I ask him how he's doing and he says he's fine. I think he's depressed."

Tom nods. "That's understandable."

"Would you maybe...would you invite him to work out with you or something? Ask him, I dunno, if he wants to spar or something? Keep at his boxing, something like that. I'm worried about him."

"Yeah," Tom says. "Of course." He doesn't leave the table straight away. "How are you holding up?"

She forces a smile and motions to her books. "I'm keeping myself busy. If I keep myself occupied, it means I'm not thinking about this situation we're in. And that feels best for me right now."

"Why don't you come and work out with us," Tom says.

Ruth flashes a wry smile. "Do you want to see me squat, Tom?"

Tom smiles back. "Well, yes, but that's not the reason. It might make you feel better. Same way you think it might make Calvin feel better."

She laughs. "I think I'm going to keep at the books. I'm already going to fall behind. I might as well do what I can to mitigate that."

Tom nods. He starts to stand. Ruth reaches out before he can get up. She places her hand on his.

"Listen," she says, then trails off. She looks at him. "I know we've already said thank you, for coming here with us, but I mean it. To put your life on hold like this, for us... We... we shouldn't have asked you to do it. We were scared, and you'd helped us, and I think maybe we expected too much from you. You don't have to put your life on pause."

"I didn't have anything else going on."

"I mean it, though. You don't have to stay here. If ever you want to leave, to move on, we'll understand. We won't hold it against you."

Tom looks her in the eyes. "I'm not going anywhere." He gets to his feet and goes to Calvin's room. He knocks on the door.

Calvin calls back. "Yeah?"

"It's me," Tom says. "Can I come in?"

"Sure."

The room smells musty. It needs aired out. Calvin has

been showering, though, and it doesn't smell as bad as it could. He's been changing his clothes, too. Right now, he's lying on the bed, on top of the covers, his hands laced behind his head.

"What you been doing in here?" Tom says. He leans against the wall.

"Nothing much," Calvin says. "There ain't much I *can* do. I can't even listen to music or anything. If you're gonna carry around phones, you should think about upgrading to ones with some internet, man."

"That's not why I carry them."

Calvin grunts.

"What kinda music would you be listening to?" Tom says.

Calvin pushes himself up so he's sitting with his back against the headboard. He thinks. "Danny Brown, maybe. You heard of him?"

"I think so. Used to have the chipped teeth, right?"

Calvin grins. "He got them fixed."

"I don't keep up. He's from Detroit, right?"

Calvin lights up at this. "Yeah, yeah he is. Sounds like you know exactly who he is."

"I've heard a few songs."

"Like them?"

"Sure," Tom says. "I've got a broad taste."

"Yeah? Who's your number one?"

"You kidding me? The Boss, of course."

Calvin frowns.

"Ouch," Tom says.

"What?" Calvin laughs. "Who's *The Boss*?"

"Bruce Springsteen."

Calvin waves a hand. "Shit, yeah, I've heard of Bruce Springsteen. Why didn't you just say that?"

"Usually I don't need to." It's good to see Calvin laugh. "Listen, you got plans for anything more productive than staring at the ceiling?"

Calvin snorts. "Plans? How am I supposed to make any plans?"

"I'm gonna work out," Tom says. "You wanna join me?"

Calvin scratches his ear. "I'm okay."

"Mm," Tom says.

"What?"

"I just expected you wouldn't want to join me, was all."

"Uh-huh."

"Figured you'd be afraid I could teach you a thing or two."

Calvin's eyes narrow. "You box?"

"I've had a few lessons, but no. I do fight, though. A lot."

"You wanna teach me how to fight?"

"Maybe we could exchange a few tips. Help each other out."

Calvin looks like he's considering it.

"It's got to be better than just lying around in here day in and day out, right? Think of your boxing. You keep lying around in here, you're gonna get slow. You're gonna get sluggish. Probably gonna get soft in the middle. By the time you make it back to Noah's, everyone else you train with is gonna be running circles round you. You don't have Danny Brown right now, but you've still got your fists."

Calvin sighs. He pushes himself off the bed. He moves slowly. "I don't know," he says.

"What don't you know?"

"I don't...I don't know if there's any point anymore. What

does it matter? It's like you say – when I get to go back home, after all of this, I won't be the same person anymore. They *will* run circles around me. The fights that Noah was planning on booking for me, they'll be out the window." He sighs. "I probably won't go back."

"You're not a quitter, Calvin," Tom says.

"How would you know?"

"I can tell. You're not a quitter. Right now, you're going through a big change, and it's affecting you. Of course it is. But it's not going to be like this forever. What you're feeling right now, it'll pass. How fast it passes, that's up to you. What you need to understand is, it's going to pass eventually whether you help it go, or you wait for it to do it itself. And if you wait, you're going to struggle. It's going to be harder than you expect, and when it's that hard you might give up again, and you're right back here, in this depressive rut. But if you come with me now, you're going to feel a hell of a lot better about yourself. And then tomorrow, when we do it again, you're going to feel better yet."

"What did you have in mind?" Calvin says.

"We go in the garage and do some push-ups, squats, sit-ups. The basics. Jumping jacks. Burpees."

Calvin smirks, a cocky gleam in his eyes. "That all?"

Tom shrugs. "Come show me what you've got, and then we'll see how far we go."

"All right," Calvin says. He stands. "Just remember, you asked for this. I'm gonna put you through your paces, old man."

"Old man?" Tom laughs. "Thirty-three, and you're calling me old? Let's go do this. We'll see who's talking smack once we're done."

45

Fred Boothe lives in a shitty little apartment in downtown Detroit. It's cheap. The neighbourhood is rundown. Fred doesn't appear to spend much time in it. The GCTF have been watching his building in shifts for the last couple of days. Carter is currently on watch with Nick. They're in the van. It wasn't hard for them to find Fred's address. Darren got in touch with people in the precinct who know who he is. Darren made sure to talk to people sympathetic to the GCTF. People who wouldn't care if Fred suddenly went missing, and wouldn't go telling stories about people asking for his address.

"This motherfucker likes to work, don't he?" Nick says. "He just ain't coming home."

"If you lived around here, would you?" Carter says.

Nick laughs. "Probably not."

It's early evening. They've been watching the building for exactly forty-eight hours now. Carter's patience has been thin since they arrived. He's sick of sleeping in HQ. He's annoyed that he can't go home – that none of them can go home. He's pissed off that he got hauled into the station again and had to answer questions about the attack in his apartment. The chief wanted the task force to take on extra men, to offer protection from the DLB. It was clear now that the reason for the two dead cops with the acronyms carved into them was a warning to the GCTF. Carter refused the help. It took a lot of persuasion to get the chief to back down. Carter lied and said he didn't want to put anyone else at risk. That managed to get through. The chief agreed to leave it for the GCTF to handle it themselves.

"I'm gonna kill them," Carter told him. "I'll kill them all."

"I wouldn't expect anything less," the chief said. "But maybe arrest a few of them, something to make it look good."

Sure, Carter can arrest a few of them. Lower down members, no one of importance. He intends to wipe out the DLB. When he finally gets his hands on Darius Walker, he's going to make it slow. He's looking forward to it. First, though, he has other problems he needs to deal with. Other people he needs to kill.

Nick taps him with the back of his hand, snaps him back to attention. "He's here," Nick says. "Son of a bitch has come home."

Carter looks. He sees Fred Boothe get out of his car and arch his back like he's stiff from spending the last two days on the move. He yawns. When he walks, it's a shuffle. He makes his way toward his building.

"Get him," Carter says.

Nick fires up the engine and spins the wheels. He blares the horn and mounts the sidewalk. People scatter. Fred spins. Carter throws open his door. It smacks into Fred's side as he tries to turn away. The impact dents the door, but

Carter doesn't care. Nick gets out and runs round to open the rear doors. Carter goes to Fred. Fred is clutching his left arm and groaning. Carter glances at the people nearby, watching what's happening. He flashes his badge. "Police," he says. "Get the fuck out of here." He sees someone start to pull out their phone. "Put that fucking phone away or I'll stick it up your ass. You wanna try me? *Move*. Get out of here – *get*!"

He pulls cuffs from his back pocket and slaps them on Fred. He drags him across the ground to the back of the van, to the open doors. Hauling him up, he shoves him into the back, then climbs in with him and slams the doors shut.

They drive back to HQ. Carter calls ahead, lets the others know they're coming. A chair is set up just for Fred when they get there. It's in a corner of the room. There's plastic sheeting spread on the floor beneath the chair, and more up the walls to catch splash. Carter grabs a handful of what little hair Fred has at the back of his head and gives it a pull, makes sure he gets a good look at the set-up. Delia, Darren, and Anthony are standing by. They're in view, too. So is Delia's toolbox, resting on the corner of the sheeting.

Carter shoves Fred down into the chair. Darren and Anthony unclasp his hands, moving the cuffs from his front round to the back, looping it through the chair. Delia plastic-ties his ankles to the legs of the chair.

Carter watches Fred with his arms folded. He has to hand it to the old man – his mouth isn't gagged, but he hasn't made a sound yet. "You know who we are?" Carter says.

"Yeah, I know who you are," Fred says.

"Calvin Styles – we know you found him. Where is he?"

Fred says nothing.

Carter nods at Nick. He steps forward and slashes his switchblade down across Fred's face. It cuts him open from his temple, down his cheek, and to the corner of his mouth. Blood runs down his face and soaks into his shirt.

"Where's the kid?" Carter says.

Fred spits blood. He doesn't speak.

"Delia," Carter says, "work him over."

Delia grins. She looks like a wolf. She goes into her toolbox and brings out a hammer. "Gag him," she says to Anthony. From behind, Anthony wedges a gag into Fred's mouth and holds it there. Delia slams the hammer down onto Fred's right kneecap, shattering it. Carter can hear him screaming through the gag.

"You think he's ready to talk?" Delia says, laughing.

"I don't think he's ready yet," Carter says. "He's old, but he's tough. Like a stringy steak. Soften him up."

Delia proceeds to work him over with the contents of her toolbox. Carter takes a step back. He watches. Blood drips from the private detective. It pools beneath his chair, splattering across the plastic.

When Delia is done, Fred is a mess. Bits of him are missing. He's covered in blood. He doesn't look like himself anymore.

"Where's the kid?" Carter says.

Fred's head hangs down. His body trembles with what has been done to him.

"Where's the kid?" Carter says again.

Anthony, still behind, grabs Fred by the hair at the back of his head and forces him to look up. His eyes are swimming in his skull with the pain, but he's still conscious. He's still aware. With each breath he sprays blood through the gaps where his teeth used to be, and where his lips are swollen and split. "You're just gonna kill me anyway," he says. "Get it over with."

Carter steps closer. The plastic crinkles under his boots. "Sure, we're gonna kill you," he says. "But it doesn't have to be tonight. It doesn't even have to be tomorrow. We can draw this out, Fred. You have information, and we want it. How long's it gonna be before you speak to us?"

Fred's trembling increases, but he's crying now. His tears cut streaks through the blood coating his cheeks. He's considering what Carter has said. Thinking over the aches and pains that now ravage his broken body. Gauging how much more he can take.

Turns out, he knows it's not much. "Fuck you," he says, but then he gives them an address.

"You telling us the truth, Fred?" Carter says.

Fred nods. His eyes are closed. He's too ashamed to speak, or to look at them.

"We're gonna keep you alive until we know for sure, Fred," Carter says. "If you wanna reconsider the address you just gave us."

"Please," Fred says, "no more..."

Carter steps off the plastic. He looks at Nick. "Give the address to the JJC," he says. "Bring them in on this. It's as much their problem as it is ours. Tell them to go in heavy."

Nick nods.

Carter looks back at Fred. Anthony has let go of his hair. He lies slumped in the chair. He makes small sounds, pained. "The JJC can deal with the safe house," he says. "While they're doing that, we've got someone of our own to visit."

46

Tom sleeps light. He always has. When James opens the door into the bedroom where he's sleeping, his eyes are already open and he's pushing himself up. "What is it?" Tom says. He glances at the time. It's after midnight. Tom sees that James is carrying his Sig Sauer.

James keeps his voice low. "Wake up Ruth and Calvin," he says. "I think I've seen someone outside."

Tom gets off the bed, sliding his feet into his boots. He's already dressed. Each night, knowing he'll be back on watch in a few hours, he's slept in jeans and a T-shirt. He grabs his Beretta and KA-BAR from the bedside table. "How many?" Tom says.

"I counted three, but there could be more. Could be nothing, but they're walking this way up the sidewalk – I've never seen anyone walk these sidewalks, and especially not at this time of night. I'm going back. Wake them up, then you cover the rear." He turns and disappears, heading back toward the front of the house.

Tom keeps the Beretta in his hand, but entering Ruth's room he keeps it low, out of sight. There's no time to knock. He goes straight to her on the bed. She's lying on her side, facing the wall, wrapped up in the blankets. Tom can hear her breathing lightly. He places a hand on her shoulder and gives her a firm shake, enough to wake her up. She turns to look up at him, and then her eyes are wide. "What is it?" she says, her voice speech-slurred.

"Get dressed and wake Calvin," Tom says. "Stay together in his room. Anything happens, I'll come and get you."

Ruth pushes herself up. The blankets fall away. She's sleeping in a loose grey T-shirt. "Is someone here?"

"Maybe. James thinks he's seen people coming this way. Better we're careful than not." Tom leaves the room, leaves her to change and go and get her brother. He goes through to the rear of the house, the kitchen. The lights are all off. He moves deftly through the darkness, avoiding bumping into anything, having mapped out the layout of the house on their first night here. His Beretta is up now as he goes to the window, looking out into the back yard. The back yard is nothing more than a lawn. There's no decoration on it. Nothing to hide behind. He watches for movement. He doesn't see any.

Tom goes to the back door. He hears a door open behind him and glances to see Ruth leaving her room. She's dressed, wearing her sneakers. She sees him and they exchange nods. She freezes a moment when she sees the gun in his hand. Forces herself to keep moving. She goes quickly to Calvin's room and enters without knocking.

Tom returns his attention to the back yard. He looks through the glass in the door. He still can't see anyone.

Slowly, he unlocks the door. Opens it, just a crack, just enough to hear the night air. It's still. He pauses. There's no one coming up the side of the house, or hopping over the fence at the rear. He can't hear any signs of approach.

He pulls the door closed again, as quiet as he can, and relocks it. He moves through the house, to the front. James is in the living room, crouching low by the window, peering out.

"Back's clear," Tom says. "They still there?"

James nods. "They've stopped. See for yourself."

Tom goes to the window and looks out. He sees the three men. They've stopped two houses down. They're in a huddle, like they're making conversation, but they're out of place here. This isn't the right neighbourhood for a sudden huddle. They're not in the centre of the city anymore, where people wouldn't cast a second glance at something like this.

"I'll feel a lot better when they start moving again," James says. "Make it clear whether they're a problem for us, or just some passersby out too late, and in the wrong neighbourhood. Who takes a huddle in a place like this at this time of night?"

Tom grunts.

"I doubt they've seen us," James says. "I doubt they know we're in a stand-off right now."

Tom looks down the road beyond the group, and the opposite way. Checks the rest of the street. There's no one else out. There aren't any vehicles, either. The other houses are mostly in darkness. There's nothing out there, just those three huddled men.

"One of them's making a call," James says.

Tom looks. One of the men takes a step away from the group. Tom sees his dreadlocks illuminated before the phone is pressed to the side of his head. His back is turned to the house.

"I don't like it," James says.

Tom grunts in agreement. "If anything changes, call me. I'm going back to the kitchen. I don't want anyone to get the drop on us."

James nods. Tom goes and checks the back yard again. It remains clear. He stands by the door, looking out the window. They need to remain vigilant. They can't be distracted by three men at the front of the house. Tom cracks the door again, listening to the night air. Other than insects, there's still nothing to hear. If the men at the front are conversing, he can't hear the dull, distant murmuring of their voices.

But then James is calling for him. "There's a car coming," he says.

Tom can hear its engine. A low hum, drawing closer.

"The three are all looking at it," James says.

Tom spins. He considers the implications of the three men looking at the car. Of the phone call. He can hear the engine, and it is not moving fast. If anything, it sounds like it might be slowing down.

And the three men are watching it.

Waiting for it.

"James!" Tom says. "Get away from the window!"

Automatic gunfire breaks the night's silence. The windows at the front of the house shatter. Tom throws himself to the ground. Bullets ping and ricochet around the house. They punch through the drywall and the woodwork. Tom crawls toward the kitchen doorway, covering his head. His Beretta is raised. He can see the front door. It's peppered with bullets. They're spraying the whole front of the house. Tom thinks there's at least two of them firing.

The automatic gunfire stops. Tom gets to his knees, but he stays low. He covers the door. He's ready to drop flat again in case the gunfire starts back up. He makes his way to the living room. He doesn't call James's name. Doesn't want to alert the men outside to his position.

He reaches the doorframe and peers inside. James is lying flat. There's blood on his torso and splashes of it on his face. It's hard to tell where it's come from. He's still alive, though. He sees Tom. He grimaces. There's blood on his teeth. "They've winged me," he says.

Before Tom can respond, he hears the screech of tyres and the roar of an engine. A car smashes through the front of the house, through the shattered window. It drives over the top of James.

Tom doesn't hesitate. He can't afford to be surprised. He fires into the car, through the windshield. The two men in the front convulse with the impact of his bullets. The passenger rear door opens. A man starts to stand. Tom fires twice. One of his shots takes the top of his head off.

The front door is kicked down. Tom wheels on it. The three men who were huddled outside, who first got James's attention, are coming in. Tom recognises the one with dreadlocks who made the call. They're all carrying handguns. Their weapons are raised, ready to fire. Tom manages to catch the man at the front, but then throws himself back, heading to the kitchen. The other two fire at him, driving him into cover. As Tom dives behind the wall, he sees the man with dreadlocks peel away from the front door, disappearing from view.

The other man advances. He empties his magazine, but

rather than pausing to reload he pulls out another gun from his waistband. Tom shelters in the kitchen, aware that the man with dreadlocks is still out there somewhere. Aware that he could be either trying to come around the back, to flank Tom, or else he's gone to grab some heavier weaponry, or call for reinforcements.

Whatever it is he's doing, Tom needs to wrap this up. He, Ruth, and Calvin need to get out of here, ASAP.

The man in the corridor is advancing, firing with every step. Tom doesn't know how many guns he's carrying. He might have something stronger than a Glock. Tom waits for an opening to return fire, but none comes.

Then, the shooting pauses. Tom can hear a struggle. Bullets fire, but they go upward, into the ceiling. Tom steps into the doorway, Beretta raised. Calvin and Ruth have emerged from the room, have tackled the man in the hallway. They're battling with him. Calvin is wrapped around his waist, pressing him up against the wall. Ruth has his arms, forcing them up, pinning them above his head. She claws at his wrists, trying to get him to drop the gun.

Tom does not have a clear shot. He keeps the scene covered, waiting until he can fire.

Behind him, the back door is kicked open. Tom spins on the sound. The man with dreadlocks enters, firing. Tom throws himself to the ground and fires back, catching him in the shins. The man falls, dreadlocks whipping around his head, slapping onto the linoleum. He's screaming. Tom keeps shooting, buries bullets up his torso and into the side of his neck. He's still.

Tom's magazine is empty. There's no time to reload, not right now, not while Calvin and Ruth are struggling with the remaining man. He rushes into the hallway. The man is fighting his way loose. He's kneed Calvin in the chest, is kicking him back. Without Calvin, Ruth is not strong enough to restrain him. He brings his arms down and backhands her across the face.

As she falls, Tom strides up. He swings the Beretta toward the man's face, but he ducks it and tackles Tom, forcing him back into the bedroom usually occupied by Ruth. Tom falls to the ground, keeping hold of his attacker, raising a leg to flip him. The man rolls through, getting back upright. Tom hops to his feet. The man still has his gun. He's beginning to raise it. Tom acts without thinking. If he thinks, it'll slow him down. Instead, he moves.

He charges the man before he can bring the gun all the way up. He throws himself at him and they crash through the window, falling to the hard, cold paving stones outside that lead up the side of the house to the back yard. Tom lands hard on his left side. He feels something crunch. A shooting pain runs up and down his arm, and the burning taste of vomit fills his throat. He ignores it. There's no other choice. The glass has cut him up, but the other man has taken the worst of it. Lacerations cover his face and blood pumps from the back of his neck. In the crash and fall, he's dropped his weapon. It's skittered across the ground, out of reach of them both. Tom grabs a shard of glass, the closest to hand, and jams it down into the front of the man's throat. He coughs and blood sprays. It pools in the hollow of his neck. Tom drives the shard down, cutting up his hand on the jagged edge of it. The man goes still. His eyes roll back in his skull.

Tom falls off him. He can't hold himself up with his left arm. He rolls, glass crunching beneath him, and uses his right to grab at the nearby fence and pull himself up. He looks through the smashed window. Calvin and Ruth are in the doorway.

"Grab your things," Tom says, wincing. His left arm hangs useless. Blood drips down his face, and from the tips of his right hand's fingers. "Meet me at the car – we need to go."

47

Lainey is concerned. She hasn't heard from Fred.

It's not uncommon. Sometimes they go weeks without speaking, but the last few days have been different. They've been busy. They're onto something. Time is of the essence, and he's been checking in every few hours. Last she heard, he said he was going home.

"Tell me when you get there," she said.

"You worried about me?" he said, laughing.

"Yes," she said, deadly serious.

Fred matched her tone. He understood. It's a serious situation. "I'll let you know as soon as I'm through the door."

"As soon as you've locked it," Lainey said.

"Soon as I've locked it."

That was five hours ago. She's heard nothing since. In no situation she can envisage should it take him five hours to get home. Even if a tip came up, a lead to chase, something that kept him from going straight home, he would have let her know.

She's messaged him three times. She's called him six. There has been no answer to any of her attempts at contact.

She's at home. She sits in her study, at her desk, the only light coming from her tabletop lamp. The curtains are drawn behind her. She stares at her phone and chews her bottom lip. It's late, but she's not tired. She's wide awake. She's wired. Fred isn't the only person she's tried to contact. As her concern grew, she's tried to contact James Strand, too. He hasn't answered, either.

She feels sick. There's a heavy feeling in her stomach. She wants to contact the police, to get them to drive by the safe house and see if everything is all right, but she can't risk them finding out where and what it is. The GCTF have too many friends, and she doesn't know who any of them are. They're out there, though, ready to feed information back to them at a moment's notice.

Outside, she hears a car door close. She leans back in her chair, peers out the corner of her curtain. She spots the car, a few houses down. Recognises a couple of her neighbours. A married couple. The man was in the passenger seat. He's unsteady as he gets out of the car. The woman was driving. She laughs as she comes round to him, holding onto his arm to keep him upright. They're both dressed up, like they've been out. To a party, perhaps. They head up to their house. Lainey lets the curtain fall back into place.

There's a knock at her door, downstairs and along the hall. A hard, pounding knock, followed by the ringing of her doorbell.

She freezes. She doesn't move from her desk. The knocking sounds like a cop's knock. She's familiar with the sound from her youth, and from ride-alongs. Her mind races. She thinks about Fred. She thinks about the safe house.

The doorbell rings again.

Cops could be here to tell her that something has happened to Fred. Except, why would they? They don't know he works for her. Of course, rumours get around. Scuttlebutt spreads. If that were the case, though, if it were about Fred, they would call. Surely, they would call. They wouldn't come to her front door in the middle of the night.

She peers around the curtain again. There are no cruisers in the street. She can't see any people, either. She gets up and leaves her study, going to the spare bedroom at the front of the house. It has a clearer view of the street. Still nothing.

The doorbell rings, and the hard knocking comes again, and she feels her heart hammering in her chest. She doesn't want to answer it. She doesn't trust it. Whoever is there, at this time of night, it can't be anything good.

Lainey goes through to her bedroom, stepping lightly, as if the people outside are likely to hear her. Her bedroom is at the back of the house. She can open the window and climb down using the trellis. It's bare now, because of the cold snap, but in spring and summer it's vibrant with vines. Before she opens the window to attempt her escape, she looks down into the back yard. There's a dark shape down there, masked and hooded. It's watching the rear of her house. Her movement at the window catches its attention. It looks up at her, and it waves.

Lainey takes a step back, feeling her heart pounding in her throat. Behind her, she hears the staircase creak. She spins. As she does so, another dark figure steps into view. This one bigger than the one out in the back yard. Again, it's masked and hooded. When the figure sees her, it smiles. It peels back its mask. Lainey recognises the man. Of course she does. She's been hunting him and his team for years.

Carter Brown.

"Didn't seem like you were going to answer the door," he says. "So we let ourselves in."

Carter steps aside. Three dark shapes flood Lainey's room, grabbing her, gagging her to keep her from screaming. They've peeled back their masks now, and she recognises them all. Delia Curtis. Anthony Felton. Darren Wong. They carry her out to the hall, down to her study, and she sees a masked man come to the top of the stairs. The dark figure from her back yard, invited inside now that she's been caught. He hasn't pulled back his mask yet, but Lainey knows who he will be. Nick Sanchez. He's the only one left. Lainey notices now that he's carrying something down by his side. A paper bag. The contents clink together.

Lainey is carried through to her study and pushed down into the chair behind her desk. She grabs at the gag, but Delia pushes it back into place, holding Lainey down in her chair while Anthony and Darren tie her into place. They're using rags. Cotton. It's soft against her skin. Lainey frowns, but then she understands. They don't want the binds to leave a mark, the kind of marks that cuffs or plastic ties would leave.

Carter stands before her. Nick is beside him. He reaches into the paper bag. Lainey's eyes narrow as he pulls out two bottles of red wine.

"You've been a thorn in our ass for a long time now," Carter says. "That ends tonight."

Nick opens a bottle of wine, then advances. When he's almost on top of her, Delia rips the gag from her mouth. She clamps her nostrils shut and holds her jaw open. Nick pours the wine down her throat. Lainey gags and splutters. Nick pauses, giving her a chance to breathe, keeping her from choking. Lainey gasps. She feels the wine running down her throat, filling her stomach. After a few deep breaths, Nick resumes.

They empty the first bottle. "Half of the second one," Carter says. "That should be enough."

Nick nods. He starts pouring again. It doesn't go on for as long this time. When he's done, Delia returns the gag, though Lainey doesn't have it in her to scream right now. Her head hangs. She feels sick. The room is beginning to spin around her. Her stomach is doing flips. Acidic bile rises in the back of her throat. She recognises the feeling that is coming over her. She's never felt it set in this fast before, but she's never drank a bottle and a half of red wine this fast, either.

"You feeling it?" Carter says. At least, she thinks it's Carter.

She tries to look at him. She can't make out his face. Everything is blurring.

"It'll be in her system already," someone says. "We don't need to hang around."

Lainey feels the binds loosened from her wrists and ankles. Strong hands haul her to her feet. She's close enough to see Carter's face.

"I want you to know what we're going to do to you," he says.

Lainey's head is swimming. She struggles to focus, to see his face and hear his words.

"All these years you've been trying to nail us," Carter says. "You pushed too hard, Lainey. How many people needed to die for this? There's a high body count behind us now, and it's just as much on you as us. I'm about to add you to that pile, Lainey."

He's keeping her upright, and he's dragging her across the floor, her feet trailing through the carpet. She feels its scrape. She tries to stand, to stop, but she's unfocussed and unbalanced, and Carter is too strong. They stop. Lainey blinks to see where they are. They're at the top of the stairs.

"It's going to be a drunken accident, Lainey," Carter says, putting his mouth close to her ear. "You got drunk, and you fell down the stairs. Careless. No one's going to suspect us of this. It's going to be all you." He leans her closer to the stairs. "If the fall doesn't kill you, I will." He pushes her back.

The world spins as she falls. She hears the thudding of her body against each step on the way down. She feels it, too. Feels the edges poke and prod into her, bruising her, potentially fracturing bones. She barely feels any pain. She hits the bottom and lies flat. It takes her a moment to realise she's still breathing.

She hears Carter speaking. "Bring her back up," he says.

Footsteps on the stairs, coming down. Hands hauling her up, two pairs of them. Carrying her by the ankles, and under her arms. Not dragging her. They need the injuries to look consistent with a fall. A scrape on her ankles or the backs of her legs might not look in keeping.

"One more time," Carter says, when she's returned to him. "Just for luck." He pushes her down again.

And again, the tumble, the spinning, the thudding. She bangs her head. She lands at the bottom. Lies flat. Breathing hard. Her eyes fluttering. She tastes vomit.

Carter follows her down. He kneels beside her. "Do you

have any last words? Do you maybe wanna lament the waste of your life? Maybe a defiant *fuck you* before you go?"

Lainey tries to speak, but she can't. The vomit rises up and spills down the corner of her mouth. Carter smirks. He reaches down with his big hands and cradles her head. He twists. Lainey hears a loud snap, and then nothing.

48

Ruth won't let Tom drive. "Your arm's broke," she says. "What good are you going to do us by forcing yourself to drive?"

He got them away from the house, though, after the attack. Tom got them clear, watching the mirrors as they went. No one followed. He saw people from the neighbouring houses turning on their lights and peering out, some of them coming out onto their lawns now that the shooting had died down. There were police sirens, and the distant glow of their approaching red and blue lights. The cops are no help to Tom and the siblings. They have no way of knowing which side they'd be on.

Ruth saw how he winced while driving. Once they were clear she forced him to pull over so she could check him out. She felt how his upper left arm was swollen, and saw how he grimaced as she felt around. She fashioned a sling for him out of one of her blouses. "I need something to brace it with," she said. "To set it. In the morning, when stores open, I might be able to get something."

Tom shook his head. “We can’t stay on the road all night. We need to find somewhere to hide out. They’re coming for us. They’re going to be looking for us. They haven’t stopped just because we got away.”

Ruth thought of somewhere they could go.

She drives now. Tom is in the passenger seat. He clenches his teeth against the waves of pain that run up and down his left arm. There’s a dull ache in his shoulder. When he looks down, his skin is purple and swollen. He turns away from it, stares ahead, focusses his mind away from the pain.

“Where are we going?” he says.

“Before our dad was a paramedic, he worked in a factory,” Ruth says. “They built cars – big surprise. When I was about Calvin’s age, I worked a few summers there. That would’ve been a couple of years before it closed down and Dad had to find a new job.”

“You know the building well?” Tom says.

“It probably looks a lot different to how I remember, but yeah, I reckon so.”

“It might not be empty,” Calvin says from the back. “Homeless, junkies – they might have made it their home.”

“We’ll deal with that when and if we have to,” Ruth says. “We’re not going to hassle them. We just need a place to hide out.”

“Did your mom work?” Tom says, trying to distract himself. “I don’t think you’ve mentioned what she did.”

“She was a secretary,” Ruth says. “Part-time, after Calvin was born.”

It takes an hour to get to the old factory. Tom feels cold. He glances at the temperature gauge. The heat is up high. When he presses his hand to a blower, it feels hot against his palm. His fingers, though, are trembling. They’re trembling on his left hand, too, and they cause ripples of pain to pulsate through his arm and emanate to the rest of his body. He lets his right hand drop from the blower. Ruth and Calvin seem fine. Shaken from the attack, perhaps, but not cold.

Ruth doesn't park in front of the factory. She pulls around the back. Keeps the car concealed. She's learnt from Tom. The factory is in darkness. The land around it is overgrown and wild. Tom looks up at the building as he gets out of the car. Some of the windows are smashed, but not all of them. One-handed, he reloads his Beretta. "Wait here while I check it out," he says.

"No," Ruth says, getting out of the car. "You're hurt, and I'm not sending you in there alone."

Calvin gets out of the car, too.

Tom doesn't argue with them. He's too sore and too tired. He feels an exhaustion sweeping over him. A tiredness he hasn't felt in a very long time. He takes a step toward the building and realises how unsteady his legs are. He takes a deep breath and tries to keep from shaking. He forces himself on, heading to a back door leading into the building. He steps inside. Ruth and Calvin follow. Ruth turns on the torch on the burner phone Tom gave her. She lights the way for him.

The inside of the factory is in good condition. Most of the machinery is still in place, and while dusty and cobwebbed, it's intact. There's no one else in the building. They check every room.

"It's cold in here," Calvin says.

Tom is glad to hear him say it. Except Calvin isn't shivering the way he is.

"When I go to get a sling for Tom's arm, I'll maybe get

some generators, too," Ruth says. "Some space heaters, to keep us warm. Some blankets. Until we can get in touch with Lainey or Fred, I guess we don't know how long we might have to hide out here." She looks at Tom. She notices how he shakes. He can't control it now. "Are you okay?"

"I'm fine," he says.

"You don't look fine. Let's sit you down." She guides him into an office, lowers him to the floor with his back against the wall. "You're shaking bad," she says.

"I can't get warm," Tom says. "It was the same in the car."

She frowns. "Do you hurt?"

He nods. "Aches and pains."

She presses a hand to his forehead. Calvin stands close by, lighting the room with his phone. He looks concerned. "You don't feel cold," Ruth says, taking her hand back. "You feel hot. You're having rigors, Tom. I think you've got an infection."

Tom frowns. He nods toward his broken arm. "From this?" he says. "That's too soon."

Ruth agrees. "It *is* too soon. You could have picked it up from something else. You've done a lot of fighting lately, right? Could be your body's been fighting it off, but now with all of this –" she indicates the broken arm and his various cuts and scrapes after falling through the window, "– it's too much for your body to deal with."

Tom feels his teeth chattering together in his head.

"You need to rest," Ruth says, standing. She turns to Calvin, taking control of the situation. "You're going to have to watch over him."

"What are you going to do?" Calvin says.

"I'm going to the hospital," Ruth says. "I need to get him

some antibiotics, and a brace for that arm. Once I've fixed him up, I'll go back out and get the generators."

Tom wants to protest, but he feels his strength ebbing away.

Calvin does it for him. "Is that safe? For you to go out so much?"

Ruth looks at her brother. "We don't have any choice," she says. "If I don't get him medicine, that infection could kill him." She reaches out and squeezes his arm. "I'll be careful. And I'll be back as soon as I can. You watch Tom. If anything happens – if he gets worse, or anyone comes into the factory – call me." She turns and leaves the office, lighting her way with the phone. Tom watches her go. His eyes are fluttering closed. He doesn't have the strength for anything else.

49

As much as Darius enjoyed his makeshift office in the basement, and despite there being no obvious signs that anyone had tracked him down, he's had to leave it behind. It's important for him to keep moving. To stay one step ahead. Right now, he's travelling in the back of an RV, conducting his business via his phone while he lies low in the bed, the motorhome in a constant state of motion through Detroit.

He's sent his mother out of town. She's staying with her sister in Flat Rock. He's told her he'll send for her when it's safe for her to come back. Darius was prepared, in case he ever needed to move his mom out, hide her. Her sister, his aunt, has always been the plan. Darius pays for her home, too, so she can't turn him down. Much like his mom's, it's not in her name. No one will be able to track them down there.

The truth is, Darius isn't sure it'll ever be safe for his mom to come back.

The DLB have been making noise. More than just the two dead cops, which has painted a huge bullseye on their backs. They've been striking at the JJC, too. Darius has been organising hit-and-runs, drive-bys, targeting their corners and businesses, anything they know of connected to or known to be friendly with the JJC. Things have gotten bloody. People have been caught in the cross-hairs. At least three bystanders that Darius is aware of have been torn to pieces in the middle of a drive-by.

Darius doesn't concern himself with this. The DLB are at war. They've been at war for a long time, and this is the hottest it's ever been. If they don't push back now, they'll forever be on the back foot. If they don't push back now, then they're sitting and waiting for eradication.

So, so far as he's concerned, a few innocent bystanders can die. The DLB have nothing left to lose. They're already marked men. Two dead cops means the full might of the entire Detroit police force is coming for them. The GCTF were already on their tails.

Darius sits up and peers out a corner of the window, keeping the blinds closed. He can't risk opening them all the way. Can't risk being seen. He looks out at the city. A city that should be his. The city that has been his home all of his life. He breathes deep. He strokes the Glock beside him on the bed. Its cold feel brings him comfort. The weight of it makes him feel safer. He uses its barrel to scratch the side of his face. He lets the blinds fall back into place.

He calls through to the two men in the front, the one driving and the one riding lookout in the passenger seat. "I'm sick of moving," he says. He's been living in the back of the RV for about four days now, but it's hard to be sure. It's difficult to gauge time when in constant motion, hiding out from the world. "All this driving around, it's making me feel sick. Find me somewhere new to hide out."

The man in the passenger seat nods and pulls out his phone. "I'm on it."

Darius and his men aren't going down without a fight. Either they win, or they take as many people down with them as they can. The DLB have already left a mark. The streets are running red with blood. Before they're done, no one will ever forget their name.

50

Tom's eyes flutter open.

Glancing around, moving only his eyes, he sees a light in the corner of the office. There's a space heater next to it, turned down low but still belching out warmth. Tom is lying on a pile of blankets, and another is draped over him. He moves his left arm a little. It feels encased. He raises his head and looks down. It's braced, his upper arm held tightly together to aid the reknitting of his fractured bones. A Velcro strap runs across his chest and under his right armpit.

Ruth sits beside him. "You're awake," she says. "You've seen your brace? We had a hell of a time getting that on you. You're heavier than you look. Calvin had to hold you up while I put it on. How do you feel? How's your temperature?" She reaches out, pressing her hand to his forehead.

Tom swallows before he can speak, his mouth dry. "How long have I been out?" he says.

"A day," Ruth says. "A full day. Twenty-four hours." She checks the time. "Twenty-seven, to be precise."

Tom starts to push himself up. Ruth places a hand on his chest.

"I told you, you need to rest," she says. "You're still going to ache."

She's right. Tom can feel the pains coursing through his heavy limbs, though they're nowhere near as severe as before he passed out.

"I got some food while I was out," Ruth says. She reaches into a bag near to her, pulls out some jerky. "You should eat. See if you can keep it down."

Tom's stomach groans. He manages to push himself up so he's seated, his back against the wall. He sighs, this slight exertion already exhausting him.

"The antibiotics will start working soon," Ruth says.

Tom frowns. "I've been taking them?"

"I was waking you up to take them," Ruth says. "Every few hours, as prescribed. You never fully came around. I don't expect you to remember."

"I don't," Tom says. "Where did you get them from? And the brace."

"I went to the hospital," Ruth says. "The one where I work when they put me on placement. I know my way around it. Know where everything is."

"Did anyone see you?"

Ruth shakes her head. "No. I was careful. I avoided cameras, too. And no one saw me – no one I know, anyway. A couple of patients here and there, but I was in everyday clothes, so as far as they're concerned I was just another patient or visitor walking the halls. I got in and I got out and I came straight back here."

"And you weren't followed?"

"I checked. I was careful."

"Where's Calvin?"

"He's on watch," Ruth says. "He's not far."

Tom opens and closes his left hand, squeezing his fist as tight as he's able. It's not as much as he'd like. There's a tingling and a weakness in his fingers. His upper arm, where the bone is broken, tingles and aches.

"When I connected up the generators, it brought back a lot of energy to the factory," Ruth says.

"What do you mean?" Tom says.

"It means some of the machines are working." Ruth grins. "And the lights. Don't worry, though – we've kept them off. Kept the place as dark and quiet as we can, and we've always had someone on watch."

"You've learnt well. What kind of machines are we talking about?"

"Conveyor belts, compactors, shredders, that kind of thing."

"All of the machines?"

"No, only the ones on the factory floor out there. I only hooked up generators in this area. The machines in the rest of the factory, they're still dead."

"Did you do much practical work when you had your summer job here?"

"Well, I was in the offices, but Dad would show me around the floor, talk me through some of the machines, show me how they worked." She smiles, remembering.

Tom picks up the jerky Ruth has put close to him. He tears some off and chews it. He hears footsteps coming toward them, running.

"Is that Calvin?" he says.

Ruth leans toward the door, trying to see. "It must be," she says, getting to her feet, looking concerned at his abrupt approach. She goes to the door and opens it to look out. Tom can see out now. Can see Calvin hurrying toward them. He's carrying something in his right hand. It's small and black. A radio. Tom can hear music playing from it, though it's turned down low and he can't make out the song.

"What's wrong?" Ruth says, seeing the look on his face.

Calvin steps into the office, holding up the radio. He glances at Tom, sees that he's awake, but something has him aggravated and he needs to address it. "Lainey is dead," he says.

"*What*?" Ruth says.

"I just heard it on the radio," Calvin says. He turns the music off. "She fell down the stairs in her house, broke her neck. Apparently she'd been drinking. Some freak accident."

Ruth covers her mouth with a hand.

"Have you heard from Fred?" Tom says.

Ruth shakes her head.

"And Lainey had a freak fall in her house?" Tom says.

"That's what the news is saying," Calvin says.

"It doesn't feel right," Tom says. "We haven't heard from Fred, and now Lainey is dead."

"You think she was killed?" Ruth says.

"It would make sense that she was," Tom says. "Same for Fred."

"We can't be sure Fred's dead," Ruth says.

"We have to assume he is," Tom says. "The safe house is hit, and we don't hear from him. Lainey is dead, we still don't hear from him?"

Ruth and Calvin's faces darken. They know he's right.

"We're on our own," Calvin says. "Right back where we were."

Tom gets to his feet.

"What are you doing?" Ruth says.

Upright, Tom gets a better look at his braced left arm. There's very little mobility in the shoulder, but he can still bend at the elbow, though it's painful to do so. "I need to go out," he says. "I need to find them."

"Are you – are you joking?" Ruth says. "You're one-armed. You're not in any condition to go anywhere or *do* anything."

"We don't have any choice."

"Uh, yes, yes we do. And your choice is to lie back down and rest. You need that arm to heal and you need to finish the antibiotics."

Tom sees the antibiotics on the ground, close to where he was lying. "I'll take them with me," he says, grimacing as he reaches down to pick them up.

"That's not the point," Ruth says.

Tom straightens and looks at her. "We can't just wait around here. They're looking for us. It's just a matter of time before they turn up. One way or another, they'll find out where we are. They have every time before."

"So what are we going to do?" Calvin says. "Run away? Leave Detroit behind?"

"Do you want to run away?" Tom says, pausing.

Calvin looks at his sister. "No," he says. "This is my home. And I don't think they're gonna be happy with just chasing us out. I don't think that's going to be enough for them. If they've killed Fred and if they've killed Lainey, they're not going to stop there. They've already tried to kill us a few times now."

Tom nods. "Good, because I'm not a fan of running away. What we're gonna do is this – the two of you are going to wait here, stay on lookout, the way you've been doing. I'm going to go and find the GCTF. I'm going to spook them. Let them know I'm still around, and I'm coming for them. Get them on edge, make them worried, make them sloppy. And then, soon as I get the chance, I'm gonna hit them." Tom looks around for his jacket. It's folded in the corner. He picks it up, but struggles to get it on. He turns to Ruth. She doesn't look happy. He holds it out to her. "Will you help me get this on?"

She stares at him, ignoring the jacket at first, but then she sighs and shakes her head and takes it from him. They slide it up his immobile left arm first, Ruth taking her time to get it over his brace. She gets it started on his right arm and then Tom shrugs it on the rest of the way.

"How's that look?" he says, studying the bulge of the brace through his jacket sleeve. "Is it obvious?"

"You can tell something's there," Calvin says. "Can't tell what it is."

"Tom," Ruth says, her tone exasperated, knowing she's not going to talk him out of this. "Tom, you have an infection. You've got a broken arm."

He pockets the antibiotics, and arms himself with his Beretta and KA-BAR. "I'm not going to let that slow me down," he says. He places his right hand on her shoulder and looks her in the eyes. "I can't," he says. "We don't have any other options." He pauses. "I'll be careful. Don't worry about me."

"If we lose you, we've lost everyone," she says.

"I'll be careful," Tom says again.

Ruth doesn't respond. She steps aside and lets him leave.

51

A couple of days have passed. Ruth and Calvin remain alone in the factory. Tom has not returned, though he's called a couple of times to check in. To let them know he's still alive, too, Ruth knows, though he never says this. And, of course, to make sure *they're* still alive, too.

She wonders, if the GCTF were to turn up before he could return, if they were to find her and her brother before Tom can find them, and they killed them both, what would Tom do then? Would he still have a horse left in the fight, or would he split Detroit? He told them he didn't like running away. Ruth doesn't think he would. She thinks he'd hang around, and continue to go after them, regardless of who they are and the help they have behind them. A broken arm and an infection haven't kept him down.

Last time they spoke, Ruth asked him how he was feeling. "How's your arm?" she said. "And what about the infection – are you hurting?"

"I'm okay," Tom said. "I can manage. You don't need to worry about me."

"That's a stupid thing to say," Ruth said, "because I'm going to worry. I feel like my life is one long worry right now. Are you remembering to take the antibiotics?"

"Yes."

"Do you promise?"

"I promise. When I get back, you can count the pills and see for yourself."

"I will," she said, almost wanting to laugh. "Don't think I won't." She paused. "When will you be back?"

"Soon," Tom said, but that was all he said.

She and Calvin have taken turns on watch. Have slept in shifts. No one has tried to sneak up on them, so far as they can see. No vehicles come down this way. There are no signs of life outside in the long grass, other than small animals and birds, but it's so cold there haven't been many of them, either. Last night, some snow fell. Not a lot, but enough to coat the ground in a fresh layer. It's helped them with lookout. So long as no footprints appear in it, they're happy.

They've listened to the radio, too. Waited for more news on Lainey's death. There has been no mention of Fred. Each of them has shared a silent, unspoken hope that something suspicious has been found as the cause of Lainey's death, but nothing has been said on the matter. Just a drunken accident, and no one seems to think any more than that.

Ruth is on watch. She sits by a window that still has glass, up high on a gangway, looking down. Looking at the fresh, untouched snow. It's thin, and it won't be around for very long. It'll either melt in the weak sunlight, or rain will wash it away. She doesn't stare at the snow too long. Doesn't want to risk getting lost in her thoughts. She looks to the distance, to the road, keeping an eye out for vehicles and anything coming this way. She looks left and right, too, across the grassland.

Below, on the factory floor, Calvin works out. He's restless. He runs laps. Does push-ups. Squats. He performs pull-ups on machinery. Shadow boxes. He pushes himself hard, until he drops to his knees in the corner and throws up. Ruth goes to him.

"Are you okay?" she says.

"You should be on watch," Calvin says, getting back to his feet and wiping his mouth with the back of his hand.

"It's clear," Ruth says. "It'll be okay for five minutes."

"It might not."

She looks at her brother, saying nothing. He's been withdrawn, distant, ever since they were moved to the safe house. For a short time, it seemed like Tom was able to draw him back out, boosted his mood with workouts in the garage. Then they were attacked, and on the move again.

He's not usually like this. He smiles. Makes jokes. Then again, this isn't how their lives usually are. Right now, there is a palpable anger coming from him. It shows in the set of his face, and it blazes in his eyes. The last time she saw him like this was after their parents were killed. She remembers those early days. She wasn't a mother, but she did her best. She talked to him. She asked him how he was feeling. They took it from there.

"Talk to me," Ruth says, hoping it can still help. "Don't just hold it in. Talk to me. Tell me what you're thinking. Tell me what you're feeling."

Calvin breathes hard. "The Gang Control Task Force are coming for us," he says. "I need to be ready for them."

"There's being ready, and there's pushing yourself to exhaustion."

"It's the only thing I can do. I can't just sit around and wait. It'll drive me out of my mind." He bites his lip.

"Is there anything else?" Ruth says.

He sighs. There is. She can tell. He can't bring himself to tell her what it is. Ruth waits. She watches him. She thinks she knows.

"It's Javon," she says.

"Javon isn't GCTF," Calvin says. "He killed our parents, Ruth. I just – I need to –" He can't find the words. Ruth sees how he balls his fists. Sees how he shakes. He coughs. "I'm going to kill him."

Ruth feels a twinge inside when he says this. It horrifies her. She knew he felt this way, but it still stabs at her when he verbalises it.

"I just – I can't wait around here," Calvin says. "I need to get out there. I need to find him. He needs to pay –"

"Tom told us to wait," Ruth says.

"Tom's looking for the GCTF," Calvin says. "He's not looking for Javon."

"He knows what he's doing, Calvin. We need to trust him. If you disappear, that's going to put everything in jeopardy."

Calvin grinds his teeth. "I'm going on watch," he says, stepping past her.

"My shift isn't over," Ruth says.

"Doesn't matter," Calvin says, reaching the steps and making his way up. He pauses halfway and turns back to her. "I need to – I need to *do* something. Something productive. I can't just wait." He turns and goes up the rest of the way, heading to the window where Ruth was sat.

She watches him go. She thinks about the look in his eye. The burning hatred. The lust to kill another man.

When she breathes, it hitches in her chest and throat. She coughs, clearing it away. Swallows. Breathes deep. She can't cry. She needs to be strong. They both do.

52

It didn't take Tom long to find the GCTF. He didn't hunt them directly. He went to the streets. Any task force was going to pay off snitches and CI's, most of whom were found in either the homeless or junkie community, or both. So he went to them. He asked around. Slipped some cash into palms until he was able to find someone who knew someone who had spoken with the GCTF.

"Shit, it's just as dangerous working *with* the GCTF as having them coming after you," the man said. "A buddy of mine, Greg, he turned me onto feeding them information in exchange for cash, right? Greg was a favourite of theirs. Anyway, just a couple of weeks ago, he up and killed himself. Well, he OD'd, but I saw the body. It looked like it was on purpose to me."

Tom listened, saying nothing, letting the man speak.

"I don't know what he saw, what drove him to it, but I know he hated whenever they called him in or came to see him. Used to be he loved it – called it easy money." The man shrugged. "I don't know what changed. They've hassled me a little, but Greg, he was soft. I don't mean that to sound too bad, it's just how he was. He wasn't strong. He couldn't handle this life, not really. Anyway, yeah, I know them."

"Do you know where their offices are?"

"They call it HQ, and yeah, I do."

The man gave him directions. An old tyre factory just off 7 Mile Road. Tom found it easily. He parked his car around the back of an abandoned building opposite their own. He's been inside the building since, watching HQ. Their cars have been present, and a van, but they've barely come and gone. Their vehicles are parked around the back, concealed. Tom can see them from his vantage point. He's familiarised himself with them. The GCTF have headed out in twos and threes, usually to get food or coffee. Tom assumes that sometimes they've done their jobs, but he has no way of knowing. He's seen enough to know that all five of them are present in the building. They've stayed overnight. It seems more like a hideout than an HQ. When night falls, they batten down the hatches. They don't leave. Tom imagines it has something to do with their problems with the DLB. The DLB must have come after them, and come after them hard.

While Tom drove around the city, trying to find out where the GCTF were, he heard on the radio about the DLB's current activities. Their careless shootings, gunning down bystanders. Tom isn't a big fan of the DLB. They went after Lewin. They came after him. They put a gun in Calvin's face. There's a litany of things they've done that Tom doesn't like. He can't forgive them just because they've potentially put the GCTF on the back foot.

Tom's phone rings. It's Ruth. "Everything okay?"

"Are you free to talk?"

"For now." The area is quiet and still. The lights are off in HQ.

"I'm worried about Calvin. He's been taking about Javon. He wants to kill him." Tom can hear the concern in her voice. "I've never seen him like this before. He means it. He wants to kill that man. The way he is, it's scaring me."

Tom understands. She's worried for her brother. You don't come back from killing a person. "Do you want me to talk to him?"

"I don't know if that'll help. I don't know what could help him right now. There's only one thing he wants, and it's terrifying."

Tom sees activity at the front of HQ. A door is opening. "Ruth, I'm sorry, but I need to go. We'll talk again soon." Tom hangs up. He watches the front of the building. Only one person steps out and heads toward a car. Anthony Felton. No one follows him. He's all on his own. He gets into a car and starts the engine.

Tom leaves the window and hurries outside to his own car. He jumps inside and fires up the engine, leaving the lights off as he pulls it around to the front. He sees Anthony's vehicle up ahead, pulling away from HQ and onto the road. The other cars remain where they are. Tom leaves his lights off and follows, keeping a distance, until Anthony pulls onto a more active road. Tom hits his lights and pulls out after him. His left arm is bent, resting in his lap. He drives one-handed, using his knees to steady the steering wheel when he has to change gear. Right now, he's wishing the car was an automatic.

Anthony doesn't appear to be in a rush. Wherever he's going, it can't be serious. Can't be work related, or extracurricular. Tom thinks it might be personal.

Eventually, they reach a neighbourhood. It's neat. Tidy. Affluent. Anthony parks in front of one of the houses. Tom has kept a safe distance. When he saw Anthony begin to slow, he turned off the lights again. He parks up at a corner and watches as Anthony makes his way up the porch steps. He rings the doorbell. The door opens, but Tom doesn't see who it is. Anthony goes inside. The door closes.

Tom waits. Ten minutes pass. He watches the house and the street. There's a car in the driveway, and Anthony's car out front. Possibly only two people inside the house. Anthony and probably a woman. Tom thinks he's hooking up. He's left HQ to see his girl. If this is the case, Tom is surprised the others have allowed it to happen.

Tom gets out of his car and goes to the house. Anthony is on his own, and Tom sees an opportunity. He's careful on his way over. Makes sure no one at any of the houses is watching him. It's clear when he slides down the side of the house and round to the back yard. He looks in the windows. The downstairs of the house is clear. Tom checks the back door, leading into the kitchen. It's locked. He goes back around the front, and tries the handle. It's locked, too. Tom rings the bell a few times, enough to make it seem like an emergency, and to be sure he gets their attention. He reaches behind himself and grasps the handle of his Beretta. He holds it in place. He hears someone coming down the stairs, then coming to the door. They're moving slowly, cautiously. Tom steps aside, out of view of the spy hole.

"Hello?" a woman calls through. "Who is it?"

"I'm here to see Anthony," Tom says. "Open up. It's important."

"Who are you?" the woman says.

Tom knows his voice will be muffled through the door, same as hers. "Carter Brown," he says.

"Carter?" she says. For a moment, Tom starts to think he may have gone too far with his bluff, that perhaps the muffling of the door is not enough. He's preparing himself to go around the back of the house and kick the kitchen door down. It looks flimsier than the front.

But then the woman on the other side starts to unlock the door. Tom pulls the Beretta out. As she opens the door, he steps into view. He makes sure she sees the gun, then presses the barrel to his lips to tell her to keep quiet.

Tom doesn't recognise her. Her eyes are wide, staring at the gun. She's wrapped in a nightgown, her hair all mussed. She's rushed down to answer the door from the bedroom. Tom points the gun in her face and steps into the house, kicking the door shut behind him.

"Who are you?" he says.

"K-Katy," the woman says.

"Call Anthony down," Tom says. "Tell him Carter is here."

She moves toward the foot of the stairs. Tom steps with her, keeping the Beretta raised. "Anthony," she calls up. "It's, uh, Carter is here. He says he needs to speak to you."

Tom hears Anthony shout back. "*Carter*?" he says.

"Yuh-yeah," Katy says.

"You sure?"

"He's right here in front of me," Katy says, looking at Tom. Tom nods.

Anthony doesn't rush. Tom can hear him moving around. "Tell him to hurry up."

Katy clears her throat. "Anthony – Carter says this is important. He's in a rush."

"I'm coming down now," Anthony says.

Tom motions with a flick of the gun for Katy to step into the living room with him. He brings her deep into the room, positions her so he has her covered, as well as the doorway.

Anthony comes down the stairs. "Where you at?"

"In here," Katy says.

Anthony steps into the living room. He's topless and barefooted, but he's wearing jeans. Tom sees that the jeans are tight at the front, like something is tucked down the back of them. He's carrying a gun.

"Over here," Tom says, pointing the Beretta at him. "Next to Katy."

Anthony raises his hands and does as he's told. "I recognise you," he says. "You're helping the kid. Hiding out with him and his sister, right?" He looks around. "You got them here with you?"

Tom glances at Katy. She doesn't seem surprised at anything Anthony is saying. "They're safe," Tom says. "Safer than you right now. You'd have been better off if you stayed back at HQ."

Anthony raises an eyebrow and cocks his head like he's impressed at this knowledge.

"Looks like your dick took precedence over your sense," Tom says. He looks the woman over. "You must've been desperate."

"Hey," Katy says.

"Who are you?" Tom says. "Full name."

She glances at Anthony. Anthony shrugs. "Katy Doerr."

"All right, Katy Doerr," Tom says. "How do you know Anthony here? You a cop? Two of you meet on the force?"

She doesn't answer.

"Do you know what Anthony and the rest of the GCTF

do?" Tom says. "I'm not talking about their official capacities. I'm talking unofficial. You probably don't care, do you? You don't look like you would."

"She's not a cop," Anthony says. He's smirking. "She's a secretary. You wanna know whose secretary she is?" He looks like he's about fit to burst out laughing.

Tom tilts his head.

Katy shoots Anthony a look. "Are you going to tell him?"

"Why not?" Anthony says. "It doesn't matter. He can't do anything with it. Lainey Wylder. That's who Katy works for. At least, she *used* to." He chuckles now.

Tom frowns. He looks between the two of them.

Anthony takes his chance. He moves fast, reaching back for his gun. Tom is not as thrown and distracted as Anthony thinks this revelation has made him. He's kept his focus. He sees what Anthony is doing. He puts three bullets into his chest. Anthony's blood sprays onto Katy's face. She screams. Tom turns the gun onto her as Anthony falls.

"You worked for Lainey?" Tom says. "That true?" He's aware, though, that Anthony came downstairs armed. He *knew* Carter wasn't here. He took his time coming down. He moved around upstairs. Did he place a quick call? Send a message? And the gunshots – did neighbours hear them? Tom can't hang around here long. He needs answers, and then he needs to go.

She nods, wiping the blood from her face. "Yes, I worked for her. I don't – I don't understand why he told you. Did you already know?"

"I've never seen you before," Tom says. "I've never heard of you, either. I met Lainey once, when she sent us to the safe house. Anthony was trying to distract me. He thought he was faster than I am." Tom stares at her. The front of her nightgown has come loose and she ties it back up, but he isn't interested in that. "How did it work? Were you already dating this asshole, and then you got the job with Lainey? Or was it the reverse – you already worked for her, and then he came along?"

She doesn't answer.

"I suppose it doesn't matter," Tom says. "You told them about the safe house."

"I found out about the safe house," Katy says, swallowing. "She never told me anything, not about you, or the Styleses. She barely trusted anyone. I had to find it out for myself."

"Did the GCTF kill her?"

She bites her lip. "I don't know."

"But you've got a good idea."

She's shaking.

Tom lowers his gun. "I have a lot to do, Katy," he says. "I'm not going to hang around here and ask you questions I can already guess the answers to. But I want you to remember this – I know who you are now. I know where you live. And I know what you've done. Your boyfriend's dead, and his buddies aren't going to be around for much longer." He moves toward the door, leaving her in the living room. He doesn't put his gun away. He listens. He's wary of her. She shrieked when Anthony's blood landed on her, but she never cried. She wasn't shaken. She's colder than she tried to make herself appear.

As he reaches the door, he hears Katy move. Hears her running to the living room doorway. Tom turns. He's ready for her. She's grabbed Anthony's gun, is holding it two-handed. She sees Tom staring back at her, and realises the mistake she's made. He fires. One bullet, between the eyes.

She falls back, landing with a hard thud. Tom puts the Beretta away and leaves the house, wiping down the handle as he goes to get rid of his prints. He didn't touch anything else. Other than the two dead bodies, it was like he was never here.

53

As morning rises, a cold sun casting its light across the city and through the gaps in HQ's boarded-over windows, Carter is feeling frustrated about a lot of things. Too many things.

First of all, he's frustrated that he and the rest of the GCTF are still having to hide out in HQ, like they're criminals on the run, instead of cops chasing them down.

Secondly, he's frustrated at their lack of progress with the DLB. Despite chasing down many leads day after day, they're yet to find out where they are. They stay on the move, constantly moving, forever one step ahead. The whole city's law enforcement is looking for them, and still nothing. If it weren't for the DLB's regular strikes against the JJC, Carter would begin to suspect that they'd fled the city.

Thirdly, he's frustrated at the JJC fucking up *yet again* when attempting to capture Ruth and Calvin Styles. Carter doesn't care how much blame they place on the mysterious stranger assisting the siblings. So far as he's concerned the blame lies entirely with them. However, going forward and with Lainey dealt with, the GCTF will be handling the siblings. If they want something done right, it's clear they're going to have to do it themselves.

Fourth, and most pressing, Carter is frustrated at Anthony. He went to see Katy last night. He still hasn't come back. He hasn't checked in, either. Carter has tried calling him. He's left messages. Nothing.

His frustration with Anthony has gradually turned to worry with the coming of the morning light.

The others are awake. They share in his frustrations, and his concerns. Delia sits at her desk, her right knee bouncing. "He wouldn't leave us hanging," she says. "If he was gonna stay over, he would've let us know. He wouldn't just shut us out like this."

Darren sucks his teeth. "You think something might have happened to him?"

"We have to consider it."

"I shouldn't have let him go," Carter says, mostly to himself.

"What was that?" Nick says, the closest of the three.

"I said I shouldn't have let him go," Carter says, louder now, clearer. "For what, just so he could get some action?" He shakes his head. "I should've told him to stay here with the rest of us. It was too risky letting him go."

"It wasn't just him," Darren says. "We needed to keep Katy happy, too."

"Fuck Katy," Carter says. "Lainey Wylder is dead. Katy doesn't have much use to us anymore."

"I know where she lives," Nick says. "I'll go there. And if he comes back while I'm out, kick his ass from me for making us worry so much."

Carter runs his tongue around the inside of his mouth, thinking. Sitting around waiting for Anthony isn't doing them any good. They can't stay here, paralysed at the thought of what might have happened. "Darren, go with him," he says. "From here on out, we don't go anywhere alone. I don't care if someone's mother dies, we don't fly solo on anything."

Darren gets to his feet. He and Nick head out of the building.

"What are we gonna do?" Delia says.

"We're gonna go get coffee," Carter says.

They leave and get in a car, Delia driving. On the way to the coffee shop, Carter finds himself looking into every vehicle coming from the other direction, whether they're the same make as what Anthony took last night or not. He keeps waiting to see his face, driving back to HQ, oblivious to the concern he's caused.

Delia was right, though. Anthony wouldn't have left them hanging like this. He wouldn't be so careless. Carter looks at his phone, but there's still nothing.

"I'm not gonna lie," Delia says, seeing what he's doing, "I've got a bad feeling. I think something's happened."

"If the DLB have done anything to him, I swear to Christ," Carter says, "I'm gonna skin those motherfuckers alive."

Delia grunts agreement. "I'll be right there beside you, elbow-deep in entrails."

They reach the coffee shop. Carter looks through the window. There's a queue, but it's only three people deep. Some of the tables are occupied, but he's seen it busier. It looks like a quiet but steady morning for them. "Wait here," Carter says. "I'll go get them."

"Thought none of us were supposed to fly solo," Delia says.

"We're not," Carter says. "You need to keep an eye on the outside, make sure no one tries to get the drop on us. You think the DLB would think twice about shooting up this place just because it's full of uninvolved people?"

"True," Delia says. "I've got your back."

Carter crosses the road, checking the vehicles and the sidewalks as he goes. He enters the coffee shop. The thick aroma of grinding coffee beans greets him. He breathes it in deep. He needs the caffeine. He didn't sleep well last night. He hardly slept at all.

He joins the line, checking the people present. Looking over the people in the queue ahead of him, behind the counter, and seated at the tables. None of the faces leap out. They're not familiar. They're not concerning, either. There's a low murmuring in the room as the people at the tables converse, punctuated by the occasional burst of laughter. The grinding of coffee and the steaming of milk provides a constant undercurrent to it all. Carter watches the door. No one comes in. He looks through the window, to where Delia is parked on the other side of the road.

He senses movement behind him. Someone joining the line, though he hasn't seen anyone new enter. Someone from a table, perhaps, coming up for a refill?

Whoever they are, they get close. Carter doesn't like it. He starts to turn. He feels something jabbing into his lower back and he freezes. Out the corner of his eye, he looks at the person sticking a gun into his back, concealing it within the pocket of their jacket. His blood runs cold. He recognises the face, though it takes him a moment to place it here, in this coffee shop, out of context of everywhere else he's seen it. It's the man they've seen with Calvin and Ruth Styles. The man helping them. The one who's prevented the JJC from getting their hands on them, and most recently killed six members of the gang out at the safe house.

"Don't make a scene," the man says. "I don't have any problem with shooting you dead right here and now, and then your friend out in the car, too."

Carter grits his teeth. "What do you want?"

"Let's take a seat."

54

Carter is big. It's clear that his mass is not natural, and Tom wonders what the drug-testing policy on the Detroit police force is like. Maybe it's different for the leader of a task force. Maybe they just don't care. If they did, Lainey likely wouldn't have been investigating them in the first place.

He stares at Tom, a scowl twisting the corner of his mouth. His body tenses and ripples, like a tiger preparing to jump. He wants to leap across the table, to grab at Tom with his bare hands. Tom holds his stare. He doesn't back down. Tom stays loose. He's not intimidated. He's faced down men just as big as Carter, and men just as scary. He keeps his hand in his pocket, on the handle of his gun, and he knows that Carter is aware of this.

"What do you want?" Carter says.

"I'm a polite guy," Tom says. "I figured it was about time I introduced myself. Plus, I wanted to see you up close. In person. I'd heard you were a big guy."

Carter says nothing.

"You *are* a big guy," Tom says, then leans closer, and lowers his voice to a conspiratorial tone. "But I've seen bigger." He winks as he sits back.

Carter shrugs. "So introduce yourself," he says.

"My name's Tom Rollins. When we're done here, you can look me up. What I want you to understand is, I know how this game is being played."

"That so?"

"That's so. I know you're not a cop, no more than I am."

Carter grins, showing his teeth. "That what you think?"

"That's what I know. That's why I gave you my name. You can't do anything with it. You're operating outside of the law, same as me."

"You think I won't use your name to put out an APB?"

"That kind of shit might fly with the handful of uniforms that you're friendly with, but an APB is a bigger deal, isn't it? It's going to raise questions, questions you don't want to answer. Because you don't want the uniforms to find me, same as you don't want them to find Ruth and Calvin. *You* want to find us. If you didn't, you wouldn't keep sending the JJC after us. You could've sent uniforms a long time ago. There's too much red tape, too much admin if you do things the right way. And then there's the questions, and the answers Ruth and Calvin – and hell, even me – might give to those questions. You can't run that risk, Carter. None of you can. It's down to you, your task force, and the JJC. That's all you have."

Carter raises an eyebrow. He smirks. "That's *all*?"

"Do you think it's enough?"

Carter works his jaw, grinding his teeth. He looks toward the window, out to where Delia is sat waiting in the car.

"Do you think she could get in here fast enough?" Tom says.

Carter turns back to him. "She's fast."

"You think she could get here before I could put a bullet through your face?"

"Not sure there's anyone who could. But do you think you can draw on me faster than I can draw on you?"

"Yes," Tom says.

Carter is a little taken aback by his lack of hesitation, but he tries to hide it. "Yeah? What makes you so sure?"

"Your hands are on the table. My finger's still on the trigger. But I know that if we were doing this Old West style, middle of the road, guns holstered and hands primed, I know I could out-draw you then, too."

Carter chuckles. "You're a cocky little fucker."

"It's not cockiness," Tom says. "Just facts."

"Just facts, huh? All right."

Tom says nothing.

"Since all the cards are on the table," Carter says, "since we both know how this thing's gonna go down, let me ask, how're Ruth and Calvin? They doing well? You got them somewhere safe?"

"They're fine."

"They nearby? Outside, waiting for you in a getaway car?"

"I'm sure you'd like that. You're thinking right now, three birds with one stone. But no. They're not here."

Carter sits back in his chair, leans his head back and regards Tom. "What do you get out of all this?" he says. "What you getting from helping those two? They ain't paying you. I know they can't afford it. They can barely afford their rent."

"You seen that *since* you tried to intimidate a young woman, or was that while you were out there?"

Carter smiles. He raises a finger in the air, waving it back and forth a little. "That's what it is, right? It's her. Ruth. You fucking her?" He holds up his hands. "Hey, man, I get it. She's a good-looking woman. I've seen her. Of course, when I saw her she had that whole deer in the headlights thing going on, but I could tell she was an attractive woman. That how they paying you? You getting to hit that, gratis?"

Tom doesn't speak for a while. He holds Carter's eye. "Some of us still believe in doing the right thing," he says. "And we don't need paid for that. We don't need a uniform or a badge to show what side we're on, either. Fact is, a lot of the time, we're better off without."

"All right, Rollins," Carter says, breathing deep, sounding impatient. "You've got my attention. You've introduced yourself. You want something else, or are we just gonna sit and stare into each other's eyes all day?"

"I think we're done here," Tom says. He makes like he's about to stand.

Carter blinks. "What? That's it?"

"There anything else?"

Carter frowns, staring at him. Tom remains seated for now. Carter nods like he's beginning to understand. "I get it," he says. "I got it now. You're trying to lure me out of here. You've got something all set up, probably just down the block and round the corner. A trap. Or else you came here, you're trying to spook me, right? Trying to show that *you* ain't scared. That you can get us any time. You want us to get frightened. To get careless. Make some mistakes. That about right?"

Tom smiles. "I told you. I wanted to meet you in person. I

wanted to introduce myself. I wanted you to know that I understand how this ends. I don't need to turn up just to show I can get to you. When that time comes, you won't see me coming."

"Yeah? What's wrong with your shoulder?"

He's spotted the bulge of the brace under the jacket. "There's nothing wrong with my shoulder," Tom says. It's not a lie.

Carter is undeterred. "Arm, then. You get hurt?"

"It comes with the territory."

Carter grins like a shark smelling blood. "It broken?"

"Not enough."

"What's that supposed to mean?"

"Means it ain't gonna slow me down. Means that if you think it's gonna help you out, you're in for a nasty shock." Tom waits a beat, then, with a smile, adds, "Anthony can tell you how much it's slowed me down."

Carter's face drops. Tom can see his mind racing behind his eyes. Carter starts to sneer. "He dead?" he says, his voice low and strained, barely suppressing a rage building within him.

"You'll know soon enough." Tom gets to his feet. "I'll see you again, Carter." He backs up toward the rear door, the same one he entered the coffee house through. He makes sure Carter can see he's still pointing the gun at him through his jacket pocket. Carter stares at him as he goes, his lower jaw jutting, his eyes burning. Tom slips out the back, onto the sidewalk behind the building.

He doesn't head straight for his car. He stays behind the coffee shop. Over the road, there's an empty office front with big For Lease signs in the windows. Before Tom entered the coffee shop, he picked the lock on its door. He goes to it now and slips inside, closing the door behind him. Pressing himself against the wall, he watches out the window, knowing that Carter and Delia are going to attempt to follow him. They'd be foolish if they didn't.

Sure enough, a moment later, Delia comes speeding around the corner in the car. The back door of the coffee shop bursts open and Carter leaps out onto the sidewalk, gun clasped two-handed. He looks up and down the sidewalk, scanning the area. Delia jumps out of the car. She's armed too. They shout to each other. Tom can hear them through the glass. He pulls himself back out of view, behind the wall. He keeps his Beretta out, just in case.

They're wondering where he's gone. Neither can see him. It's like he's disappeared. They don't waste time here. By now, they're thinking about Anthony. About what Tom said about him. They jump back into the car and they speed away.

55

Tom returns to the factory. Ruth wraps her arms around him, then checks his temperature and insists on taking off his jacket so she can look at his arm. Calvin stands close, wanting to know what he's seen.

While Ruth checks him over, Tom updates them on what has happened. Ruth is very quiet while he speaks, though he can tell she's listening. Her brow furrows when he mentions the killing of Anthony and Katy, and how Katy sold out Lainey to the GCTF.

"So you saw Carter?" Calvin says. "You spoke to him?"

"Yeah."

"Why didn't you kill him there, like you did with Anthony?"

"If I'd had the opportunity to kill him I would've taken it," Tom says, "but it was a room full of other people. I don't take those kinds of risks, not if the other person isn't already holding a gun to my head. And with Anthony it was different. I saw a chance, and I took it."

"All right," Calvin says, looking like he can accept this. "What now?"

"Well, I've had a lot of time to think and plan while I've been watching the HQ. Now that I've got them all riled up and pissed off, it's time I find where Javon is."

Both siblings freeze at this. Ruth looks toward her brother like she knows what he's going to say.

"Then I'm coming with you," Calvin says, his face dark, his tone firm.

Tom remembers what Ruth told him on the phone.

"How are you gonna find him?" Calvin says.

"There's been a lot of activity lately. The DLB have been hitting them hard. I'll correlate where most of the attacks have been occurring, pinpoint which corners are JJC."

"I know the corners," Calvin says. "I've been watching them."

"When I first met you, you were questioning a DLB member on who Javon was," Tom says. "How do you know who controls what corners?"

"I heard things while I was watching," Calvin says. "I heard names. I heard acronyms. Just because I didn't know who Javon was, doesn't mean I hadn't heard of the JJC."

Tom considers this.

"I don't want you to go," Ruth says to her brother.

"It's going to save you a lot of time," Calvin says, looking at Tom.

"Maybe he *should* come with me," Tom says, talking to Ruth.

Ruth doesn't look happy. "Can I talk to you?" She takes Tom to one side, away from Calvin. They go into the office. Ruth closes the door and then wheels on him. "Okay, first of all, you're not well enough to be going around like this. You still need to recover."

"There's no time for that," Tom says.

"Tom, you have a *broken arm*. You have an *infection*. I don't understand why this isn't getting through."

Tom pulls the blister pack of antibiotics from his pocket. "I've been taking the pills," he says. "I've nearly finished the course."

"That's beside the point!" Ruth throws up her hands. "Listen, you're a grown man. I can't stop you and I can't tell you what to do. But I told you my concerns about Calvin. I told you that because I *don't* want him to go out there – I wasn't implying that I wanted you to *invite* him."

"Listen," Tom says, "no matter how much Calvin might want to believe it, he's not a killer."

"How can you be sure?"

"Because I know. You need to trust me on this, Ruth. He's a fighter, sure, but he's no killer. If we try to keep him here, out of the way, it's not going to work. He'll tear away, he'll go out there on his own, the way he did when I first met him."

"So what are you suggesting? Scare him straight?"

"In a sense."

Ruth doesn't say anything. She turns away. "Do what you have to."

Tom leaves the office. Calvin watches him. "Let's go," Tom says.

"I'm coming with," Ruth says, following him out of the office. Her face is as dark and firm as Calvin's now. She stares at her brother. "If you're going out there, you're not going without me." She takes Tom in with her gaze. "Either of you."

56

Javon is in his apartment. He stands at the window, staring out at the city before him. *His* city.

And now, the way things are, the way the war with the DLB has turned, he can't go out into his city. It's too dangerous for him. It's too dangerous for all of the JJC, but Javon has told them that as far as they're concerned, it's business as usual.

Javon tents his fingers, pressing the tips up against his lips, mashing them back against his teeth. He breathes deep. Everything is on hold. Everything has come to a screeching halt. He doesn't like it. Things were moving along well, things were getting hot with his investors, but now he's had to put everything on ice. He can't host them. Can't take them to his clubs. His clubs have been getting hit. The last thing he needs right now is for an investor to get caught in a crossfire.

It would be impossible to cover up the death – or deaths – of people not caught up in the gang life. Especially if they were shot to death in one of his establishments. Javon has had his secretary put out that he's been out of town on business. He told her to keep it vague, say he was down in Chicago for at least a couple of weeks. One week has passed already. He didn't expect things to take this long. The DLB have put up more of a fight than he anticipated. They've shown themselves to be more vicious, and more resourceful, than he ever gave them credit for.

Tyrell is on his way up. As he enters the apartment, Javon turns to him. "You got any good news for me?"

He can tell from the look on Tyrell's face that the answer is no. "Guess that depends on what you want to know about."

"We still got problems with the DLB?"

"No, but we bagged a couple of them."

"Uh-huh. You found the Styles brother and sister yet?" The Styleses are the least of their problems right now. They're an issue, there's no doubt, but the GCTF can deal with them. They're a bigger headache for Carter and his crew.

"No," Tyrell says.

"So there's *no* fucking good news," Javon says.

"Didn't you hear me? I said we bagged a couple of DLB's."

"Unless one of them was Darius Walker, I don't really give a shit."

"It wasn't Darius Walker. We still ain't been able to find him. He's a slippery motherfucker."

Javon grunts. "This should've been over by now. It should never have gotten to this stage to begin with."

"I *told* Carter not to go after the man's mama."

"Carter was taking a proactive approach," Javon says,

giving Tyrell a side eye so he knows exactly what Javon thinks of the approach he has taken.

"And I told *you* that you needed to take this thing more serious from the get-go." Tyrell breathes deep. He's agitated. He raises a hand to the back of his head and starts fiddling with his cornrows. "I've done what I can. The GCTF went off half-cocked and now we're suddenly fighting on two fronts. We ain't got the men to spare for their bullshit."

"The GCTF are – and always have been – important to us."

Tyrell rolls his eyes.

"What? You don't agree?"

"Man, they're *cops*. Fuck cops. Fuck all cops."

"Not if they're useful."

Tyrell rolls his eyes again.

"You gonna keep rolling your eyes at me?" Javon says. "You're acting like a bitch, you know that? You been acting like a bitch for a long damn time now."

"A bitch? That's what I am this week, huh?"

"Yeah, it is. That's how you've been. What, you think I'm gonna sugarcoat it? You've become a colossal pain in my ass, Tyrell. You think I ain't got enough problems right now without you always up here complaining?"

"Complaining? Man, I'm the only one giving it to you *straight*. You got your priorities wrong, and I'm the only one who'll tell you. The JJC is dying, and it's starting at the top."

Javon waves a hand.

"You don't care?"

Javon doesn't answer. The truth is, he doesn't, not really. He knows they remain necessary, but the sooner he can move on from them, the better.

Tyrell shakes his head in disgust. "The JJC is the only

real thing you ever built. All of *this*," he indicates the apartment, "it's changed you for the worst. It's made you soft. It ain't fucking real, man. What was real was when we were out on the streets."

"We were out on the streets *dreaming* of reaching this point," Javon says. "And you think this is fake? Jesus Christ, you're a dumbass, ain't you? The only thing that was ever real was our dreams, and I've been accomplishing mine. You ain't just a bitch, Tyrell, you're a *jealous* bitch."

Tyrell's hands ball into fists. His arms shake.

"You gonna take a swing at me?" Javon says.

Tyrell breathes deep. He opens his hands. "Nah," he says. "I don't think I am. Used to be, I would do anything for you, man. Now, I don't even wanna look at you. I don't wanna be anywhere near you." He turns away, shaking his head. "You enjoy your ivory tower, man," he says, heading toward the exit.

Javon flips the bird to his retreating back.

Tyrell leaves. Javon stares after him, at the space he previously occupied. He returns to the window, to his view of the city.

Tyrell will come back. Javon doesn't know when – it could be later today, it could be tomorrow. Hell, it could be a couple of days, but he *will* return. He'll make some attempt at straightening things out, though they'll likely end up arguing again. Maybe next time will be the time they finally come to blows. Whatever happens, though, Tyrell always comes back.

Of course, whenever he decides to show back up, Tyrell remains an issue. When the problems with the DLB are resolved, the Tyrell problem is next on the agenda. Until then, much like the rest of the JJC, Javon has to continue to rely on him.

He presses his forehead against the cool glass and closes his eyes. Silently, he keeps telling himself this will end. His problems will go away. Things will get back on track. The investments will be made. The contracts will come through. He'll accomplish this current set of dreams. And then? Well, then he'll have to find some new dreams. Javon has always been ambitious. Working out where to go next has never been a problem for him.

57

They couldn't find Rollins after he left the coffee shop.

"The smug prick," Delia said. "Smug son of a bitch. He ain't gonna be smirking when we catch up to him."

It didn't take them long to look into him. To find out all about Tom Rollins – or at least all that is available to know. From what is available to read, Carter has a feeling a lot of things have slipped through the cracks.

They're in HQ. Nick whistles through his teeth. "CIA, huh?" he says. "Most likely black ops? And that shit in Texas? I remember hearing about that on the news. What's he doing all the way up here?"

"He clearly gets around," Darren says. "Texas was a few years ago now. He could've gone anywhere after that."

"I don't give a shit who he is and what he's done," Carter says. "Now we know who we're up against. Now we know how to handle him."

"We gotta find him first," Delia says.

"Anthony would've been able to find him," Darren says,

clutching his hands together, popping his knuckles. "Now we know who he is, he could've got some facial recognition shit up and running. We'd track him down like *that*." He clicks his fingers.

Nick and Darren found Anthony and Katy dead in Katy's home, shortly after Carter had his meeting with Rollins. Carter was unsurprised. Part of him had hoped Rollins was bluffing, but it was a small part. Carter saw the look in his eyes. Rollins isn't the kind of man to lie. He doesn't need to. He can back up his words.

Despite the obvious signs of gunfire, no one had called the cops on Katy's street. Carter told Darren and Nick not to call it in. "Leave them as they are," he said. "We don't wanna have to deal with this right now. Once the bodies are found, we can come up with an excuse then. Blame it on the DLB or something."

Darren runs both hands down his mouth. "It doesn't feel right," he says, "leaving Anthony out there like that."

"No other choice," Nick says. "Carter is right. We got enough on our plates."

"He's gonna pay for what he did," Carter says. "We get hold of him, we bring him back here, and we make it *slow*. Fred Boothe got it fast compared to what we're gonna do to this prick."

"But how do we *find* him?" Darren says.

Carter is sick of hearing the question. "Listen to me," he says, staring at them each in turn. "He's hurt. He's trying to hide it, but something is up with his left arm. Either he's broke it, or dislocated his shoulder, judging by where he had the cast. He's not at one hundred percent. He can talk a big game, but that's all he's got – *mouth*. Going forward, we stick together. All four of us. The only chance he has of picking us off is if we're separate, like Anthony was. We stay together."

"But how's that gonna help us find him?" Darren says.

"We don't need to find him," Carter says. "He's made his intentions clear. He's coming for *us*. So long as we stick together, we don't have to go looking for him. We just need to be ready for him."

58

Calvin gave directions to a few different corners. Tom passed by them, getting an idea for them, working out which one would be best to grab someone from. Each one was heavily manned and guarded. He saw how the men on the corners were clearly concealing weapons, and how they watched every vehicle and pedestrian that passed by with furtive, suspicious eyes.

Tom picked a corner at random. They were all much the same in terms of manpower, but he chose the one with the clearest escape route. He went after the big guy guarding the stash. He left Ruth and Calvin down the block, where it was safer. He drove up, mounted the sidewalk at the last second and spun the steering wheel, slamming the rear side of the car into the guard. When Tom hurried out of the car to get him, he saw that the impact had broken his left leg. He was screaming, and reaching for a concealed weapon. Tom kicked him across the jaw, dazing him, then took the Colt Mustang he was trying to pull and threw it into the gutter. He threw the guard's cell phone after it. Tom bundled him into the backseat, moving fast. He could see the other guys on the corner down the block realising what had happened after hearing the impact. They were starting to rise up, to pull their guns. Tom was back in his car and driving before they could fire a single shot.

He was able to go fast, but it all happened slower than he would have liked. The broken arm is holding him back. As much as he doesn't want to, he has to admit it.

He picked up Calvin and Ruth then took the broken-legged corner boy into an abandoned warehouse. He left Ruth out in the car on guard, not wanting her to see what happened. He took Calvin in with him, wanting him to see. Wanting to gauge his reaction. Wanting to put him off.

The corner guy was JJC. With his broken leg, it didn't take Tom long to find out what he wanted to know. Namely, where Javon is. Where he lives. How to get inside.

When he looked back at Calvin, the kid's face was ashen. He looked like he could be sick. He was staring at the broken leg. He'd seen what Tom had done to it – pressing his boot into the worst of the break to get answers. Tom left the corner guard alive. By the time he'd be able to get to anyone who could help him, they'd have already been to see Javon.

Tom parks the car outside of Javon's building. He looks at Ruth. "You coming in?"

Ruth looks at her brother. "Are *you*?"

Calvin's lips are pursed. Already, Tom can see he could be having second thoughts on why he has come here. He nods, though.

"Then I'm coming in," Ruth says.

"The two of you are gonna hold back until I've cleared the apartment," Tom says. "I don't know what kind of security he might have in there with him. If I have to go in there shooting, I want you both clear of it. The guy I spoke to, he said he didn't think there'd be anyone. He said Javon is barely in the streets anymore, and he's gotten lax because of it. But he could've been lying to me, trying to lull us."

It's easy enough for them to get into the building. The front requires a key card and a security code, but the guard from the corner told them that if they go around the back the card reader there is broken and it's just a regular lock. Tom is able to pick it. The door leads them into a stairwell. They take the stairs up to Javon's floor, all the way at the top. The guard said there are two ways into Javon's apartment, up the elevator, or up the stairs. The elevator requires another key code. Only Tyrell gets to use the elevator. Everyone else in the JJC has to use the stairs. Javon doesn't want too many people knowing the code.

Tom goes on ahead, leaving Ruth and Calvin in the stairwell. The door into Javon's apartment is locked. Tom picks it. It leads through to a small, plain corridor. There's nothing on the walls, or the ground. Tom makes his way toward the door at the end. There's no lock on this one. Tom is cautious opening it, keeping his Beretta up, peering inside. From what he can see of the apartment beyond, it's clear. He steps inside. As he scans the area, he sees a man standing at the far end, his back to the room, looking out of a window.

"I knew you'd come back," the man says without turning. Tom can hear the satisfied smirk in his voice. "Using the servant door, huh? You must *really* be contrite."

Tom looks around, makes sure they're alone. There's no one else present in the space between Tom and the man at the window. He can't hear anyone behind the other doors he can see. The apartment is quiet.

"Ain't talking?" the man says.

"I think you've got me confused for someone else."

The man spins, brow furrowed. He's Javon Johnson. Tom expected as much. He looks Tom over, no doubt surprised to see this stranger in his home. He straightens up, smiling. "I recognise you," he says. "I know who you are."

Tom walks toward him, gun raised, remaining wary of the closed doors around them. They don't open. He can't hear anyone getting close, bracing themselves to listen in and emerge in an ambush when the time is right. Javon doesn't call out for help, either. "Javon Johnson," Tom says.

Javon holds out his arms. "At your service." He takes a step to the left.

Tom shakes his head. "Stay where you are." Javon is unarmed. If he was moving, it was likely an attempt to get closer to a weapon.

Javon stays where he is, keeping his arms raised. "You've got me at a disadvantage," he says. "You know my name, but all I know about you is your face, and the fact you've killed a lot of my men."

"You haven't spoken to your buddies in the GCTF?" Tom says. "You wanted my name, you could've asked them."

Javon grunts. "I guess we've all been busy with our own shit lately. We don't talk as much as we should."

"I'm of the opinion you talk too much."

"That so? Let's see, what's that in regard to? The raid at the safe house? I know someone got killed out there, and he was one of yours, because he certainly wasn't one of mine."

Tom steps closer.

"Easy now," Javon says. He looks like he wants to back up, but the window's behind him. There's nowhere for him to go.

The door into the apartment opens. Tom assumes it

must be Calvin and Ruth, but he spins on it nonetheless. He needs to be sure. It's the siblings. They raise their hands. "We didn't hear any shooting," Calvin says. "We figured it had to be clear."

Tom hears movement. He spins back to Javon. He's running. Tom fires. With the infection and the broken arm, he's slower than usual. His first shot is wide. He drops his arm and aims ahead of Javon as he races toward a door. He fires. The bullet catches Javon through the right thigh. He goes down, clutching at his leg. He lies on the ground, blood running through his fingers while he curses.

"Is that him?" Calvin says. Ruth tries to hold him back but he shakes her off and hurries through the apartment, trying to get to Javon, to see him properly. Tom holds an arm across his chest, keeping him from getting too close. "Let me go, Tom. He's right there. He's right fucking there!"

"What are you going to do to him?" Tom says.

"I'm gonna kill him!" Calvin takes a step back so he can look properly at Tom. "You know what I'm gonna do!"

"All right," Tom says. "How are you going to do it?"

Calvin hesitates at this. "I'm going to – I'm going to kill him..."

"How?" Tom says. "You don't have any weapons. Are you going to beat him to death with your hands?"

Calvin looks at Javon. Javon is looking back at them. He sees Calvin and he sees Ruth. He knows who they are. He knows why they're here. His past sins, catching up with him. He tries to push himself back across the floor, slipping in the blood pumping out of his leg.

Tom holds out his Beretta to Calvin. "You could shoot him."

Calvin stares at the gun. While he hesitates, he keeps one

eye on Javon, making sure he doesn't get too far away. Javon is staring back at them, watching the gun. Behind them, Ruth watches, too. Her eyes flicker toward Javon and the spreading blood. Tom wonders what is going through her head. What is going through both of their heads, so close to the man who killed their parents.

Calvin reaches for the gun. He bites his bottom lip. His reach is tentative, his fingers trembling as they come close to the handle. They brush against it and he takes his hand back as if burned. He closes his hand into a fist, still staring at the weapon. His arm drops down to his side. He looks away, back at Javon.

"Do you know what you did?" Calvin says, his voice cracking. Javon stares back at him. He's in pain, but that's all his face shows. "Do you even care?"

Calvin's words seem to get through. Javon starts laughing. "You want the truth, kid?" He turns his head and spits. Blood continues to pulse out of his leg. His trouser leg is soaked through. "The truth is, until recently, I ain't given you or your sister or your dead fucking parents any thought at all."

Calvin stares at Javon. His breathing hitches. Tom can see his teeth tightly clenched through his cheek. Calvin breathes deep. He turns away. He looks at Tom.

"Take your sister and wait in the stairwell," Tom says.

Calvin walks away.

Ruth catches Tom's eyes. She nods, too, and then places an arm around her brother's shoulders when he's close enough. They leave the apartment together. Tom waits until they're gone.

Javon is laughing through his pain, clutching at his leg.

"So what was that? You doling out some kind of life lesson to the kid?"

Tom shoots him through the head. He puts the Beretta away and pulls out his KA-BAR, approaching the cooling corpse, stepping around his spreading pool of blood. He uses the knife to cut open the front of Javon's shirt. Into his still warm flesh he carves DLB, and follows it up with the first line of an address. When the JJC find the dead body of their leader, they're going to come looking for revenge. They're going to assume it's the DLB.

Tom will be waiting for them.

He's going to take Ruth and Calvin back to the factory, and then head to the address he's given and wait. This ends soon. If Javon's body is found early enough, this could end tonight.

They won't know what's hit them.

59

Carter wakes to the sound of his phone ringing. He looks around. It's dark in HQ. Nick is on guard. He's by the door, turning back at the sound of the phone's vibrations.

Carter checks the number. It's Tyrell. "Hello?"

Tyrell is breathless. Carter hears him swallow before he speaks. He gulps. "Shit, man – *shit* –"

"Tyrell," Carter says, "what is it?"

"Fuck, man, *fuck* – they've killed him. He's dead. They've killed him right here in his home."

Carter feels his blood run cold. "Who's dead, Tyrell?"

"It's Javon," Tyrell says. "We – we fell out earlier. Man, it felt like that's all we ever did lately. I was going back to him, to try and make it right. I didn't know how it would've gone – hell, we might've even ended up hitting each other. But I needed to try, right? I couldn't just leave things how they were. But then I walk in, and there he is, he's dead, and those sick fucks, they've carved their name into him, same as they did with those cops –"

Tyrell is rambling. Carter cuts him off. "Javon is dead? When did it happen? Tonight?"

Nick has overheard. He leaves the door and comes closer to listen in. He stands to the side, arms folded. Carter turns the phone away from his ear a little so Nick can hear better.

"Yeah, it was tonight. I only left him a few hours ago – like, five hours? I just needed to cool down. And you know, when I went back, I was full of hell, man. Those five hours, I didn't calm down any. I went back, and I was ready to have it out with him all over again. He'd changed. He refused to see it, but he had. But I walked in, see him lying dead, and all that anger, it just left me. I just felt...*regret*."

Carter doesn't care about Tyrell's feelings and his sudden realisations. "Did you say the DLB killed him?"

"Yeah, yeah, it was the DLB. Like with those cops. I said that. They carved their names into him, and an address."

Carter perks up. He notices Nick do the same. "An address?"

"Yeah, they cut that into him, too. An invite, I reckon – a threat. Gonna try and lure us in. Try and ambush us."

"What are you gonna do?"

"Well, we're gonna go out there. I've put the call out, told everyone we're gonna meet up and then go along there."

Carter and Nick exchange glances. "You just said it could be an ambush."

"Yeah, it could be, but they killed Javon, man. And if they wanna fight, and they're stupid enough to tell us where they are, we'll see them there. We *know* it's gonna be an ambush, man. If we know that, we're ready for them."

"If you say so," Carter says. "Give me the address."

Tyrell tells him. "Why? Are you planning on coming along?"

"We'll be there. But also, I'll make sure the area is kept quiet, and that patrols know it's likely to get noisy and they should steer clear for a while."

"Good thinking. We're setting off in five minutes. I'll see you there."

Carter hangs up. "Wake them up," he says to Nick.

"Why do we need to be there?" Nick says. "It sounds like the JJC are ready to deal with one of our problems tonight – why do we need to go?"

"Do you trust them to deal with things properly? I'm not willing to sit around and wait for a call just to hear them say they've fucked up again. Wake Delia and Darren. Tyrell said they're heading out in five minutes. We'll wait fifteen, let them get started. If things get messy, we can deal with the aftermath."

"This doesn't sound like the DLB at all," Nick says. "So far, they've been careful. Staying in hiding, always on the move. Now they're calling out the JJC like this?"

"They called us out by killing two cops, knowing it would bring the full city's force down on them," Carter says. "Just because they're careful most of the time doesn't mean they're not likely to slip up and do something stupid."

Nick hesitates. "Crazy about Javon," he says.

Carter grunts. His mind has been racing since Tyrell dropped that bombshell.

"How do you feel?" Nick says. "I know you had big plans – we all did – and we needed Javon for them."

Carter grinds his teeth. "We'll find a way to adapt," he says. "There are always other options. Now wake them up. I ain't gonna tell you again."

60

The address Tom carved into Javon's body was for a rundown area. Tom got the location from Ruth. Told her he needed somewhere rundown, quiet, where no one else was likely to be. Somewhere with plenty of hiding places. He scoped it out on the way to confront Javon. It was perfect for his needs. It used to be a couple of warehouses and a factory. Ruth said the factory burned down a long time ago. The warehouses are still blackened. The three buildings formed half of a box shape. They'll give the JJC something to search through when they get here.

Tom lies flat nearby, behind a low wall, waiting. Overgrown grass surrounds him, giving him something to hide in. The ground is damp and he's smeared the dirt over his face as camouflage. Already, it's been a long night. It's been a long day. He's tired, and his eyelids are heavy. He pinches himself to stay awake. Tenses his muscles to keep the blood flowing through his body. The infection is still working through him, and at moments – like now – he can feel it. He pops an antibiotic, swallowing it dry. His broken arm aches and itches simultaneously. He rubs at his left shoulder, trying to bring himself some relief. He's parked his car a mile away, out of view across the harsh, overgrown terrain. It's behind a bush, out of view. If he looks back, he can't see it.

There's no guarantee that Javon's body will be found tonight. If it's not, he'll have to make himself comfortable here in the dirt and grass tomorrow, and wait until the JJC do find the message and finally turn up. He potentially has a long couple of days ahead of him, but he can live with that. They're closing in on the endgame now. Soon, this will all be over. Ruth and Calvin will be able to return to their lives. Tom can move on from Detroit.

On his way here he bought a lighter. He feels it in his right pocket, digging into him when he shifts his weight. The JJC will likely arrive en masse. He can't face them head-on, especially not in his weakened state. He's going to have to sneak. He's going to have to be careful.

It shouldn't be difficult. Tom is always careful.

This area is quiet. The few hours Tom has been here already, he hasn't heard a vehicle. He hasn't heard a voice. He hasn't seen any living thing, save for a few birds circling in the darkness overhead, probably hunting. Now, though, he can hear cars coming. They're coming fast. Their engines are loud and roaring, bumping over the unmaintained, potholed road. Slowly, Tom looks back. He sees the cars coming this way. He counts five, their headlights blinking as they approach, bouncing up and down and disappearing momentarily behind bushes and trees.

If they had sense, they wouldn't have driven all the way here. They would have stayed back, at the end of the road. Tom had anticipated they would approach on foot and he would sneak away, back to their vehicles. This way works, too. The JJC are all worked up. They're angry. They're not thinking straight.

The lead car comes to a stop and the men inside get out. They leave their doors open, something to hide behind in case they're attacked. There's a man with cornrows who seems to be in charge, barking out orders. The other four cars pull up alongside them, parking haphazardly. They don't keep it a neat line. Tom can't make out what the man with cornrows is saying. He points and gesticulates and shouts. The men are armed with submachine guns. From where he is, Tom can't make out the models. It doesn't matter. All he knows is that he doesn't want to be on the end of their fire.

The men begin to spread out, searching the area, heading for the buildings. They're cautious, watching the windows. They split into three groups. One set goes into the burned-out remnants of the factory, and the other two go into the old warehouses. Some men stay with the cars, at least one of them standing by each vehicle. They turn their heads, looking around, checking that no one is trying to sneak up on them from left or right, or from behind. The man with the cornrows stays with the cars, standing in front of them, pacing back and forth. Occasionally, he looks back, looks toward the road, like he's expecting more men to show up. Tom can't hear or see anyone else approaching.

Tom waits until they settle, until the men by the cars are all watching the buildings and their heads aren't so much on a swivel, getting lax, no longer anticipating an ambush from the sides or behind.

Tom takes out his KA-BAR and leaves his hiding area behind the wall. He stays low, crawling over the wall at first, before getting up to a crouch. He makes his way toward the cars, watching the men, making sure they don't turn and look back at him. He clears the space as fast as he can. He ducks behind the car the man in cornrows was in. If he's giving the orders, that likely means he was Javon's second-in-command. It means he's in charge now.

Tom lies flat. He crawls under the car. The gas tank is at the rear. He sticks the KA-BAR up into it, and fuel spills out around his hand. He takes the knife back and rolls away from the flowing fuel. It runs along the ground, heading back the way Tom came. He looks between vehicles, makes sure no one is looking back at him, and then goes to the car on the left. He punctures the gas tank at the rear, careful not to get the flow of gas all over himself. He leaves the vehicle to the left of this one, and instead creeps to the one to the right of the first. On his way, he looks toward the buildings. The man with the cornrows has stopped pacing. He's shouting.

"They there? You see anything?"

A faint voice calls back. "It looks clear."

Another adds, "I don't see anyone."

Tom punctures the third gas tank, then backtracks toward the wall. He moves quick, but backwards this time, and with his Beretta in his hand. No one turns. They're all distracted by the men searching the buildings, and the seeming lack of DLB presence.

Tom reaches the wall and hides behind it. The trail of fuel is pooling close to him. The gas from the three tanks has spread across the tarmac and joined together, mingling on their way down the slight incline. Tom puts the Beretta down but keeps it within easy reach. He buries his right hand in the dirt, trying to soak the worst of the fuel from it. He rubs dirt over it, getting it as clear as he can. He sniffs. It still smells like fuel, though not as bad as it did. He takes the lighter from his pocket.

The man with cornrows is pacing again. Stomping his feet now. Throwing up his arms. He's shouting not at the men, but out into the darkness. "Where you at? We're here! Where you at?"

He's calling to the DLB. The DLB are not here. The DLB don't know anything about this meeting.

Tom needs to cripple the JJC. The DLB are a problem for another time. Dealing with the GCTF is one thing, but if the JJC are still around then Ruth and Calvin will never truly be safe. He needs to ensure their future safety, for after he's left Detroit.

Someone says something to the man with cornrows. The man with cornrows wheels on him. His face is lit by the headlights, and Tom can read his lips enough to work out what he says: *I can see that they're not here.*

The men who searched the buildings are making their way back to the cars now. They're still cautious, but not as much as they were before. They're starting to think this was all a joke at their expense. The DLB mocking them. None of them looks happy.

The man with cornrows laces his fingers atop his head, looking back at the buildings. He turns, giving up. After a moment, he motions to the men to get back into the cars. None of them have noticed the fuel that has spilled from the backs of their vehicles and is still pumping into a small pool near to where Tom lies.

When most of the men are back inside the cars, Tom hears another vehicle approaching. He looks back, sees it making its way slowly down the road. He recognises the car. He's seen it a lot lately. It was parked outside of the GCTF's

HQ. The JJC must have contacted them. Told them what had happened to Javon. The GCTF have come to help.

The man with the cornrows is not inside yet. He sees the car, too. He waits for it to come closer.

Tom can't wait for the GCTF to get any closer. They might spot the fuel on the ground, get the JJC to scatter. He buries his fingertips in the dirt, coating them, shielding them, and then flicks the lighter. The man with the cornrows spots the light out of the corner of his eye. He turns to it. Tom rises from cover. He drops the lighter into the puddle of gas. It ignites instantly. Tom dives back from it. He lies low behind the wall, peering over. Sees how the man with the cornrows' eyes grow wide, watching as the gas catches and the flame speeds across the ground, toward the cars, and up into their tanks.

Tom pushes his face down into the dirt and covers his head with his one good arm as the cars explode. He feels the heat whoosh above him, prickling and singeing the hairs on the back of his neck.

When it calms, Tom pushes himself up. He can't see the man with the cornrows anymore. More than likely he's been blown clear in the blast, and his smouldering remains have landed somewhere close to the old warehouses. Not all of the JJC were caught up in the explosion. Most of the men in the two cars parked further out, the two that Tom did not pierce, have survived, though the cars have rolled. The men are crawling around. Some are stumbling, looking burnt and dazed.

Tom looks back at the GCTF. They've stopped halfway down the road, pausing at the sight of the explosion. Tom wasn't expecting them to turn up. He knew it was a possibility that the JJC would alert them as to what happened to

Javon and tell them the address. Tom was planning to deal with the GCTF at HQ. He was going to trap them inside and burn the building down. Despite what he told Carter, he's too weak for a direct confrontation. He accepts his limitations, and the broken arm and infection have imposed a heavy limitation upon him.

The GCTF's car starts to turn, its headlights strafing across the wasteland until they're pointing his way. Tom grits his teeth. They've seen him. The light from the fire had already picked him out.

He turns and starts running, heading toward his hidden car. The ground is too uneven for the GCTF to follow him this way – there are remnants of old buildings, like the low wall Tom was hiding behind while he waited for the JJC to turn up, that will tear the underside off their car.

Tom's ears are ringing, but he can hear the groans of the surviving JJC. He leaves them behind. The GCTF have not yet realised that the ground is inhospitable to their vehicle. It doesn't take them long to find out. Tom glances back as he nears his car. He sees that a couple of them have gotten out, are following him on foot. When Tom jumps into his car and turns it around and they see it for the first time, they turn and run back to the car. They'll have to find another way to follow. If they get back to the main road in time, they could potentially catch him up. Tom has time to get ahead of them, to lose them, but he's not sure if it's enough. His mind is racing, wondering if this is the best option for him, or if he should allow them to follow.

Again, he reminds himself he's too weak. A direct confrontation is not in his best interest. Looking to his right, across the field, he can see the GCTF reversing back up the road. They're going fast. On the main road, too, their car will be faster than his. Chances are, they're going to catch him up.

Tom slams his foot down on the accelerator and clears the area. In his mirrors, he sees the bobbing headlights of the GCTF. He leaves the road and merges with another, slipping into the traffic. The GCTF follow him down. They weave in and out of the traffic. They have him in their sights. They're not going to let him get away.

Tom thinks. Considers his options. Despite his misgivings, a direct confrontation is looking like his only choice.

He pulls out his phone and calls Ruth, watching his mirrors. Ruth answers fast, like she's been waiting for his call.

"Ruth, I need you to listen very carefully," Tom says. "You and Calvin have to get out of the factory, get clear of it, and find somewhere safe to hide. I've got the GCTF on my tail. Before you leave, kill the lights but turn on all the machinery that you can. I need it loud in there – it'll give me some sound cover, and it'll distract them."

"Wait a minute, Tom – they're coming here?"

"Get out of there and run." Tom hangs up. The GCTF are sticking to him. Tom puts his foot down, tries to put some vehicles between them. The GCTF stay close. They aren't going anywhere.

61

Tom knows the ground around the factory better than the GCTF do, and he's able to get clear of them as he nears it. The GCTF can't miss where he's going, though. He skids the car to a halt and jumps out, running inside. It's in darkness, as requested, and he hears the mechanical thud of old, rusting machinery. The whir of a conveyor belt. The grinding of a compactor. The metal on metal of the shredder, like knives being sharpened. Tom runs into the shadows. He heads up top, to the walkway above, and presses himself against the wall when he gets there. He gasps for breath. He hears his heart pounding. His arms feel like they've been strapped with twenty-pound weights. His legs are wading through treacle. He gets close to a window and looks out, peering down, keeping the mass of his body concealed away from the glass in case they spot him and start shooting.

He sees the GCTF pull to a stop. They don't park directly by his car. They saw the explosion at the warehouses, and they anticipate a similar kind of ambush. Nick approaches the car. He checks it over. He pulls out a switchblade and goes around, popping all four of the tyres, preventing an escape. The four gather round at Carter's motioning. He gives them instructions. He points toward the factory. They're all carrying handguns. They're wearing vests. They don't come storming carelessly in. They're careful. They separate. They don't all come through the same door Tom did. They spread out. There are four sides to the building and they're going to enter through each one. If there's no door, they'll use a window. If the machinery wasn't running, Tom would probably be able to hear glass smashing.

Tom steps away from the window and braces himself. Darren is coming through the front. Delia went to the west side of the building, and Nick and Carter headed to the east. There's no way for Tom to know which of them will come in through the east and which will come through the rear.

Darren steps cautiously, Smith & Wesson M&P held out ahead of him. He has a torch. It's held out beside the gun. He shines it around the darkness, searching the corners. He hasn't looked up. He hasn't spotted the stairs and the gang-plank. The machinery is distracting him. He winces against its pounding, cocks his head to try and hear beyond it, under it, through it.

Tom raises his gun, steadying his tired arm on the railing in front of him. He takes a deep breath, making sure his aim is true. The torch is making Darren an easier target. Tom fires twice, the noise disguised by the machinery. One bullet goes wide, but the other finds its mark, punching through Darren's skull. Blood sprays and he goes down, landing hard, the torch rolling away across the ground.

Tom doesn't descend instantly from the walkway. He waits, keeping the area covered. His eyes have adjusted to the dark. He doesn't see anyone approaching, either with or without a torch. He makes his way down, leaning against the railing, keeping the Beretta raised. He can hear his heart pounding in his ears. His body does not usually protest against him like this. He's pushed himself too hard. It makes its complaints known.

He goes to the torch and turns it off, but he keeps hold of it. It dangles down by his side in his left hand. He presses himself to a wall close to an opening that leads through into the east side of the factory, where either Nick or Carter is. There's no machinery running through there, and Tom doesn't want to leave its noise behind. At the same time, he doesn't want to wait for all three remaining members of the GCTF to converge on this part of the factory at the same time. Gritting his teeth, he slides against the wall and heads through into the east.

As he rounds the corner, a boot slams into his chest and knocks him down. Tom skids across the ground. He tries to roll onto his left but puts all of his weight onto his broken arm. It screams at him. Tom bites down on his lip to avoid a scream of his own.

Nick bears down on him. Tom raises his Beretta, but not high enough. His bullet connects with the Kevlar. Nick grunts but he keeps pushing, dropping his weight and knocking the Beretta out of Tom's hand. He gasps with the impact of the bullet in his vest, but he fights through. He pulls out his switchblade, popping the knife. Tom has to fight him off one-handed, gripping at his wrist and keeping the knife out of his face.

"I saw you shoot Darren, you dumb fuck," Nick says through his teeth. Tom can barely hear him over the pounding of the pumping pistons of the compactor nearby.

"You stupid asshole, you should've stayed up there. But you came down here. You made it easy for me."

The knife comes closer. Tom looks up, toward the pistons. He sees them. They're close. Keeping hold of Nick's wrist, he shifts his weight and gets a boot under Nick's torso, pressing it into his midsection, then rolls through and flips him overhead, toward the pistons. Nick's right leg lands between the pistons as they part. He isn't able to pull it free as they slam together, crunching through bone and flesh, mangling his leg.

He screams, the scream loud enough to pierce the sound of the grinding machinery. He drags his leg free, but it's useless. Bone is bent and twisted at the wrong angles, and punches through his skin. Blood pours profusely from the wound.

"Oh, shit," Nick says, hyperventilating. "Oh my God, oh *fuck...*"

On his knees, Tom wraps his right arm under his jaw, and twists hard and fast, breaking his neck. Nick's head thuds on the ground.

Before Tom can catch his breath, he feels a new boot come up and kick him in the ribs. He rolls onto his back, the air knocked out of him. He struggles to breathe. Feels the oxygen strain down his thin throat, unable to fill his lungs. The boot comes down again, stomping in the middle of his chest, almost cracking a rib. Tom coughs. He gasps. He looks up to see Delia. She kicks him across the face. Blood flies out of his mouth. On the other side of him, Tom sees Carter, his thumbs hooked through his vest.

"You goddamn son of a bitch," Carter says, looking over Nick's body.

"He got Darren, too," Delia says, unable to contain her fury.

Carter looks around the factory. "This where you've been hiding out, huh? I'm surprised these machines ain't been stripped for scrap."

"Just a matter of time," Delia says, staring at Tom, struggling to hold herself back. She wants to kick him again.

Tom swallows blood. He tries to push himself up but he's too weak.

"I wanna hurt him," Delia says. "I wanna hurt him real bad."

Carter grunts. "We're gonna. No quick death for this piece of shit." He crouches close to Tom's head. "Maybe you should've shot me in the face when you had the chance, huh?"

Through it all, Tom has managed to keep hold of the torch, gripping it in his left hand. Even when he rolled onto his arm, the pain just made him grip it tighter. No one seems to realise he's holding it. Reaching across with his right hand, pretending he's trying to roll, he grabs the torch. He swings it in a backhand, catching Carter in the temple, knocking him off balance.

"Damn it!" Delia says, laying a boot into Tom's back. She kicks him again and again, then takes the torch from him and throws it across the factory floor.

Carter gets back to his feet, spitting. He presses a tentative hand to his right temple. There's blood there. The torch cracked him open. A trickle of it runs down the side of his face.

"What do you wanna do with him?" Delia says.

Carter looks around. A grin splits his face. "Haul him up onto the walkway," he says. He turns and heads across the factory while Delia grabs Tom by his good arm and drags him across the floor, toward the stairs. Tom tries to struggle, but he doesn't have much energy left.

When Carter reappears, he's carrying a long-rusted chain. Delia sees it. "What's it for? We gonna hang him?"

"Something like that," Carter says. "You see that shredder over there? We're gonna lower him into it, nice and slow. Let it chew him up."

Delia laughs. She likes the sound of it. "Hell yeah," she says.

62

They drag Tom up the steps. They're not gentle with him. Carter has wrapped the chains around his neck, hauls him up that way. The links dig into Tom's throat. It feels like it's going to tear his head from his shoulders.

Delia follows up the stairs at Tom's feet. If he grabs at the rail she kicks at his fingers. If he gets snagged on a step she kicks him loose and keeps him on his way.

When they reach the top and things level out, the drag feels a little smoother. Tom kicks back at Delia, but she's stronger than him right now, and she kicks harder.

Carter stops when they reach the space above the shredder. Carter crouches down, holding Tom up like the chain is a noose. "You know what those shredders are for? They're for waste. All the metal pieces of the car that they don't need. It's fitting, ain't it? It's for getting rid of waste, and that's exactly what we're gonna use it for."

Tom blows blood from his lips. It mists onto Carter's face. Carter flinches, but he doesn't recoil from it.

"When we find the kid and his sister, what do you think we're gonna do to them?" Carter says. "We're gonna do the same thing to them as we're about to do to you. All the waste, all of the *shit* that has been bringing us these headaches lately, it's gonna be shredded away into nothing. Just a big red puddle that we can mop away."

They patted Tom down before they brought him up the stairs. They found his KA-BAR and discarded it. He has nothing left. Just his limbs, and they're not on his side right now. Carter isn't even close enough that Tom can bite at him, and the chains are keeping him back.

Carter starts to drag him up to his feet. He pulls at his left arm, just to see him hurt. Tom grimaces. He doesn't make a sound. Won't give him the satisfaction.

"I'm gonna hook it under his arms," Carter says. "You make sure he doesn't try anything stupid."

"He's already a stupid son of a bitch," Delia says.

Tom doesn't have much left to give, but he readies himself. He's let them think he's weaker than he is. Has let them drag him around. As they bring him up to his feet, and Carter starts to lower the chains down his front to loop them under his arms, Tom makes his move. Carter is behind him. Tom feels his breath on his neck as he comes in close. Tom throws his head back, butting him in the centre of the face. He lashes out at Delia, kicking at her legs. He knocks her left leg back, catching her unprepared and knocking her onto her front. He spins, swinging with his right elbow, catching Carter between his shoulder and jaw. He sees Carter trying to bring up his gun and Tom kicks out again, knocking it out of his hand.

Every muscle in Tom's body screams in agony. His blows aren't landing with as much impact as they usually would.

He does his best to ignore the pain. To push through. He thinks on what Carter said – if they kill him, they kill Calvin and Ruth. He's all that stands between the siblings and their death.

Delia is back to her feet. She advances on Tom. He raises his right arm to defend himself as best as he can.

He hears footsteps pounding down the walkway behind Delia. She hears them too. She starts to turn. Two unexpected shapes charge out of the darkness. Ruth and Calvin. They're close. Tom doesn't know where they came from, but they must have been creeping up. Now that they've seen Tom in action, causing a diversion, they've sped up. They barrel toward Delia. She tries to raise her weapon but they're too close. They throw themselves against her, pressing her up against the railing. Ruth pulls on her arm, pushing it back, trying to disarm her.

Delia, with her other hand, grabs at the front of Calvin's shirt. She pulls him closer and headbutts him, bloodying his nose. He stumbles back, reaching to the wall behind him to keep himself up. Tom sees Ruth still struggling to take the gun from her. Tom takes a step forward, to help, but Carter grabs him by the ankle and sweeps his legs from under him. Tom lands on his front, twisting to avoid his left arm taking the impact. His chest and chin take most of it.

Delia grabs a handful of Ruth's hair and pulls her back, trying to raise her upright. Ruth cries out, but she struggles against the pain. She looks at Tom. Their eyes lock, just for a moment. Ruth pushes down, presses her head between Delia's legs. Her hair slips out of Delia's hand. Delia pounds at her back, not understanding what she's doing, assuming she's trying to take cover under her body. Instead, Ruth throws herself up, lifting Delia from the ground, flipping her over the railing.

Too late, Delia realises what is happening to her. She drops the gun now, her arms waving, hands grabbing for the railing. She's already too far from it. She falls through the air. She lands in the shredder.

Tom has never heard a scream like it. It's thankfully brief. She lands head-first. Blood sprays, coating the walls and the ground. The machine continues to chew up the rest of her body.

Carter doesn't scream her name. He doesn't stare at her body being ground down and spat out. He sheds no tears. She's already dead, and he moves on from it. All of his team are dead now, and there's nothing he can do about it. He feels nothing.

Except vengeance.

He's already on Tom, grabbing at his throat. The plan is no longer to lower Tom slowly into the shredder. There's no time for that. No longer time for torture. Ruth and Calvin are present now, too, and he has to deal with them as well. He needs to kill Tom fast.

Tom's one good arm is not strong enough to keep him at bay. Carter grabs his throat and squeezes, but more than that, he raises his head and slams the back of it down into the walkway. Tom hears the metal grill beneath him rattle. His eyes lose focus. Carter is strong. He sees the veins bulging in his unnaturally large biceps. Calvin and Ruth try to intervene. Tom is dazed enough for Carter to let go. Tom can't see what he does. Everything is unfocussed. He must hit them – he can feel the vibrations of the walkway beneath. He dimly hears Calvin grunt, hurt, and Ruth cry out. Before he knows it, Carter's hands have returned to his neck. Tom's right arm scrabbles. He can't breathe and he can barely think. He has one function right now – survival.

His hand lands upon the rusted chain. He grabs the chain and moves fast, before Carter can slam his head down again. One more, and he's out. Carter will be free to slam his skull into mush. Tom whips the chain across his face. It lashes him across the nose and mouth, and his right eye, causing him to fall back, temporarily blinded.

Still breathless, Tom raises a leg and kicks at his chest, knocking him back, creating some space. He keeps moving. He can't afford to wait. Carter is hurt, but not as bad as he is. He'll recover faster. Tom whips him again, bringing the chain down on the top of his head, splitting his scalp. Tom wraps the chain around his fist and throws himself at Carter, punching him, falling through, feeling his jaw break under the blow.

Panting, he pushes himself up. Carter is still alive. Tom can't see Carter's Smith & Wesson nearby. It might have rolled off the edge, be on the ground somewhere below. All Tom has is the chain.

He wraps it around Carter's neck, looping it three times. He doesn't tie a knot. It's tight enough. Carter fights back against him, but the blows from the chain have dazed him, and now he's weakened. He's in the same position as Tom was, has just one focus. He's not thinking, just battling. Just surviving. He kicks at Tom, same as Tom did to him, but Tom has the chain and he keeps hold of it as he falls back. He's able to keep his feet. He drags Carter up to his. Tom finds himself close to Ruth and Calvin. Calvin's eye is swollen. Ruth bleeds from her nose and the corner of her mouth. Carter sees them together. He spits blood, his jaw hanging loose and misshapen. He stares at the three of them. There's hatred in his eyes. He charges.

Tom sidesteps him, bringing up a knee and driving it into his midsection, then ducks down and repeats Ruth's manoeuvre – he gets under Carter's bulk, and flips him over the railing.

Carter falls through the air, but he's nowhere near the shredder now. Tom still has the chain. It's long. It's long enough for Carter to hit the ground. Tom twists, wrapping the chain around himself, and throws himself flat to the ground. Ruth sees what he's doing. She throws herself on top of him, on top of the chain. Below, the chain is pulled taut, Carter's body still three feet from the factory floor.

Through the noise of the machines, they hear his neck snap.

63

The GCTF are dead. The JJC are in tatters.

Ruth and Calvin have returned home.

It's been three weeks since that night in the factory. Tom has been staying with them. He was badly beat up after that night. It turned out, they never left the factory like he told them to. Tom wasn't mad. They saved his life. Instead of fleeing, they found an office to hide out in and they lay low. They'd heard some of the battle, though the machinery had disguised the sound of most of it. They'd seen Delia pass by in the dark. She didn't see them. They'd waited, then come to explore, to see what was happening. When they saw Delia and Carter with Tom up on the walkway, they knew they had to help him.

After, Ruth and Calvin took the GCTF car and used it to drive Tom back to their apartment. They put him into Ruth's bed. He was already unconscious. A combination of pain, blood loss, and general exhaustion. The infection was still working him over, and Ruth worried his refusal to rest had allowed it to reignite.

She and Calvin went back to the factory and tidied up. They buried the three bodies they were able to outside in the scrubland surrounding the factory. What was left of Delia they mopped up. They cleaned up all of the blood. Got rid of the weapons, save for Tom's Beretta and KA-BAR. They removed the generators and lights, all traces that they had ever been hiding out there. They bought four new tyres for Tom's car, and together they changed them. They drove the GCTF car to a quiet part of the Detroit River under cover of darkness and pushed it in.

Tom slept through it all. He slept for two days. He remembers waking up, feverish, seeing things that weren't there – Carter and the rest of the GCTF, in the room with him. He saw people he hasn't seen in a long time – his father, his brother. Alejandra. Cindy. Hayley. Zeke and his family. But mostly, he's seen people he has killed. The ghosts of them, looking down on him. Like they expected him to cross over, to join them, and they were waiting for him.

Tom didn't give them the satisfaction. His fever broke. When he finally opened his eyes, only Ruth was beside him, a damp cloth close at hand. The bedsheets were wet. He'd sweated through them.

"You've only got a couple of days left on the antibiotics," she said. "We'll see how you're doing when they're gone, but I think I might have to put you on another course."

She didn't. Tom has always healed fast.

His arm took its time, though. Ruth took him to the hospital, to a doctor she was friendly with, and had it put in a proper cast. "It'll help it heal better," she said. Tom asked how much it cost. Ruth told him it was off the books. She owed the doctor a huge favour for keeping it quiet, but she doubted he'd ever call it in.

Tom is with Ruth in the living room. She's on the sofa behind him, her legs drawn up beneath her, her books spread open around her. She's studying. Tom stands by the window, looking down, watching the area below the building. Calvin is at boxing. Every night, when it's over, he comes straight home. Ruth doesn't worry about him. He's not looking for trouble. They found the trouble. They dealt with the trouble. Now, Calvin looks only to his future.

"Are you going to take a seat?" Ruth says.

Tom turns. She's smiling at him.

"You've been standing there a long time," she says.

"Just want to make sure."

She nods. She understands this.

Tom has watched the news. They've checked online together, and looked in newspapers. The explosion that decimated the JJC was blamed upon the DLB. The disappearance of the GCTF, however, has led to more theories. Some think they were killed by the DLB too, and their bodies disposed of. Others, however, have become aware of Lainey Wylder's investigation into the GCTF's practises in the past. With her recent death, they've wondered if this was the GCTF, attempting to clear up loose ends, and now they've fled. They've wondered how Anthony Felton and Katy Doerr tied into all of this – if they were perhaps loose ends, too. If maybe the GCTF also killed them. If maybe Anthony was talking to Lainey, revealing GCTF secrets – Katy was her secretary, after all.

No one has a clear answer, though. Without evidence, they're all theories. Without the bodies of the rest of the GCTF, no one can know for sure.

"How's your arm?" Ruth says.

Tom leaves the window. He sits on a chair close to her. "It's not itching anymore," he says.

"That's good."

"When can I get the cast off?"

"Another week, at least. Four to six weeks for a break."

"I've always healed fast."

"I don't doubt it, but we'll need to get you checked before the cast comes off. You don't have anything to rush for now. You can rest."

Tom looks toward the window. "When it comes off, whether it's next week or the week after, I'll be moving on."

Ruth doesn't say anything.

"I've stayed here long enough," Tom says. "I needed to make sure you're safe, and you are. No one's come by the apartment. No one's watching it. No one's following you or your brother. You're clear."

"I understand," Ruth says. "We'll miss you when you're gone. We appreciate everything you did for us, Tom, more than we can ever say."

"You don't need to say anything," Tom says. "That's not why I did it."

"And we appreciate *that*, too."

"If anything comes up, you have my number. Don't hesitate to call it."

Ruth nods. "Where are you going to go next? Do you know?"

"Never do."

Ruth smiles.

What Tom doesn't tell her is that he still has some business left in Detroit. That once the cast is off his arm, he might be hanging around the city a little while longer, depending on how long it takes him to find who he's looking for. There's a loose thread that needs cut. Ruth and Calvin won't know he's still here.

Tom sits back in the chair. It's hard for him to relax, especially when he knows he's not one hundred percent. He tries to settle into the comfort of the cushions. He breathes deep. Ruth holds her hand out to him. She smiles at him. She has a very sweet smile. Tom returns it. He takes her hand. They sit in silence.

EPILOGUE

For most of his adult life, Darius Walker hasn't had a fixed address. He wonders if he ever will. He's not so sure. He's used to this transient way of life now. It's kept him alive. When it's kept him breathing, it's hard to turn his back on what he knows works.

Even with the JJC mostly gone and the GCTF missing, Darius won't rest on his laurels. He's not living in the back of an RV anymore, and he's glad of that, but he's spent the last few weeks in his most current temporary home and he's getting antsy. Ready to move on. To find somewhere else to stay.

The home is in someone else's name, of course. Darius isn't a fool. He knows the cops are still looking for him. It hasn't been long enough for the heat to die down. It will, eventually. They'll always be looking for him, but sometime soon they won't be looking so hard. Eventually, they might even become friendly to him, like the GCTF were for the JJC. For now, Darius concentrates on building up his empire. A lot of the survivors from the JJC have come over to the DLB. His ranks are swelling. His path is clear. Detroit is his.

The house is small. It's sparsely furnished. It has a sofa and a television, but everything in it is just for show, to look good should anyone come by. Darius spends most of his time in the living room, his desk in the window so he can see out, watch for anyone coming that he needs to be alarmed about. There isn't much action out on the street, though. Old folks taking a walk around the block. Kids on bikes. It's a quiet neighbourhood, similar to where his mom used to live. She's still with her sister. Darius isn't sure he can ever let her come back. He can't let her be used against him again.

He's not alone in the house. He always has a guard with him. The man is sitting on the sofa behind him, staring at his phone. Darius thinks he's watching porn.

Darius hears a noise. It comes from under the house, in the basement. Darius turns. He and his guard lock eyes. "Did you hear that?" the man says.

"The basement?" Darius says.

The guard reaches behind himself, into his waistband, and pulls out his Glock. He leaves the living room, heads through into the kitchen. Darius stands, follows him. The guard goes down into the basement. Darius waits, watching the open door.

A couple of minutes pass. The man doesn't return. He doesn't call back up the stairs. Darius doesn't call after him. He starts to turn, planning to leave the house and call in reinforcements from outside. He isn't taking any risks.

"Where you going?"

Darius freezes in the doorway. He turns slowly. A white man stands at the top of the stairs, pointing a Beretta at him. "What do you want?" Darius says.

The man steps out of the basement, closing the door behind him. "To see you. Do you know how long it took me to find out about you, Darius Walker? Do you know how long it took me to find you?"

Darius frowns. He doesn't know who this man is.

"I knew that when I destroyed the JJC there would be a power vacuum in Detroit," the man says. "I knew that when I killed the GCTF, some other crooked cops would step in to take their place. I know that every city is going to have its problems. The bad people of this world are a hydra. You cut off one head and two more are ready to take its place. So I know that when I leave Detroit, someone is going to take the place of Javon Johnson. I know that someone is going to take the place of Carter Brown. But not you, Darius. I can't let it be you."

Darius's eyes flicker down toward the gun. "Who are you?"

The man doesn't respond. "You're too careless, Darius. You've killed too many people in the streets, people who had nothing to do with the JJC. And you came after me. You came after friends of mine."

"Man, I don't even know who you are," Darius says. "I don't know who your friends are."

"My name is Tom Rollins," he says. "I wouldn't expect you to know. My friends are Lewin Spinks, and Ruth and Calvin Styles. I wouldn't expect you to know their names, either. I wouldn't expect you to know the names of the people you gunned down. I don't expect you to care."

Darius clenches his jaw. He straightens up. "You're right," he says. "I don't."

Rollins nods. He fires three times. Darius feels each of the bullets hit him in the chest. He falls back and lands flat in the living room. Darius tastes blood. He hears Rollins leaving out the back door. Briefly, he wonders how he got down into the basement. He wonders how long he was there, waiting.

Darius starts to laugh in the back of his throat. He stayed in one place too long. He should have left sooner. Kept on the move. Three weeks was too long. He got comfortable.

He closes his eyes and he laughs until the last breath leaves his lungs, and the sound dies in the back of his throat.

ABOUT THE AUTHOR

Did you enjoy *Full Throttle*? Please consider leaving a review on Amazon to help other readers discover the book.

Paul Heatley left school at sixteen, and since then has held a variety of jobs including mechanic, carpet fitter, and book-shop assistant, but his passion has always been for writing. He writes mostly in the genres of crime fiction and thriller, and links to his other titles can be found on his website. He lives in the north east of England.

Want to connect with Paul? Visit him at his website.

www.PaulHeatley.com

ALSO BY PAUL HEATLEY

The Tom Rollins Thriller Series

Blood Line (Book 1)

Wrong Turn (Book 2)

Hard to Kill (Book 3)

Snow Burn (Book 4)

Road Kill (Book 5)

No Quarter (Book 6)

Hard Target (Book 7)

Last Stand (Book 8)

Blood Feud (Book 9)

Search and Destroy (Book 10)

Ghost Team (Book 11)

Full Throttle (Book 12)

The Tom Rollins Box Set (Books 1 - 4)

Printed in Great Britain
by Amazon